# A KISS FOR A HERO

"He can't get down," Lorna said.

Jonathan crossed his arms. "Of course he can. Kittens have been climbing trees since the world began."

"Look at him; he's terrified!" She gestured at the kitten, who was indeed looking somewhat uncomfortable in its perch. "He will get tired and fall out. He'll be hurt."

Jonathan stripped off his jacket and swung himself onto a limb. The tree branched often, and it wasn't a particularly difficult climb, but the kitten seemed to have gotten itself rather higher up than he had originally thought.

"Jonathan! Do be careful!" she called out in alarm.

Ignoring the violent protests of his body, he snatched the kitten from its perch. The tiny animal clung to his cravat. He arrived on the ground wearing the kitten something like a large, furry medal on his chest.

"Why did you do that?" Lorna chided. "You could have been killed!" She collected the kitten in her arms. "I'm perfectly capable of taking care of things on my own."

"I know," he said, acutely aware of her closeness. "But I wanted to do it for you."

"But you don't like cats, Lord Griffith."

"But I like you," he said softly.

"You do?"

"Yes." He wondered if, since he had specified that he would not kiss her again in a rowboat, if kissing her right now would be considered a breach of contract. . . .

—From "The Black Kitten" by Catherine Blair

# BOOK YOUR PLACE ON OUR WEBSITE AND MAKE THE READING CONNECTION!

We've created a customized website just for our very special readers, where you can get the inside scoop on everything that's going on with Zebra, Pinnacle and Kensington books.

When you come online, you'll have the exciting opportunity to:

- View covers of upcoming books

- Read sample chapters

- Learn about our future publishing schedule (listed by publication month *and author*)

- Find out when your favorite authors will be visiting a city near you

- Search for and order backlist books from our online catalog

- Check out author bios and background information

- Send e-mail to your favorite authors

- Meet the Kensington staff online

- Join us in weekly chats with authors, readers and other guests

- Get writing guidelines

- AND MUCH MORE!

**Visit our website at
http://www.zebrabooks.com**

# MAGICAL KITTENS

## DONNA BELL
## CATHERINE BLAIR
## JOY REED

## ZEBRA BOOKS
Kensington Publishing Corp.
http:www.zebrabooks.com

ZEBRA BOOKS are published by

Kensington Publishing Corp.
850 Third Avenue
New York, NY 10022

Zebra and the Z logo Reg. U.S. Pat. & TM Off.

First Printing: September, 2000
10 9 8 7 6 5 4 3 2 1

Printed in the United States of America

# CONTENTS

*To the original Aidaworks crew:*
*Jack & Sylvia, Rochelle, Suzann,*
*Jane, LeWayne, Marjorie, Elyshia,*
*Carol, Schelle*

# THE RELUCTANT WARLOCK

*Donna Bell*

# ONE

"Felix Baring, so good to see you safe and home again. And now you are Sir Felix. Your father would have been so proud."

"Thank you, ma'am."

"No, we must thank *you* for protecting us from the little Corsican monster. But here you are, home again, safe in the bosom of your family. I daresay they are delighted the war is finally over."

"Indeed, my lady, we are all glad to have Napoleon back in captivity. How fares your family?" inquired the dark-haired gentleman on horseback, keeping his young gelding under wraps with some difficulty as the lady's plumed hat fluttered in the breeze.

"All grown up since we last saw you. Why, the youngest, Amy, is eighteen now and made her bow into Society last spring," she added, her expression suddenly becoming predatory as she studied him.

Sir Felix shifted uncomfortably in his saddle, and his smile became forced. "Eighteen," he said quietly. "Time does have a way of getting away from us, doesn't it?"

"Yes, yes, and though you may accuse me of motherly prejudice, I must admit that Amy was quite the belle of the Season last spring. But you know how young ladies are, at the time, she was in no hurry to settle on one gentleman."

"Of course," he murmured politely, wondering how he was supposed to know anything about young ladies, having had only a younger brother.

"Now, perhaps . . ."

The lady let the possibilities dangle in the air for a moment. Rather like the sword of Damocles, thought Sir Felix Baring. He essayed a nervous smile before maneuvering his horse to one side in order to escape.

But the lady feinted to her right and leaned toward him again, declaring purposefully, "I am holding a small soirée in two weeks' time, Sir Felix. It will be an intimate affair, of course. I'll send you a card. Do say you will come."

"I am sorry, Lady Harkness, but . . ."

"Oh, but surely you can spare an hour or two for old neighbors. Amy will be so disappointed if you do not come."

Felix reflected privately that since Amy had no idea he was home from the army, she would suffer no pangs of disappointment. Out loud, however, he acquiesced and was finally allowed to move along.

His aunt had the right of it, coming to London had not been very wise, not for a man such as he who craved only peace and quiet. Shaking his head at his own foolishness, he turned the restless gelding toward the elegant town house he had taken for the autumn.

His butler and his groom met him on the front steps, fairly tripping over each other as they hurried to his side.

"I am so sorry, sir!" exclaimed the distraught butler, wringing his hands like a nervous old woman.

"I tried t' stop 'im, guvner, but wot could I do? I asks ye? 'E pulled a pistol on me!" wailed the groom.

"Who the devil are you talking about?" demanded Felix, turning just in time to catch in his arms his wild-eyed aunt.

"Oh, Felix, thank the Lord you have come! That dratted boy! Oh, my palpitations! I shall faint!"

Felix sighed and turned back to the house to usher his whimpering aunt inside. "What has Oliver done now?"

"He has taken my baby! My Francis!"

"Now, now, Aunt Felicity, Oliver wouldn't hurt your baby. He'll be fine!"

"He also took one of your mother's silver napkin rings!" put in the butler, following close on their heels.

"Surely we can spare one napkin ring, Winchester," said Felix.

"And 'e took yer team and curricle, sir," added the groom reluctantly. "Th' new one. They just delivered it this mornin'."

Sir Felix Baring dropped his aunt's arm and turned the full force of his catlike gaze on his groom. "He . . . took . . . my team?"

The groom swallowed hard and nodded. Felix turned on his heel, retracing his steps to the street, where a young groom still held his horse in readiness.

"I will kill him," said Sir Felix, swinging back into the saddle with a feral growl.


"Strolling along the Serpentine on such a fine autumn day makes me proud to be an Englishwoman," said the lady with salt and pepper hair, bowing her head slightly as she leaned toward her petite companion, a young woman in a modish walking costume whose golden blond curls were only partially obscured by a small straw bonnet.

"I would have said it makes me glad to be alive," said the blonde, her voice flavored with a hint of amusement.

"Oh, yes, certainly, Gilly, but to be English, on English soil . . . why, one can't help but . . . Oh, my! How rude!" exclaimed the older woman as a horse and rider thundered past.

"It seems others are not as intent on enjoying this proper

English afternoon as we are, Rose," said the beauty, her amusement bubbling forth in a musical laugh.

The two ladies continued their walk, the elder stopping to sample the fragrance of some late-blooming flowers.

"Only look, Rose, that young man has a kitten in his curricle," said her pretty companion.

The tall but slightly built young man in the curricle nodded a greeting and reined in his restless team. His green eyes locked on the pretty young woman, and a nervous flush tinged his cheeks. As the ladies paused, smiling, the kitten began to squirm.

"Good afternoon, ladies," squeaked the youth, holding the reins in one hand and taking his other hand off the kitten long enough to sweep an oversize, curly-brimmed beaver from his head.

The drum of hooves made all of them turn to watch the rapid return of the black-haired demon whose pale green eyes glittered with rage.

"What the devil do you think you're doing, Oliver?" shouted the devil on horseback, his mount skidding to a stop and sending a cloud of dust swirling about them all.

"Now, Felix, I . . . wha . . . oh, no!" yelped the young man, standing up on the box to retrieve the dropped ribbons while the kitten let loose a long yowling sound, wiggled free from its silver collar, and flew across the glossy backs of the plunging team.

Felix lunged for the ribbons just as the black kitten skittered off the backs of the pair and up the nose of his gelding, who took great exception to this treatment, screamed his protest, and reared up to dance on his hind legs a moment before kicking out from behind and unseating his unseatable rider.

Felix landed with a hard thud, his language scorching the cool autumn landscape as it spewed forth. The black kitten dropped onto his lap, its fur standing on end and its back arched, and proceeded to dig its claws into Felix's breeches.

Pain silenced Felix, but his hands reacted with a quick swat that sent the kitten flying yet again.

"Wretched man! How dare you frighten this poor little thing! What a bully you are!" shouted the pretty blonde, who caught the black furball and clutched it against her round bosom.

Then, to punctuate her words, the angelic beauty rapped Felix sharply on the head with her parasol, breaking it in two. The cracking sound made her gasp, but she kept the kitten firmly in her grasp and marched away, her gait stiff with disapproval.

With a loud sniff and a, "Well, really," her companion followed in her wake.

Silence reigned for a moment.

Sir Felix Baring managed to scramble to his feet and stand erect, although his first instinct was to double over from the feline assault on his manhood.

"Are, uh, you all right, Felix?" asked the youth, his voice trembling with fear and sympathy. Or was that laughter?

Felix's gaze came to rest on his brother. He shook his head, amazed at his own ability to restrain his desire to strangle the tall young man.

"You've not suffered any permanent harm, I hope."

"Ride Pickles home. I'll take the curricle," Felix managed to say through gritted teeth.

"Well, I . . . Yes, of course, Felix. See you at home," said Oliver, hopping to the ground and taking the reins from his brother. Swinging up easily on the gelding's back, he looked down on his brother and said, "I . . . I'm really sorry, Felix. I just wanted . . ."

Felix waved his hand, and his brother nodded and turned the horse toward home.

Felix climbed into the curricle, his brand-new curricle, noting the claw marks in the smooth leather, he blinked once slowly and picked up the ribbons. As if the contretemps had overset them as much as it had their master, the pair of prime bloods walked sedately home.

"Ahhhh," breathed Felix, sinking down in the copper tub of steaming water. "Much better."

His valet handed him soap and a sponge, but Felix waved them away, saying, "Not now, Waverly. I just want to soak my bruised backside until the water cools."

"Very good, Sir Felix," said the extremely proper servant, backing out of the room.

"Ahhh." Felix sighed again, commenting to the empty room in general, "Such a good fellow. Always knows when to leave a man alone."

Boom! The door crashed against the wall, rattling the glass in the windows across the room. Felix snatched a towel from the nearby chair, his bruised body screaming in protest at the sudden movement.

"Felix! Felix! How could you! I demand you get up right now and go find those kitten-nappers! My baby, my poor baby!"

"If you will tell me how I am to accomplish that, Aunt Felicity, I would be only too happy to do so. But seeing as the kitten-napper did not bother to leave her calling card . . ."

"What difference does that make?" his aunt demanded, waving her arms frantically, the scarf in one hand flying back and forth, accenting her agitated state. In her other, she held a silver stick that she used to punctuate her speech.

"I have no way of knowing where to look for Francis," he added calmly. "And in case you haven't noticed, Aunt, I am in the middle of my own room, in the middle of my own bath."

"Oh, I take no notice of such things. Besides, who do you think used to change your . . ."

"Say no more, Aunt, but please allow me to get dressed before I call out the Bow Street Runners."

"Why on earth would you wish to do anything so nonsensical, Nephew? You have no need to take such measures," she said, looming over him, her stick almost touching his chest.

Felix shook his head, knowing what was coming next. But try as he might, he could not convince his eccentric aunt that he was not, nor was he likely to become, a warlock.

"All you need do, Felix, is concentrate your powers. How often must I tell you? And if you feel it is beyond your current capabilities, then we will work together."

"But Aunt, I have no powers."

"You know in your heart that is not true, Felix. You simply choose not to use them. But how can you be so heartless? You don't even care about your own father!"

The injustice of this made Felix half rise in the chilly water before he remembered his delicate circumstances. Sinking back down, he protested, "You know I cared very deeply for my father, Aunt, but Francis—for all that you named your kitten after your brother—is neither your brother nor my father."

"How can you say so? Of course he is! We have spoken together on several occasions. That little kitten is your father all over again! All you need do is look into his eyes," she exclaimed.

"Please be reasonable, Aunt, surely your other six cats are enough to keep you company."

"I have four cats! And now only three! That a nephew of mine could be so insensitive!" she declared dramatically, turning on her heel and stalking toward the door, a cloud of silk scarves billowing about her.

"I only hope your father is not being tortured! If he is . . ." she said, muttering spells and incantations under her breath as she disappeared, leaving the door to his bedroom wide open, making him shiver as a chilly draft from the corridor penetrated the room.

"Devil take her," grumbled Felix, stepping out of the tub and striding across the room to shut the door, only to run into his valet, white-faced and wide-eyed, but carrying two cans of hot water.

"I cannot possibly continue on in this household, Sir Felix," squeaked Waverly, marching to the tub and pouring the steaming liquid. "I must resign."

"Waverly, I cannot allow you to leave. I can't possibly do without you," said Felix through gritted teeth.

Though the finicky valet was somewhat mollified, he gave a little shiver and said, "But your aunt . . ."

"My aunt is a very eccentric lady who gets up to peculiar starts from time to time," said Felix, returning thankfully to his bath. "She is not, however, a witch, and she cannot cast a spell upon me, or you, or anyone else for that matter, no matter how very much she pretends she can. Please, Waverly, for my sake, try to ignore her."

"I will do my best, sir, but if she should shake that wand of hers at me again, I simply can't remain."

"I understand, Waverly. I shall have another talk with her. In the meantime, do you think you could hand me some soap?"

"Oh, of course, sir. I am so sorry," bubbled the valet.

"Think nothing of it. And Waverly, please try to remember my aunt's 'wand' is nothing but a stick she painted silver."

"I shall endeavor to remember, sir, but it is rather difficult when she waves it so convincingly."

"Rose, do you think we really should go to this masquerade tomorrow night? I know the Beauchamp family are high sticklers, but a masked ball? It is not what I am accustomed to attending," said Miss Gertrude Gillingham, her button nose wrinkling in distaste.

Her companion said firmly, "It is just what you need for your first real outing on your return to Society, my dear. As you know, I do not count that card party or attending the theater. This will be perfect, and you need have no reason to be shy since no one will know who you are behind your mask."

"I am not so shy as all that," said Gilly, lifting her chin defiantly. "I am trying very hard to put myself forward . . . a little."

The older woman smiled affectionately and asked, "Is that why we have been back in London for one month and have accepted only a handful of the invitations that have come our way?"

"Touché," murmured Gilly, ever truthful.

Her countenance fell, and Rose said bracingly, "You know it is what Mr. Ward would have wanted. He would not have liked the thought of you living out your life in solitude."

Gilly gave her friend a sad smile and nodded. "I know, I know. It is more difficult than I imagined it would be, smiling and enjoying myself when . . . but you are right. He would not have wanted me to spend my life in mourning, and to be perfectly candid, I find it is becoming more and more difficult."

"To go out in Society?" asked Rose Pargeter.

"No," said Gilly quietly. "I find it increasingly difficult to remember I am in mourning, even to call to mind Mr. Ward's face. I know you are shocked, but there it is."

"Shocked? Not at all, my dear," said the elderly lady. "I have been wondering when you would be able to admit the truth. After all, it has been almost two years now. I know you were fond of Mr. Ward, but I didn't think you were so deeply attached as to go into a decline over his untimely demise. Had you already been wed . . ." she added, leaving the words unsaid.

A thoughtful silence ensued. Finally, Gilly rose, saying firmly, "Then we should go upstairs and try the attics to see if there is something suitable for our costumes."

"An excellent suggestion," said Rose, linking arms with her godchild. "I've a mind to go as someone rather daring, perhaps a pirate captain, or maybe as Medusa. I think I could make a suitably snakelike headdress."

"Rose, with your fair skin, you could never be a convincing monster, you are too like a fairy princess."

"Ah, now you are trying to flatter me, but I promise you, I shan't be taken in. I know what you want, missy. You want me to go and fetch the remainder of that box of bonbons to give us the strength to complete this onerous task."

"That does sound good," agreed Gilly, grinning up at her godmother, who adored chocolate above all things.

"Very well, wicked child, chocolates and costumes are the order of the day!"


"Oliver, you cannot remain shut away behind closed doors for the rest of your life. Being sent down from university is not the tragedy you paint it. I was sent down any number of times."

"That is all well and good, Felix, but I am not you. I am not the answer to the prayers of the cricket team, the polo team, or any other team. Give me an ancient tome to translate, and you shall have it immediately. But I have come to the realization, painful as it may be, that I am completely out of my element here in London. I have absolutely no knowledge of how to go on in Society. I either run the risk of blending in with the wallpaper or, when I try to be unique, to carve a niche for myself, I appear an utter fool."

Felix studied his self-pitying brother for a moment, resisting the inclination to tell him to get off his backside and go out and play. But Oliver had grown up while he was away fighting Bonaparte. His situation was more delicate than that now; it required more finesse.

One characteristic Felix had prided himself on as an officer in the 95th Rifles was that he always knew the best way to encourage his men. If they needed a swift kick in the pants, he gave it to them. If they needed him to sympathize with them, to admit he was as dogged weary as they and just as sick of the rain and muck and hunger, then he did it. He had always been able to gauge the best way to inspire them, to lead them.

Lead them. That's what Oliver needed. He didn't need to be pushed, he needed to follow until he felt sure enough of himself to strike out on his own.

"You know, Oliver, I received an interesting invitation to a masquerade. I was thinking of attending, but Aunt is barely on speaking terms with me at the moment, and it's not the sort of thing one wants to go to alone. Do you think you might see your way clear to going with me?"

Oliver brightened perceptively; then his eyes narrowed, and he said, "You're only saying that to bring me out of the doldrums."

"If you don't wish . . ."

"Very well, I'll go."

"Good bo—ur, man!" said Felix, turning to go. "It is tomorrow night. We'll leave around nine o'clock."

"Felix, what costume should I wear? I mean, I could go as Copernicus or Plato, perhaps Sophocles," said the young man, his quick mind churning out possibilities, each historical figure duller than the last.

"I understand, Oliver, that the usual costumes are pirates, knights, and Greek gods."

"I see, something a little more daring. What will you wear?"

Felix, who until moments before had had no intention of attending this ball or any other, paused at the door and shrugged, replying, "I think I'll just wear a domino and a mask."

"A bit lackluster, don't you think?"

Felix grinned and said, "Well, there you have it, Ollie. I am the dull one of the family; just ask Aunt Felicity. Why, I can't even work up enough determination to be a warlock."

The door closed, and Oliver murmured, "A warlock? Not a bad idea."

Oliver wouldn't tell anyone what his costume was to be, preferring to spring it on his brother and aunt after dining together. When he was satisfied with his appearance, he hurried down the stairs, pausing at the door to the drawing room where they were chatting.

He swept into the room, bowing before them in a flurry of black silk with a tall, cone-shaped hat perched on his blond curls, making him appear seven feet tall.

"What do you think?"

"Blasphemer!" snapped his aunt.

"Excellent!" laughed Felix.

"How can you say so, Felix? The boy is mocking us!"

"I didn't mean it that way," said Oliver hastily. "I, uh, I meant it as a compliment, Aunt, truly I did!"

She pointed her silver wand at him and said, "Eye of frog and black bat's brain, tell the truth or go insane." She watched him closely for a minute before nodding, satisfied that he was, indeed, telling the truth.

"Just make sure you wear that costume with pride, my boy. It should be Felix wearing it, but he's too stubborn. I'll say a little incantation to make your evening enjoyable, shall I?"

"That would be most welcome, Aunt. Thank you. Felix, are you ready?"

Felix smiled at his brother's boyish eagerness and rose, bending to kiss his aunt on the cheek.

"Are you certain you'll not go with us? It promises to be a special evening."

"No, no, you two run along. I'm just not in the mood for socializing anymore," she said with a sigh for her elder nephew's benefit. Felix rolled his eyes heavenward and motioned to Oliver to accompany him, picking up his black domino and mask from the chair by the door.


The long line of carriages moved slowly toward the lighted portico, Gilly's heartbeat picked up speed each time they plodded forward. She let down the window to allow more air inside the lumbering carriage, and Rose pulled her shawl closer.

With a nervous smile, Gilly fastened the glass again and said, "Coming tonight is rather more daring than I thought, Rose. I can't help thinking how much more pleasant it would be, sitting side by side on your sofa in front of a cheery fire."

"Comfortable is not always a desirable feeling, my dear child. You're just experiencing a case of the fidgets. You'll settle down once we arrive."

"I do hope you are right," said Gilly doubtfully.

The carriage came to its final stop, and a footman threw open the door, letting down the steps and holding out his hand to help them descend.

No turning back now, thought Gilly miserably, wishing she had chosen to wear a domino instead of the white, flowing costume of a Greek shepherdess. She fixed a stony smile on her face, adjusted her half mask, and left the sanctity of the carriage. She supposed this must be how a condemned prisoner felt, leaving the relative safety of his cell.

She swallowed a nervous giggle and turned to watch her godmother's struggle to descend from the carriage dressed as the Virgin Queen, a misnomer if ever there was one, since her godmother had buried three husbands.

Smoothing her voluminous skirts, Rose squared her shoulders and said, "Let us find some champagne, child. This white paint has frozen my face and dried out my mouth, and we haven't even gotten inside yet."

They made their way into the ballroom, which was teeming with costumed guests, too many for the crowded dance floor to hold. The balcony doors had been thrown open, and there were several sets of couples outside struggling to perform the steps of the quadrille on the uneven flagstones of the terrace.

Gilly shrank against the wall, wishing she could step behind the wallpaper and hide. But her godmother pulled her forward, and they edged through the crowd toward a footman carrying a large silver tray. When they reached it, Rose picked up two glasses of champagne and handed them to Gilly.

Then she turned and picked up two more for herself, saying, "Drink one quickly and the other slowly."

Gilly smiled, the sweet expression lighting her eyes and animating her face for any observer to see, even behind the half mask.

"Dutch courage?" she said loudly, not that anyone could actually hear her, but Rose nodded, and the young man next to her, dressed in a ridiculously tall hat, grinned at them.

"May I have the honor of the next dance, divine shepherdess?" asked the young man.

Gilly hesitated. She had come here to dance, and yet the prospect of making polite conversation while remembering the steps was rather too daunting.

"I . . . I shall try my best not to step on your toes," added the young man, his pale green eyes pleading with her.

"I would love to," said Gilly.

Her response erased the youth's doubts, and he said artlessly, "Thank you. I really do appreciate your taking a chance with me, this is my first ball, you see."

"Your first? I would never have guessed," said Gilly kindly.

"Well, I try not to look too excited, you know. Looking bored seems to be the fashion," said Oliver. "Oh, that seems to be the next set. I'm sorry, I don't know what it's to be."

"Sounds like the boulanger," said Gilly, taking his arm.

"Boulanger?" said Oliver in strangled tones.

"Do you not dance the boulanger, Sir Wizard?"

"Well, I have seen it done, and I tried it once, but I'm not sure . . ."

"Come along. We'll muddle through together. I'm afraid you've chosen a partner with two left feet. I shall try, however, not to disgrace either of us."

They began to move through the steps, Oliver counting the rhythm out loud while Gilly tried to keep up with his awkward attempts. His foot came down heavily on the tip of her slipper, narrowly missing her toes.

He turned crimson and stammered, "I am sorry, madam. I hope I haven't crippled you!"

With a jolly laugh, Gilly assured him, "You didn't even touch my toes, Sir Wizard. And I think you're doing splendidly."

Grinning from ear to ear, Oliver proceeded to regale his partner with tales of his former attempts at dancing, laughing at himself with ease. Joining in, Gilly reflected that she could not have picked a better partner than her wizard; she had completely forgotten her own self-consciousness.

The music finally came to an end, and they promenaded around the floor, making little progress because of the great mass of people.

"Tomorrow Lady Beauchamp's ball will be touted as a *sad crush,* and she will be in alt," said Gilly. "Thank you for my dance, Sir Wizard," she added.

Oliver bowed over her hand, saying, "The pleasure was all mine, Lady Shepherdess. But I feel I must correct one misapprehension, I am not a wizard. I am a warlock . . . well, that is what my costume is supposed to represent."

"A warlock?"

"Yes. I'm afraid my aunt was right, I don't think I quite have the look of one, being blond. Now my brother, he's a natural, being dark-haired and rather fearless-looking. Not that I think he really is a warlock, mind you. I am not as foolish as my aunt."

"Your, uh, aunt thinks your brother is a warlock?" asked Gilly, backing away.

"Well, Aunt Felicity is a bit eccentric, she thinks she's a witch, too, but we pay her no heed, I assure you. I mean, I've never seen a single one of her spells work," said Oliver.

"I see. You really must excuse me, sir, uh, Warlock. I think my godmother is calling me."

Gilly turned and fled. How did she always find these strays? Or rather, how did they always find her? She needed to be more careful in the future. A warlock, indeed!

There was a shifting of the tide as the musicians struck up the next song. Knights in shining armor and swashbuckling pirates took Grecian goddesses and buxom milkmaids in their arms as the waltz began.

Gilly's progress came to a halt as she found herself being propelled backwards, toward the dance floor. Though she struggled against the ruthless tide, she felt someone grasp her hand, and she was pulled toward a man with black, wavy hair and green eyes that glittered behind the slits in his mask. Her attention was drawn to his full lips as he ran his tongue across them. Resisting the urge to lick her own lips, she focused once again on those catlike eyes.

"We might as well surrender," he said, lowering his head to speak into her ear. "We'll never make it out alive," he added, grinning.

"I suppose not," she said breathlessly as she felt him slip his arm around her waist. His touch robbed her of her voice, and she studied the broad, domino-clad chest, refusing to meet his eyes.

She had never danced the waltz with a gentleman before, but she agreed with all she had heard about it being scandalous and sinful. She was crushed against his broad chest, and she could well believe, were she not a virtuous lady, that such deportment might lead to impure thoughts. No wonder some mothers refused to allow their daughters to dance the waltz. Why, they were so close, she could feel the beating of his heart, the warmth of his breath on her cheek.

Gilly chanced a quick glance around her. Most of the other couples were not quite so close together as they were. She wriggled in his grasp, but he held her fast.

"Quite a crowd here tonight," he said, looking down at the top of her head, where a cluster of blond ringlets bounced with each step.

"I suppose you enjoy masquerade balls?"

She nodded.

"One meets all manner of people at these things."

Again the silent nod.

After several frustrating minutes, he said, "I was under the impression that you and my brother were engaging in a sparkling conversation when you danced a moment ago. What's the matter? Has the cat got your tongue?"

She glanced up for a mere second before dropping her gaze again and saying, "Your brother? You mean the warlock?"

"Yes, the warlock. He's a little shy; I was surprised to see him so animated. I thought to myself that it would take a very experienced partner to set him at ease while he danced. You must be very good at setting young men at ease. I would guess you're quite a talented young woman."

Gilly frowned. Talented young woman. Not lady.

"You are very bold, sir. I don't think I approve of your tone—or your choice of words."

"If I have offended, I beg your pardon, madam. But now

that I am closer, I can see that you are not a young girl, and knowing how shy my brother is, I can only assume . . . Everyone knows that, by its very nature, a masked ball is less exclusive in its guest list. All sorts of people may be present. Oliver is such an innocent, I wouldn't wish for him to fall victim to the first pretty face he sees."

"You beg my pardon on the one hand and choose to insult me in the next breath, sir? A pity you are not the gentleman your brother is."

Her breasts were heaving indignantly against his chest, and Felix eyed the smooth, ivory flesh appreciatively. But he had a task to perform and needed to keep his purpose in sight if he wanted to steer this lightskirt away from his naive brother.

He dragged his eyes back to her pink-cheeked face and drawled, "If I were as green as my brother, then I daresay our conversation would progress a trifle differently. But I am not a good-natured, gullible lad just up to Town for the first time. Now, if you have some . . . shall we say, *business* to conduct at this ball, then you have my blessing, even my best wishes, madam. But pray, do not make the mistake of thinking my brother would be an easy mark. He is not without protection."

"You think I'm some sort of . . ."

"Lightskirt? Yes, I'm afraid I do. The game is up, you have been found out," said Felix bluntly.

"Why, I . . . you coxcomb! You are no gentleman! Good evening, sir," seethed Gilly, wrenching herself from his embrace and fleeing.

Whistling quietly with the music, a pleased Sir Felix Baring made his way toward the refreshment rooms.

Her cheeks flaming, all Gilly could think about was escaping. She finally discovered her elusive godmother, mask discarded, ensconced comfortably in the midst of several of her bosom friends.

"Rose, we must leave immediately!"

Rose smiled at her companions and said, "Ah, the dramatics of the young. Won't you excuse us for a few minutes?" She stood up and took Gilly's arm, propelling her away from her coterie.

"Gilly, really, I know you are no green miss, but surely you don't wish to occasion gossip."

"Of course not," said Gilly, tears springing to her eyes at the mild reproof.

Her godmother was immediately repentant. "There, there, child, I didn't wish to upset you."

Bowing her head, Gilly waved her hand to indicate that this was not the true cause of her distress. "It isn't you," she sniffed.

Rose hissed, "Did someone offer you an insult, my dear?"

Taking a deep breath, Gilly said, "I don't wish to talk about it."

"My dear girl, did someone take liberties with you? I did warn you to be cautious tonight. Men are notorious for taking advantage of a little mask to make advances which they might normally not make. You really can't blame them. Still, they should not take liberties."

Gilly shook her head, beginning to feel silly. Perhaps she had misunderstood the man's comments. Perhaps he hadn't meant anything by them.

"No," she said at last. "I'm not quite certain what he meant, but he did upset me."

"Whatever did he say? And who said it?"

"I don't wish to repeat it. If I misunderstood, I would hate to cast aspersions on the man's reputation."

"But who was it?"

"I . . ." Gilly's eyes widened as the man in the black domino came into view. She turned away while Rose searched the crowd eagerly, but no one stood out from the masses.

"If you'll take my advice, Gilly, you'll only dance with those whom you know."

"But how can I know them when they are all masked? This was a terrible idea!" she hissed.

"I had forgotten how long you have been away in the country. Everyone is unfamiliar to you, but I can tell who many of the people are. Why, how do you think I found my friends?" she asked, pointing to her group.

"That's all well and good, but Rose, I cannot identify anyone. They all look the same!"

"Come here," said Rose, taking her by the arm. "This is Osgood Pemberton; I will introduce you to him and tell him to keep an eye out for you. You know his mother, one of my oldest friends. He will see to it you are well looked after."

"How mortifying," murmured Gilly, fixing the inevitable smile on her face for the introduction to the stiffly proper Mr. Pemberton. He bowed over her hand and asked very prettily for the next dance.

This dance was nothing like the last, the quadrille allowed for little intimate conversation, and when Gilly and Mr. Pemberton did come together, his comments were so innocuous, they bordered on the boring. Gilly told herself that she didn't mind in the least, but her eyes searched constantly for the man in the black domino with the dark, waving hair and the green eyes.

When the music ended, Mr. Pemberton said ponderously, "There is my good friend, Lord Chester. Allow me to present you to him, Miss Gillingham. He will be a most unexceptionable partner for the next dance."

"You are too kind, Mr. Pemberton," said Gilly.

The next two hours were spent in a steady progression of steady, unexceptionable partners making steady, unexceptionable conversation. Though she glimpsed her persecutor from time to time, he had no chance to approach her. In fact, he made no effort to approach her.

Excusing herself from yet another of Mr. Pemberton's well-meaning friends, Gilly once again sought her godmother, whispering desperately, "Rose, we simply must leave."

This time her godmother acquiesced, and they were soon on their way home, Rose chattering about the latest on-dits she had garnered, and Gilly responding from time to time with a quiet "yes" or "no."

When she was finally secure in the haven of her own bed, Gilly reviewed the evening in her mind. She realized she had been anxious about this first real outing, but she had overcome her fears. She had even enjoyed her dance with the young man. From that point on, however, the evening had taken on a bizarre, nightmarish quality, from the outlandish accusations of the warlock's black-haired, cat-eyed brother to the ponderous solemnity of Mr. Pemberton and his monotonous line of acquaintances.

"Oh! Blackie! You scared me, you naughty little puss," said Gilly, pulling the small kitten closer and beginning to scratch it behind the ear. Blackie's quiet purring made Gilly smile, and her racing thoughts quieted.

Suddenly, she sat straight up in the bed, the startled kitten let out a mournful yowl and leapt into the air and skittered across the room.

The warlock! His brother! That's who they were! She closed her eyes and could almost hear the crack of her umbrella over the handsome gentleman's head.

Was that what he had meant about her trying to . . . to ruin his little brother? Did he think she had arranged that meeting in the park? No wonder he thought her a conniving female!

Grinning, Gilly sank back down in the soft feather mattress. It was all a terrible misunderstanding, she thought. She had known there had to be a simple explanation.

Slowly, her smile faded and a frown marred her smooth brow. It still didn't explain away the youth's assertion that his brother was a warlock. Or thought he was a warlock. Or their aunt thought so.

"Argh!" groaned Gilly. How she wished she had never seen the young man and his dratted bully of a brother!

"Meee . . . ooow."

Gilly patted the bed, and the kitten returned, snuggling against her.

"At least I have you, Blackie," she whispered.

She also had dreams of green-eyed men who alternately kissed her and insulted her. The next morning, she awoke bleary-eyed and dispirited. It had not been a very auspicious beginning for her return to Society. On the brighter side, she thought, things had to improve.

They couldn't get any worse.

# TWO

*Double, double, toil and trouble,*
*Add two lovers, stir and let bubble . . .*

"I'm telling you, Felix, if you do not find Francis by week's end, I will summon my gypsy friend, Ismelda."

Felix and Oliver jumped as the door slammed on their aunt's words. They exchanged horrified expressions and shivered.

"Not Ismelda, Felix! You cannot allow her to send for that old witch!" exclaimed the dramatic Oliver, raking his hand through his blond curls.

"She's not a witch any more than Aunt is, but we most certainly don't want her in London. She would rob us blind," grumbled Felix.

"I'm not worried about that. I'm more concerned with being poisoned if she should decide we need one of her famous potions to 'protect' us. You remember the last time? I suffered the worst gastric distress of my entire life. At first I thought I would die, and then I prayed I would!"

"As I recall, she said it was the demons running around your stomach, looking for a way out," said Felix, chuckling and earning a scowl from his brother. "Very well, I'll ask around. Surely someone has seen that young woman about. Look through these invitations and decide which ones might attract such a female."

"Such a female? What the deuce do you mean by that, Felix. As I recall, she was a very fetching thing," said Oliver.

"A very fetching thing," mimicked Felix before adding, "with a large, hard umbrella."

"Aside from that, I'd say she was a diamond of the first water, I just don't remember any details. I'm not even certain I would recognize her if I saw her," said Oliver.

Felix, after a thoughtful moment, said, "As I recall, she was a tiny thing with golden hair, a small mouth, and eyes the color of the summer sky in the country."

Oliver turned his amazed scrutiny on his brother, who colored up—a rare event—and cleared his throat before rising and mumbling something unintelligible about needing to pay his tailor an urgent visit.

Felix did visit Weston in Conduit Street to choose a new coat and to Hoby's to pick up his boots, which were finished, but these activities required so little energy and time, he decided to call in at Gentleman Jackson's Boxing Salon. He was greeted warmly by several acquaintances before being invited to step into the ring by the robust Mr. Belford, who fancied himself Jackson's best pupil. Two rounds later, Belford was lying on the mat, wondering what had become of the light.

Felix left the ring after ascertaining that, not only would Mr. Belford soon be good as new, he now held Sir Felix in higher esteem than before. Still, a restlessness assailed Felix, and he turned into the park for a gallop, not thinking about the fact that it would soon be thronged with people, making any rapid progress almost impossible. Though he didn't care, the sight of the black-haired, black-browed man thundering along on his black steed made heads turn, especially the female ones.

So wrapped up in his thoughts was Felix that he passed by the one female who occupied his thoughts.

Miss Gillingham, upon recognizing the man of her nightmares, turned away quickly so that he might pass her by, hoping that her green gown would allow her to blend in with the shrubbery. She breathed a sigh of relief when he had passed and fought against the tremor of nerves that danced up her spine.

"Warlock, indeed!" she said, causing her maid, who was trailing behind her, to look around sharply.

"Beg pardon, miss?"

"Oh, nothing, nothing," replied Gilly, quickening her pace.

There was no such thing, especially here, in London, on a beautiful day in autumn. She was certainly not one to believe such a farradiddle. She recalled her nanny's tales of witches and goblins that loved to terrify little girls, especially on All Hallow's Eve. But she was grown now and no longer believed in such fairy tales. Still, from time to time, Gilly looked over her shoulder as they made their way back home, foregoing the visits to the shops she had originally planned.

When Gilly heard the door close behind her, she expelled a deep sigh of relief.

"Is something the matter, miss?" asked the butler.

"No, Parsons, nothing is the matter. Where is Mrs. Pargeter?" she said, handing her cloak to the butler.

"In the drawing room, miss, having tea. Shall I send in a fresh pot?"

"Yes, thank you, Parsons," replied Gilly, entering the drawing room and joining her godmother on the sofa.

"Good afternoon, my dear. You're looking a bit windswept," commented her godmother.

"It is a trifle breezy," said Gilly, smiling as Blackie left the warm lap of her godmother and hopped onto her lap instead. "Have you missed me?" she cooed, scratching him behind the ear. He leaned into her fingers, purring loudly. When she stopped, he turned around twice before settling down on her skirts for a nap.

"You'll get black cat hair all over that lovely gown," protested Rose.

"Just like you?" asked Gilly.

"Ah, but I'm not expecting visitors."

"Neither am I," said Gilly, though she reached up and patted her hair.

"But a young lady is always ready, should the occasion arise. By the way, I thought we would attend Lady Forbes's ball this evening. She is a particular friend of mine, you know."

"Among fifty other particular friends," said Gilly with a knowing laugh. "I warn you, Rose, I shan't dance with Mr. Pemberton, I don't care how close you and his mother are. The man's a dead bore. And so are all his friends!"

"Very well, then you may choose your own partners, perhaps you'll find another like the man last night," said her stiff-lipped godmother.

"I do beg your pardon, but they were so prosy. I know they are worthy gentlemen, dearest Rose, and certainly much more admirable than the fiend at the masquerade ball . . ."

"But you would rather take your chances with the fiend," laughed Rose, her good humor restored. "So what shall you wear for your fiend?"

Gilly settled on a silk frock of a deep blue color that brought out her eyes in a most becoming manner. The high-waisted bodice fitted her like a glove, and the full skirt fell in a pleasing bell shape. Rose supplied her with a necklace of gold filigree that twinkled with tiny diamonds. In her blond hair, she wore two short ostrich feathers dyed to match her gown.

She looked at the pleasing image in her mirror, squared her shoulders, and lifted her chin. Tonight, she vowed, she would radiate confidence, poise, charm, and wit.

"Gilly, are you ready, my dear?" called her godmother.

The frightened mouse staring back at her in the mirror squeaked, "Coming!"

Felix leaned against the wall and surveyed the crowded ballroom. Every short blond head that bobbed past him earned a scowl, though they had done nothing to warrant such an expression.

Oliver sauntered by and commented, "Any luck?"

"No, nothing. I don't understand where she can be hiding. I could have sworn her rank would set her among the Ton, but perhaps I misjudged the quality and cut of her gown. After all, I am not usually in the petticoat line. Maybe she's of the demimonde."

"No, she was definitely well-bred, don't you remember that dragon of a chaperone?" said his brother.

"Ah, yes, the chaperone," murmured Felix, shifting his scowl to the cluster of chairs against the far wall, a veritable stronghold of dragonly matrons. "You know, Oliver, maybe I've been looking for the wrong person," he said, pushing off from the wall and marching toward the chairs.

Gilly, who had refused to dance with Mr. Pemberton and, therefore, could not dance at all without offering insult to this worthy gentleman, was surrounded by Rose and her many friends. She had been watching the warlock's scowling surveillance of the ballroom, secure in the knowledge that he would never think to look for her there—not, of course, that she thought he might be searching for her. But now, here he was, his black gaze, intent and dangerous, flitting from one knot of matrons to the next. A tremor of exhilaration scampered up her spine, and she bowed her head, her mind working feverishly, one moment willing him to pass her by, the next, willing him to speak to her.

Felix spied her immediately among the older women, her

golden hair glimmering in the candlelight as she refused to meet his eyes. Who was she trying to fool with that shy miss pose? The little termagant certainly wasn't fooling him!

He bowed before her and said coolly, "Good evening, miss. A word with you, please."

"I beg your pardon, sir. I don't believe you have been introduced to this young lady," said Rose.

Felix dragged his eyes away from the girl's trembling hands and said, "You will pardon me, madam, if I feel an umbrella breaking over my head constitutes some sort of introduction."

"Well, really," said Rose, while her cronies leaned closer, eagerly gathering each line for future repetition.

Gilly chanced a glance up at the scowling gentleman, then wished immediately she had not. When she had been busy rescuing the kitten in the park, and when his face had been obscured by the half mask at the masquerade, she hadn't been thinking properly. Now, in the light of a hundred candles, there was no denying it, never had she seen such a handsome man—or such an angry one! Gilly ducked her head again and tightly clasped her shaking hands in her lap.

"You will not foist me off with any of your maidenly airs, miss," said Felix, wondering at the same moment why he suddenly felt like the villain in an overacted melodrama. But it was too late now, and he added, "I demand you return that dratted cat immediately!"

Defiance flashed in Gilly's blue eyes as she looked up and pronounced bravely, "Never, sir, will I hand over that poor, innocent creature! Why, you probably only want Blackie for one of your spells!"

"My . . . spells?" demanded Felix, almost bereft of speech.

"Yes, or you'll tie a stone around his poor little neck and drown him!"

"Drown him? What the deuce . . ." Blinking at the injustice of her accusation, Felix was suddenly aware of the curious

eyes spearing him from all sides. He hadn't been born yesterday, he knew when to cut line, and this was definitely the
time to retreat. With a growled, "Don't tempt me," he stalked
away.

Gilly sank back in her chair, her face pasty and her pulse
beating a drum. Rose patted her hand and fluttered her fan
back and forth vigorously, muttering, "Well, really," time and
time again.

After Gilly's color had returned, Rose said, "I should take
you home."

"No, no, I'm fine, Rose. I have no intention of going home
just because of some bully."

"Not just any bully," whispered Lady Pemberton, her head
nodding ponderously and sending three long ostrich feathers
bobbing up and down.

"Well, that is all he is to me, and I have no intention of
allowing him to scare me away," said Gilly defiantly.

"I'm glad to hear it; Osgood was saying that he hoped you
would change your mind about dancing, Miss Gillingham, that
you would be feeling more the thing after a little rest. And
look, here he comes now."

"How delightful," murmured Gilly.

Gilly accepted Mr. Pemberton's invitation to dance, knowing that she was opening the floodgates. And just as she
feared, Mr. Pemberton's friends flocked to her side, each demanding a dance. Her face ached with smiling politely. During
the buffet supper, they surrounded her, and though she told
herself to be thankful that she was not a wallflower, she felt
positively petrified with boredom by the time they had finished.

Escaping to the sanctity of the ladies' withdrawing room,
she reveled in the few minutes of silence.

When she returned to the ballroom, her group of swains
had disappeared, and she lurked on the edge of the dance

floor, ducking behind guests who were observing the dancers, trying to be unobtrusive. It didn't work.

"They'll find you," said a deep voice, making her jump.

"You startled me, sir."

"I only meant to warn you," said Sir Felix, a smug grin on his face.

"I have no idea what you are talking about, sir. Nor do I intend to stand here and indulge in such an improper conversation," she replied haughtily.

"Very well," he said, backing up so anyone looking in their direction would be able to spot her easily.

"Villain!" she hissed, ducking behind a pillar.

He chuckled and leaned back to whisper, "If I didn't know better, I would think you were hiding from those worthy gentlemen who have been at such pains to entertain you tonight, Miss, uh . . . Now, what is your name again?"

"Gillingham," she ground out through gritted teeth.

"Miss Gillingham. That's right. Well, Miss Gillingham, have you thought any more about returning my property to me?"

"No, I haven't, sir. Nor do I plan to," said Gilly, amazing herself with her own temerity.

"In that case . . . Mr. Pemberton, isn't it?" called Felix. Gilly cringed and closed her eyes.

"Yes? I'm afraid you have me at a disadvantage, sir," came the ponderous reply.

"No, no, we haven't been introduced formally. But we do have a mutual acquaintance in Miss Gillingham. Well, where is she? She was here just a minute ago," he said, turning and reaching for her hand, dragging her out from her hiding place. "I asked her for a dance, but she told me she was hoping that *you* would ask her for the next dance. Lucky fellow."

Mr. Pemberton puffed out his chest and said, "I am indeed. Miss Gillingham?" He offered her his arm; pasting a smile on her lips, she placed her hand on his sleeve. As he led her away, she stuck out her tongue at her tormentor.

"Tell me, Nephew, did you find the kitten-napper?" demanded Aunt Felicity when Felix walked in the door. He cut his eyes at his brother, and she exclaimed, "Aha! I knew you would find her. So we'll go and get Francis tomorrow?"

"It's not that simple, Aunt," said Felix.

Chuckling, Oliver earned himself a scowl from his brother and a rap on the knuckles with his aunt's fan, but he would not be denied. "No, Aunt, it is not nearly so simple. It seems Felix so frightened the chit that she refuses to return your kitten."

"Why, that is the most absurd thing I have ever heard! Felix? Frighten a kitten-napper?"

"I'm afraid it is so. She said something ludicrous about my casting a spell on the kitten or some such rubbish. I begin to doubt the girl's sanity."

"Well, we shall see about that," said his aunt, rising and making for the door with a militant gleam in her eyes.

"Where are you going?" demanded her nephews in unison.

"I am going to that ball to demand the return of your father!"

They were before her at the door, gently turning her back toward the sofa.

"Really, Aunt, it is too late to go to the ball," said Felix.

"And you're not dressed for it," added Oliver.

"And you declined the invitation," put in Felix.

"Bah! As if I care about that! I am Felicity Baring, I am welcome everywhere!"

"Of course you are, Aunt, but it is very late, and you would have to change, and we have no way of knowing if Miss . . . if the girl is still there," said Felix, relaxing slightly as his aunt leaned against the back of the sofa.

"What is her name?" she demanded suddenly.

"Her, uh, name?"

"Yes, her name," said his aunt, peering at him intently.

"I . . . I'm afraid I don't know. I didn't think to find out," he lied, feeling his cravat tighten beneath her relentless gaze.

"That was not very clever, my boy," she said finally. "I can see that I will be forced to take matters into my own hands."

"Not the gypsy," whispered Oliver.

"No, I have decided I will accept every invitation we receive until I discover this kitten-napper and bring her to justice! And you, Felix, will accompany me to identify the culprit!" Aunt Felicity rose and sailed majestically toward the door, a flurry of silk scarves waving farewell to her dismayed nephews.

"Now you've done it," muttered Oliver, when the door had closed on their eccentric relative.

"I don't care," replied Felix, rising and seeking refuge in the closest decanter of port. "If Aunt Felicity wants to confront her kitten-napper, let her! I'm washing my hands of the whole matter."

Oliver's laughter goaded Felix to add mendaciously, "And you can help her! If it weren't for your foolish scheme to take that blasted cat on a carriage ride, none of this would have happened! So *you* can go with Aunt Felicity! And *you* can help her confront that beautiful little she-devil!" Throwing a final scowl at his brother, Felix stormed from the room.

"Whew," murmured Oliver, idly scratching the ear of the black and white cat that hopped into his lap. "Brother Felix must be forming quite a *tendre* for this nameless little chit; I don't know when I've ever known him to pronounce a girl beautiful." He turned the cat's face so she faced him and asked, "Have you, Brunhilda? No, I didn't think so. I must say, this time away from my studies is proving most entertaining after all."

"I don't care what you say, Rose, the man is a menace! I declare I have never been more frightened!" said Gilly when they were sharing a cup of tea the next morning.

"Now, Gilly, he only wants his kitten back," said the sensible older woman.

But Gilly would have none of it, replying, "Perhaps if he had come to me with a civil request, I would have been happy to give the little dear back to him. But as things stand now, I dare not! Indeed, should I give him back, I would fear for Blackie's life!"

"Heavens, Gilly, do say you haven't been taken in by that rubbish his younger brother said to you at the masquerade."

"Well, I daresay that is an exaggeration, but it is unsettling, all the same. What's more, I told you what that man said to me at the masked ball. . . ." She gave a delicate shudder and shook her head, adding, "No, I don't see how I can turn Blackie over to the beast now!"

"Hopefully, we shan't meet him again. Surely he will not attend the small card party we have been invited to tonight. And tomorrow, the Harknesses's ball will be such a sad crush, we should be safe there."

"I hope you are right, Rose. I don't think I could bear another such encounter. By the way, what did your friends have to say about the matter? Were any of them acquainted with the man?" Although Gilly affected only a casual interest, she waited intensely for her godmother's response.

"Althea thinks he is the late Francis Baring's son. And I agreed that his eyes are the same odd shade of green, almost gold. She said he was knighted for bravery or some such thing."

"His father?"

"No, this one. He is Sir Felix Baring."

"Meow," said Blackie, hopping into Gilly's lap and rubbing his chin against hers before sitting on his haunches and staring up at her as if about to speak.

"You, sir, have been the cause of a great deal of trouble. Perhaps I should have named you Trouble instead of Blackie."

"Meow," came his mournful reply.

"It's a shame he can't talk and tell you whether he wants to remain with you or go back to the black-browed warlock," said Rose with a youthful giggle.

Blackie turned around twice before settling onto Gilly's lap for a short nap while she stroked his soft fur.

"I think this says it all," murmured Gilly.

Gilly sat up and threw the pillow across the room with a growl of frustration. For the past few nights, her sleep had been punctuated by wild nightmares about the despicable Sir Felix Baring tormenting her in ways she could not describe to another living soul. Had her dreams been of murder or mayhem, she would have laughed at them, but they were of soft, whispered conversations that she could not quite make out, looks that bespoke a depth of feelings unlike any she had ever experienced, and delicious touches that thrilled her in ways she had never known.

Now he was even disturbing her lie-down, a rest she most desperately needed if she was to look her best for the Hark-nesses's ball—not that she was worried about being unable to attract any eligible *partis*—not with the ever-present Os-good Pemberton in attendance. Lord Pemberton had assured her at the card party that he would be looking out for her, and with him lurking over her, no other gentleman dared to approach her. He allowed his friends to dance with her, but otherwise, he guarded her like a dog with a bone, sitting by her side and frowning down at any gentleman he didn't approve.

Sir Felix had not attended the card party, but he had been by her side in her thoughts. And when she did manage to banish him from her consciousness, another nagging voice mocked her, wondering why a man she certainly couldn't like was so unrelenting in occupying her mind.

"Oh, bother," she said to Blackie as he watched her run a brush through her golden curls. In the glass, she could see her ballgown hanging on the hook in the dressing room. It was a deep amethyst gown with a low décolletage and tiny, puffed sleeves. Rose had warned that it looked too much like a mourning gown, but Gilly had embroidered tiny gold flowers along the neck and hemline, and she had purchased long gold gloves and gold slippers to complete the ensemble. For a necklace, she had a choker of gold ribbon with a single amethyst in the center. No, the effect was nothing like mourning; if anything, it was a daring costume for an unmarried lady, even though she was three and twenty. Gilly thought it the most elegant gown she had ever owned, just looking at it made her smile, made her quiver with excitement and anticipation about the ball to come. She rose and gave the bell-rope a hearty pull, suddenly anxious to begin the night's adventures.

"For heaven's sake, Aunt, surely we don't need to attend all three in one evening. I mean, the Harknesses's ball will be quite enough for me."

"Felix, I declare you are older than I am. If I am willing to go to a rout, a card party, and a ball in one evening, then I don't see why you should cavil. And what about you, Oliver, my boy. Don't you want to go to all three? Or are you as fragile as Felix?" she demanded, leaning forward so the carriage lights made her eyes shine like embers.

"No, Aunt. I mean, yes. What I mean is, Aunt, I really don't relish the thought of attending three different affairs, especially when all you really want to do is find this elusive kitten-napper."

"Exactly," said Felix. "I think we should just go to the ball. Everyone who is anyone is bound to be there, sooner or later. If we try to make all three, we may simply be chasing the kitten-napper about all evening and never catch up. The ball, however, is bound to lure them."

"You have a point, my boy. I'm glad to see you're thinking. Or did you perhaps receive some message from Francis," said their aunt, regarding her nephew with an intensity that made him grimace.

"Perhaps I did," he rejoined, causing her to cackle gleefully. "One more thing I have been wanting to say to you, Aunt."

"What is it, dear boy?"

"Would you please refrain from waving your, uh, wand around when Waverly is in the vicinity? I really do not want to find myself without a valet, and he has been with me forever."

"I don't know what you're talking about! I never threatened him, I just used it to encourage him to see that you dress with a little more flair, Felix. I mean, what do you call that thing you are wearing tonight?"

"I call it a coat, a waistcoat, pantaloons, and a cravat," he replied. "What would you have me wear? A cassock and a wizard's hat?"

"Certainly not! That would make you look ridiculous! But is there any reason you can't dress with a little more color? Why, look at Oliver."

At this, Oliver shifted uncomfortably in the opposite seat.

"What about him?"

"Well, his coat is a lovely shade of purple. And that waistcoat, quite the work of art," she added with a smile for her younger nephew. "Next to him, can you not see how dull your black and white must appear?"

"I was hoping for dignified," said Felix. "I'm sorry if you don't approve of my attire, Aunt, but I am aiming to please myself, not anyone else."

"And you are pleased with this?"

"Completely. Now, will you please leave my valet alone?"

"As you wish, Felix. Only get back my Francis, your father, and you may dress as you please," said Aunt Felicity.

"Thank you. Ah, here we are," he said with relief.

Felix helped his aunt up the high steps and escorted her to a group of acquaintances. Leaning close to her ear, he whispered, "I will look for the lady, when I have located her, I will try and manage an introduction for you so you may have a quiet word or two."

Clutching at his hand, she said, "Thank you, dear boy. I know you think me a bothersome old lady, but I have been nearly frantic with worry over your father."

"I know, Aunt. But I'm certain we'll be able to work things out with the lady in question. Just enjoy yourself. I'll be back soon."

Felix searched through the various bands of chaperones, but the elusive kitten-napper was nowhere to be seen, nor was her chaperone, a daunting sign. He judged the wide marble stairway leading into the Harknesses's ballroom the best vantage point and climbed to the third step to scan the room.

"There you are, Sir Felix!" exclaimed Lady Harkness, pulling in her wake her youngest daughter. "You remember Amy, of course," she added, pushing the girl toward him.

Amy gave him a winsome smile, which reminded Felix of a sick goat he had once had. She was a tall girl with wispy blond curls that framed her face, a charming look, no doubt, if he was interested, which he was not.

"Good evening, Sir Feliths," she lisped.

"Good evening, Amy. How delightful to see you again. You

have much changed from the little girl in a torn frock with her front teeth missing."

A musical trill of laughter, very likely achieved through hours of practice, greeted this observation, and mother and daughter gazed expectantly upon him. Felix refrained from snorting his disgust as he fulfilled his social obligation and asked the girl for a dance.

"Only look, my dear. You have the waltz free," smiled the mother.

"How delightful. Until then," said Felix, backing away with a half bow.

He nearly tripped down the steps, colliding with a solid object and latching on to prevent an embarrassing tumble. Turning hastily to beg pardon, Felix found himself gazing into the blue eyes he had been searching for so diligently.

"You!" breathed Gilly.

"You!" echoed Felix. "Just the person I was looking for."

"I . . . that is, I believe my godmother needs me. Excuse me."

"Wait!"

But it was too late. The crowd had swallowed her up once more. Frowning furiously, Felix pivoted and demanded of the startled Harkness girl, "Do you know that young lady?"

With a practiced pout, she lisped, "That ith Gertrude Gillingham, a spinsther from the country."

"Thank you," said Felix, hurrying away to find his aunt.

"She's here," he said in hushed tones. His aunt looked about them expectantly, and Felix shook his head. "I mean she is at the ball. I spoke to her, but she got away before I could bring her to you."

"What is her name? Did you find out?"

"Her name is Gillingham," he replied, unable to keep the girl's identity a secret any longer. "But you can't just rush up to her, Aunt. You'll frighten her."

"Frighten her? Nonsense!" she said. Pursing her lips and

frowning, Aunt Felicity murmured, "Gillingham? I knew a Gillingham once, I wonder if she could be his daughter. Thank you, my boy, I will take it from here."

Suddenly uneasy, Felix warned, "Please, Aunt, we don't want to make a scene—especially over a silly thing like a kitten."

Aunt Felicity favored him with a haughty sniff and snapped, "I cannot believe you still do not accept the fact that Francis is . . ."

"I know, I know. I only meant that we don't wish to spoil the Harknesses's ball. After all, they are our neighbors."

"Nonsense, my boy. This ball could do with a bit of livening up," she said with a wicked grin, but she shook her head at his look of horror and added, "Don't worry so, Felix. While you know there is no love lost between me and our hostess, I have no intention of making her dull ball memorable."

With this, Felix had to be satisfied. He turned to watch as couples began to take to the floor again. It was the waltz and Felix, ever one to do his duty, excused himself to find Amy Harkness.

"I wath afwaid you had forgot," said this young lady as he led her onto the dance floor.

"Certainly not," he replied crisply.

"Good, because I would have been tho dithapointed," she replied with another wide-eyed stare.

"It is most extraordinary, Amy, I mean, Miss Harkness, but I don't remember you having a lisp when we were growing up."

She giggled, a natural sound this time instead of the musical trill. "That ith because I didn't. Don't you know? Lisping ith the fashion, Sir Felix."

"Well, it's a demmed silly fashion."

She responded with a wounded look that made Felix want to kick himself. After all, if the chit wanted to make a fool of herself, he certainly didn't care. But he couldn't bear to play the bully, and he forced a smile.

"That is, Miss Harkness, I think you'll find most gentlemen prefer rational conversation over such gibberish when conversing with a pretty young lady."

Her face began to glow attractively at this latest compliment, and Felix restrained a groan. The last thing he needed was to set up a flirtation with a child like this.

With what he hoped she would take as big brotherly advice, he added, "You just try talking sense to the next young man you meet, Amy, and I wager you'll have him sitting in your pocket in no time."

"How kind of you to say so, Sir Felix," she responded with a maidenly blush.

Really, she was quite a pretty girl if she would just be herself. She had not the beauty of Miss Gillingham, of course. Where Amy Harkness's coloring was like a watercolor, Miss Gillingham's was the vibrant splash of blue and gold in a summer landscape. He wondered suddenly what she looked like when she was smiling, it would be nothing short of spectacular, he fancied.

"Sir Felix? Shouldn't we be moving a little faster?" squeaked Miss Harkness, gazing up at him adoringly.

He was holding her much too tightly for propriety, and their progress around the floor had all but ceased. Other couples passed by in a whirl, and Felix, with a grin at his own foolishness, set her away from him and began to twirl her through the mass of dancers with great energy.

He asked about her brothers, her mother, her father. He asked about the pony she had loved so when she was a child. He made innocuous comments about the weather, the latest on-dits, anything to keep from asking himself what the deuce he was about to allow a girl he didn't really know to dominate his thoughts. Miss Gillingham had a great deal to answer for!

The music finally came to a halt, and Felix returned Miss Harkness to her mother, sketching a hasty bow before he retreated.

His gaze went immediately to the knot of matrons where his aunt had been seated. She was gone, and he scanned the assemblage for that telltale headdress of black sprinkled with tiny silver stars. He frowned when he spied her, for she was just disappearing through the terrace doors.

Felix hurried across the room, threading his way through the squares of couples just standing up for the quadrille. When he stepped onto the terrace, there was no sign of his aunt. The evening was too chilly for most of the guests, though a few couples had braved the cool breeze for a few minutes of privacy. In the garden beyond, gay lanterns fluttered here and there.

Seeing a movement, Felix hurried down the stone steps and along the garden path. He could hear his aunt before he could see her; they were separated by a thick row of shrubbery.

"Blast," he muttered.

"So you see, my girl, you really must give my brother back to me."

"I keep telling you, Miss Baring, I do not have your brother!" came the shrill reply.

"But you do, Miss Gillingham. That kitten you took is Francis, my late brother!" exclaimed Aunt Felicity, her patience ebbing. "My nephew will attest to this, or he should. He is, after all, a warlock, too, just like Francis was."

"A warlock?"

"Yes, and I am a witch, but that is neither here nor there. Really, Miss Gillingham, you must give me back my brother."

"I'm very sorry, Miss Baring, but I don't think I can do that. Blackie is just a sweet little kitten; I simply can't approve of his being made into a warlock."

Looking for a break in the bushes, Felix grinned at this. Here was the same girl from the park, the girl who had defiantly told him that she would never return his kitten. He liked her much better than that shy thing who couldn't find the courage to look up at him.

But Felix's amusement was short-lived as his aunt replied, "Then Miss Gillingham, I shall be forced to measures I don't usually like to employ. Eye of bat, knee of . . ."

"No, Aunt!" shouted Felix, crashing through the greenery.

"Felix!"

A shrill scream issued from Miss Gillingham, and she picked up her skirts and fled.

"Felix!"

"Not now, Aunt!" he said, following in Miss Gillingham's wake.

He caught up with her in a secluded corner of the garden. Flanked on one side by a high fence and on the other by an ornamental pond, there was no escape except past him.

Breasts heaving from her precipitous flight, Gilly watched his approach warily.

"I don't believe in witches and warlocks and such!" she declared, more to convince herself than him.

"Of course you don't, Miss Gillingham. Neither do I."

She frowned. "But you are one. I mean, your brother and your aunt think you are."

"No, no, not my brother. Oliver knows better."

"But your aunt . . ."

"My aunt is a dotty old lady who has nothing better to do than play at being a witch. I assure you, Miss Gillingham— that is such a long name for someone as petite as you are—I assure you, my aunt is no more capable of casting spells than I am."

When this admission didn't have the desired effect, Felix added, "I mean, no more capable than you would be."

He reached for her hand, but she backed away.

Exasperated, Felix said, "Don't be foolish, Miss Gillingham. I merely want to escort you back to the ball. I can't very well leave you out here by yourself."

"I . . . I can find my way," she replied.

Frowning, Felix said, "Don't be foolish. You might trip and fall. Allow me to . . ."

Gilly took one more step away from the sweet ogre of her dreams; it was one step too many.

"Oh!" she screamed as her foot slipped on the edge of the ornamental pond. She reached out for him, but it was too late. With a splash, she sat down in the cold water.

"Are you all right?" asked Felix, reaching out to pull her to her feet.

She didn't move. Anger lit her eyes, he could even see it in the moonlight.

"I did warn you," he said. Felix crossed his arms, putting one hand up to cover his mouth so she could not see his grin.

Gilly snatched her hand back, continuing to glare up at her nemesis. "I suppose you'll say you cast a spell over me and caused me to fall into the pool!" she snapped.

"I wouldn't dream of it, Miss Gillingham. I think you managed this all on your own," he said, a small chortle escaping.

"Beast! Help me out of here!" she commanded furiously.

"Your wish is my command, my fair lady." As light as a feather, he thought, as he pulled her up.

She came to rest against his chest, and Gilly gave a grunt of satisfaction in knowing she was soaking his black coat and wilting his starched cravat.

Felix's eyes narrowed to slits as he studied her rebellious face. The effect was quite ruined when her teeth began to chatter. Removing his damp coat, he placed it around her narrow shoulders before leading her back toward the house.

"No!" she exclaimed, wrenching out of his grasp. "I can't go through there!"

"Don't be nonsensical. It is the shortest way to the carriages."

"But everyone will see us!"

"And do you care so much for that?" he asked derisively.

"No! I mean, yes. But a lady has to care about appearances."

"Well, then we will just stay out here and allow you to freeze, shall we?"

"I shan't freeze," she said, throwing back her head to glare at him again, but once again a fit of shivering overtook her, completely ruining the point she was trying to make.

"Enough!" Felix picked her up, tightly clamping her wiggling body against his chest as he headed for the bright lights. She ducked her head against his chest, mumbling vows of dire consequences against his saturated shirt.

Ignoring all the exclamations and curious inquiries, Felix didn't pause until he reached his carriage. His sleepy footman sprang to open the door, and he thrust Gilly inside, turning to give instructions to the footman to find his brother and apprise him of the situation.

When Felix climbed in, he found his drenched kitten-napper huddled in the corner, her teeth chattering so that he was moved to tell the coachman to "spring 'em."

Gilly tried to move away from him when he began rubbing her arms vigorously, but Felix pulled her roughly into his lap.

"Please, Miss Gillingham. I am only trying to warm you." He pulled the lone carriage rug over her and continued his efforts.

"On the Peninsula, one of the worst combinations was cold and damp. Men died from it regularly. Not that I think you will, of course," he continued conversationally. "No, you'll soon be in front of a warm fire, tucked up in bed. . . ." On this thought, the carriage grew silent.

Finally, the chattering stopped, and Gilly lifted her head from his chest, saying a weak, "Thank you."

"You're welcome," he murmured, momentarily diverted by the fragrance of her hair. Felix lifted one golden curl and asked, "Lavender?"

She nodded, leaning back farther to gaze into his eyes.

"I've always liked lavender," he said, his eyes on her lips before he captured them for a warm, gentle kiss.

A second's hesitation was erased as she returned the pressure of his mouth, tentatively at first, then with more ardor. A moment later, Felix pulled away, his breathing ragged.

The carriage slowed, then halted, and the lights on either side of her godmother's front door filled the carriage. Felix hastily set her back on the seat and hopped to the ground when the footman opened the door.

"Thank you for seeing me home, Sir Felix," said Miss Gillingham, as regal as a princess as she offered him her hand to bow over.

When she began to shrug out of his coat, he said, "Keep it, Miss Gillingham; I'll get it later. I do hope you will come to no harm from this evening's mishap, and I do apologize . . . for everything."

Gilly stiffened at this and turned to go. With each step, she wracked her brain for some witty rejoinder, some tidbit that would bring him back again.

He was still there, watching her progress. She could feel his eyes on her.

Suddenly, she looked over her shoulder and favored him with an impish grin. "My friends call me Gilly, you know," she called and then disappeared into the house.

With a shout of laughter, Felix climbed into the carriage and whistled his way home.

# THREE

*Is she kind as she is fair?*
*For Beauty lives with kindness:*
*Love doth to her eyes repair*
*To help him of his blindness,*
*And being helped, inhabits there.*
　　　　　　　　　—WILLIAM SHAKESPEARE

Gilly ignored the look of surprise on the servants' faces and danced her way up the stairs and to her room, where she divested herself of the sodden coat, placing it lovingly over the delicate chair at her escritoire. She hummed quietly while her maid dressed her for bed, tutting over the state of her clothes.

"Achoo! Achoo!"

"Tch, tch, you really should have a soak in a nice, hot tub, miss, as well as a hot cup of tea with a dash of rum in it."

"Whatever you think best, Betsy."

After wrapping her mistress in a wool blanket, the maid hurried away to see to the preparations for the bath. Gilly floated toward the bed, hopping up on it and flopping back with a contented sigh.

What a lovely kiss it had been, not that she had ever kissed anyone like that before. Certainly her fiancé hadn't attempted to kiss her on the lips, settling instead for a chaste peck on the cheek or on her forehead. This was prescribed behavior, according to her governess, and Gilly had never questioned it. Had she known how delightful it was to kiss and be kissed, she and Mr. Ward might have . . . but no, she couldn't imagine the staid Mr. Ward kissing her like Sir Felix had.

And then, as if his own behavior had shocked him, he had apologized, letting her know that he truly hadn't meant to behave in such a shocking manner, but had been unable to restrain himself. After all, there she was, so close at hand, shivering in that dark, enclosed carriage. How could he help himself?

Gilly sat up, frowning and biting at her lower lip.

Betsy returned, still tut-tutting, and led the way to the dressing room, where the fire now roared and the steam from the copper tub beckoned invitingly. Gilly allowed herself to be helped into the warm water, but her mind was too troubled to appreciate the luxury of her bath. Betsy set about washing her mistress's hair, rinsing it with bucketful after bucketful of warm, scented lavender water.

The fragrance recalled Felix's words, and Gilly felt tears spring to her eyes; she whisked them away impatiently.

"Betsy, you are married, are you not?" she asked.

"Yes, miss, to John Tubbs at home."

"Don't you miss him when you come to town with me?"

"O' course I do, but I wouldn't let anyone else look after you, miss."

"Because it's your job?"

"No, miss, because I want to. I've been with you too long, why, you're almost like my own daughter, though I'm too young to have a grown child, of course," said the woman proudly.

"Of course," agreed Gilly. She was silent for a moment while her mind worried away. Finally, she asked, "Do you believe in love at first sight?"

"Oh, yes, miss. My mum and dad, they met on a Sunday

at chapel, and he asked her t' marry him the next day. They had ten children and never a cross word. I think the only time my dad ever got angry with my mother was when she died before him." The maid wiped her eyes and turned to pick up the large towel that was warming by the fire. It enveloped the petite Gilly with warmth. Betsy set about toweling the golden hair and then brushed it by the fire until it was almost dry before plaiting it.

Soon Gilly was dressed in a warm flannel nightgown and tucked up in bed with the promised cup of tea, laced with some sort of rum or brandy.

Watching Betsy straighten the room, Gilly gathered up her courage and asked casually, "What do you think about kissing?"

The abigail shook her finger at her mistress and said, "I knew more went on tonight than you said, miss, or you wouldn't be asking such silly questions."

"But Betsy, if I don't ask, how am I to know? I mean, you remember my old governess, Miss Nelson. She warned me never to allow a man to kiss me, not until I was wed. And I have lived by that . . . until tonight."

Betsy broke off her tidying and said quietly, "As to what that Miss Nelson said, miss, I have always been of the opinion that a girl needs to know a little something—not too much, mind you—in order to make up her mind about a fellow. A kiss is not such a great thing."

"Oh, I think it is a very great thing!" exclaimed Gilly dreamily.

The maid laughed and shook her finger at her mistress again. "You mustn't allow a kiss to rule your heart, miss. Love should come first."

With this, Betsy left the room, pausing at the door to add, "Wait until morning before you decide what that kiss meant. It may look very different to you in the light of day. Now, you just get a good night's sleep."

"Thank you, Betsy."

Gilly continued to lie in her warm bed, but sleep was elusive, and she welcomed her godmother's entrance with relief, popping up in the bed again and patting the side of it.

Rose Pargeter had buried three husbands; if anyone could help Gilly sort out her strange feelings about that kiss and the apology, then surely it was Rose. And couldn't they talk about all manner of things? But Rose's reaction startled Gilly.

"Kissed you? The scoundrel! Well, he shall marry you, my girl. I will see to that! I will write to your father immediately and I shall pay a call on this rake first thing in the morning!"

"Oh please, Rose, you mustn't! I never meant for you to do all that!"

"But the man has to pay for his sin! And I understand from Agatha that he is worth a tidy sum, too," she added with a grunt of satisfaction.

"I don't care if he is as rich as Croesus, Rose, I will not marry the man just because he kissed me!"

"But he is honor bound!" her godmother protested.

"I don't care what he is! And besides that, he apologized for everything!"

This admission gave Rose pause, and she pursed her lips, favoring her goddaughter with a look of pity.

Gilly frowned and demanded, "What is wrong?"

"He offered you an apology for everything?" she asked.

"Yes," whispered Gilly, leaning closer, a worried frown wrinkling her forehead. "What do you think he meant by that, Rose? I must admit, it has me puzzled."

"Well, he probably just came to his senses and remembered he was supposed to be a gentleman," replied Rose.

"You're making that up; you don't think that at all," moaned Gilly, flopping back against the pillows and pulling the counterpane up under her chin. "It means he's sorry he ever met me, and sorry he ever kissed me, and even sorry I have his aunt's dratted cat!"

As if she had conjured up this little ball of fur, he leapt onto the bed and began purring for all he was worth, rubbing his chin against hers and kneading the edge of the covers.

Gilly reached out and cuddled him, saying, "Never you mind, Blackie. I have no intention of handing you over to the ogre."

"Perhaps you should," said Rose, reaching out to pet the kitten and pat Gilly's head. "I mean, that way you would never have to see him again—the ogre, not Blackie."

"I don't want to give up Blackie, but I feel certain his aunt, who is probably unhinged, will never give up. She thinks Blackie is her late brother, she even calls him Francis. Is it any wonder I ran away from her?"

"There, you see, it might be better to return him and be rid of the whole family!" said Rose. "Think about it, my dear. I'll let you get some sleep now. Good night."

"Good night, Rose."

Sleep? How could she possibly sleep with that kiss and the apology that followed hanging over her head? For what offense or offenses had he been apologizing? Did he mean he was sorry to have kissed her?

This disturbing possibility led to the next conjecture: perhaps she had done such a poor job of it, he wished he hadn't bothered. Surely that wasn't the case, surely he had received some measure of pleasure from their kiss. Judging from the profound effect their kiss had had on her, surely he could not have remained unmoved.

Gilly did just as her godmother advised and spent most of the remaining hours before dawn thinking of nothing else but that kiss, Sir Felix's apology, and whether she should return the kitten, never seeing the Baring family again.

Never see Sir Felix Baring again; the very idea made her ache with yearning. Hugging the sleeping kitten, whose eyes reminded her so forcefully of Sir Felix, she could almost be-

lieve he was a warlock. He had certainly succeeded in bewitching her!

"Felix, where did you disappear to?" demanded his aunt,
sailing into his private sitting room after a cursory knock on
the door.

Waverly, turning down the covers in the bedroom, gave a
little squeak of dismay and scurried to close the adjoining
door.

"What is the matter with him?"

"I believe, dear Aunt, that you have bullied him once too
often and he now refuses to so much as look at you."

"Fainthearted twit," she murmured before rounding on her
nephew again, her wand menacing him as she pointed it at
his nose. Felix reached up and wrested it from her grasp.

"I believe I have been bullied once too often, too," he said
dryly. "I will keep the wand."

"Felix, how could you? Would you turn against your own
aunt?"

"No, only against this absurd notion that you are a witch.
I know you believe it," he added hastily, putting up his hand
to deter her rebuttal, "but you must admit it has caused us
nothing but trouble this evening. If you had merely reasoned
with Miss Gillingham instead of frightening her half to death,
you might have your precious kitten home with you right now,
and I would have . . . well, never mind."

"Whatever is the matter with you, Felix? I have never
known you to be so dispirited. Are you sickening with something?" she asked, placing the back of her hand against his
forehead just as she had done when he was a child.

With a nostalgic smile, Felix took her hand and kissed it.
Shaking his head, he threw off his sudden despondency and
said, "Never mind, Aunt. Don't let my mood distress you, it
will pass as quickly as it came."

"I do hope so, I hate to see either one of my boys in the doldrums. And Oliver . . . well, only wait until you see him."

As if on cue, Oliver waltzed through the open door and plopped into the nearest chair, one long leg dangling over the arm. With a foolish grin, he said, "Hullo, all. Wasn't that a perfectly brilliant ball?"

"Well enough, Brother, though parts of it were a trifle too exciting for me. But that is not, I presume, what you're referring to, is it? Do tell us exactly what it was about this particular ball that made it so brilliant?"

"Oh, everything. The champagne, the night air, the music."

"Oh, good. I was afraid you might have done something foolish like forming a *tendre* for some chit of a girl."

"She's hardly a chit of a girl," said Oliver dreamily. Sitting up suddenly on the edge of his chair, he enthused, "She's quite a beauty and like to be the belle of the Season next spring. I vow, I should snap her up quickly before some other chap discovers her. I mean, with that gorgeous blond hair and those blue eyes, she won't last long on the old Marriage Mart."

"Marriage!" exclaimed their aunt. "You're much too young to be wed, Oliver!"

"Blond hair and blue eyes," said Felix, frowning fiercely. What the deuce was his little brother about, falling in love with the same girl he had?

Felix's eyes widened at the thought. He, Felix Baring, in love? It was absurd, to be sure. He couldn't possibly be in love with Miss Gillingham, or rather, Gilly. He hardly knew her. Why, they hadn't exchanged more than two dozen words. No, to even consider such a possibility was absurd, absolutely absurd.

"Just who is this paragon?" asked Aunt Felicity.

"Amy Harkness, of course," breathed Oliver, causing his older brother to snort with relief. "Didn't you notice? We danced together twice. I would have made it three times, but her mother wouldn't allow it. Instead, she slipped away, and we met in the garden."

"An illicit tryst? I don't think much of a girl who cares so little for her reputation. Besides, Oliver, you are entirely too young."

"I am not!"

"Yes, you are," said Felix. Rising, he shepherded his bickering visitors to the door of his sitting room, adding firmly, "And I am too old for such nonsense so late at night. Go to bed, we can certainly discuss all this in the morning."

"But Felix, what about Francis?"

"In the morning."

"And Amy, I mean, Miss Harkness. What should I do about her?"

"Nothing for tonight, Oliver. Just go to bed, get some sleep."

"Sleep? Who can sleep at a time like this?" asked his brother as he shut the door.

Felix had no plans to sleep, of course. He walked to the window and threw it open, welcoming the chill, autumn air on his face. In all his years as a soldier, he had never ached for a woman the way he did now.

He expelled a hollow laugh. He had never had to ache; having been a presentable sort of fellow, he had been able to quench any aches rather easily. But this was different.

Closing the window, he retraced his steps and sat down in front of the fire. How he wished he was as young and foolish as Oliver, able to admit his love, to enjoy it. Instead, he was the cool-headed one, the rational one. His head told him he couldn't possibly love Miss Gillingham on the strength of one broken umbrella and a good soaking in an ornamental pond. Love took more than that . . . didn't it?

But Felix had never been one to wallow in despair. Perhaps he had gone about this all wrong, but there was nothing to prevent him from waging a campaign and winning the lady who had stolen his heart. He would court her, he would woo her.

Spying his aunt's silver wand on the chair, he grinned. If all else failed, he'd put a spell on her!


"Sir Felix Baring to see you, miss. He asked for a word in private."

"Thank you, James. Please show him into the study."

"Do you think that is wise, my dear?" asked Rose.

"Wise or not, I must speak with the man and give him my decision about the kitten."

"And what is your decision?"

"I have no idea," replied Gilly, smoothing the rose-colored morning gown and biting at her lower lip before walking with measured tread toward the door.

"Good morning, Miss Gillingham," said Felix, bowing before her. He smiled as the butler carefully left the door open and began tidying in the hall, humming loudly.

"He only wants to be sure of the proprieties," said Gilly, indicating the two chairs near the fire. "Won't you be seated, Sir Felix?"

"Thank you. I hope you suffered no ill effects from last night's, uh, events."

"None," she replied. Gilly bowed her head, suddenly too shy to meet his gaze.

"My aunt said to tell you how very sorry she is for frightening you with her nonsense."

"That is very kind of you, Sir Felix," said Gilly, looking up and smiling shyly. "But she didn't really say that at all, did she?"

Felix gave a rich laugh, and Gilly giggled.

"No, she said nothing of the kind. Your godmother has no doubt told you all about my eccentric aunt. But truly, there is no harm in her, despite her belief in witches."

"And warlocks?"

"And warlocks," he said quietly, his eyes darkening as he regarded her intently. "It is a beautiful afternoon, Miss Gillingham. I know I should have written you a note inviting you for a drive for tomorrow or the next day, but I was wondering if you might like . . ."

"I would love it," she said, bestowing a radiant smile on him. "Just give me a few minutes to fetch my bonnet. In the meantime, won't you come into the drawing room and meet my godmother? I am far too old to have to ask her permission, of course, but I would like for the two of you to meet formally."

"I would be delighted," said Felix, relieved that the visit was going so well. Perhaps, he thought, it would not be such an arduous task, convincing Miss Gillingham that she really needed to be his.

"How do you do, Sir Felix?" said Rose, very much on her dignity.

"It is so good to finally meet you," he replied, bowing over her hand.

"Sir Felix has asked me out for a drive, Rose. I'll just go and fetch my hat. I'll be right back," said Gilly, eyeing the two uneasily.

When she was gone, Rose Pargeter motioned Felix to a chair.

"I can't help but wonder, Sir Felix, at your motives for asking my goddaughter out for a drive."

"I thought it a perfect opportunity to enjoy the fine day, Mrs. Pargeter, and a pleasant way to make up to her for any embarrassment my family might have caused her in the past."

"You will forgive me if I find that difficult to believe."

"I beg your pardon?" he rejoined.

"I think it much more likely that you are only trying to diddle her out of her kitten," said the matron.

The kitten in question jumped into Felix's lap and began to purr loudly.

"This is my aunt's kitten," said Felix, stiffening.

"Not anymore. Gilly is quite attached to it, and so am I. Furthermore, I do not approve of gentlemen who steal the virtue of gently bred ladies in dark carriages."

Felix shifted uncomfortably on the chair, but he didn't deny the charge, although a mere kiss was hardly the same as a seduction. But Society had very strict rules.

With a nod to acknowledge her hit, she continued, "It is not that my Gilly is a complete innocent. After all, she was engaged for several months."

"I had no idea."

"Oh, yes. Sad story. He died, you know. She's only just come out of mourning, though it has been almost two years. Quite devastated, she was."

"I didn't realize, Mrs. Pargeter, and I do understand your concern. I assure you, I have only the deepest respect for Miss Gillingham. She must have loved him very much."

"Oh, yes, quite," said Rose, determined to say as little as possible on that subject. "But here she is again. Do enjoy your drive, children."

With a cheery wave, Gilly took Felix's arm. They were silent as they drove through the streets to the park. Gilly searched her brain for some tidbit of interesting conversation, but rejected all the possibilities. It had been so much easier sitting in his lap in the darkened carriage, she thought, eyeing that portion of his anatomy and then coloring up prettily when he detected her scrutiny.

"It is rather awkward being together like this in normal circumstances, isn't it?" said Felix, willing her to look up at him again.

"Yes, quite."

"Tell me a little about yourself, Miss Gillingham. I take it you do not live in London year-round."

"Oh no, I am from Wiltshire. My father has a small estate there. My mother passed away when I was a girl. Rose has been like a mother to me since then. She usually spends the summer at our home, and I would come to London for the Season. Until recently, that is."

"Yes, she told me about your fiancé. I am sorry for your loss. It must be very difficult for you."

"Difficult?"

"Mrs. Pargeter said you were in mourning for two years."

She shot him a quizzical glance and said, "At the risk of sounding cold and unfeeling, I must confess I was not really mourning my fiancé for two years."

"No? Then it wasn't a love match?" asked Felix with a wide grin before adding hastily, "That is, I'm sure it is none of my concern. It is just that we, you and I, have not been accustomed to following the usual social conventions. I'm afraid I forgot my manners."

She giggled, looking at her hands folded neatly in her lap before peeking up at him with an impish grin. "You have the most delightful way of understating the matter, Sir Felix."

Something about those blue eyes, shaded by the brim of her bonnet, struck a chord of memory, and he frowned. Then he shrugged and said, "Well, if we look back at our history, Miss Gillingham, it is easy to see that our relationship has been anything but conventional. Let's see, it all started with the umbrella and the kitten-napping, as my aunt is wont to call it."

Gilly gave a gurgle of laughter.

Felix resumed, "And then that first ball, where I demanded that you give me back my cat. Very poorly done on my part, I freely admit. Finally the next, where I backed you into the pond before carrying you through a crowded ballroom and into my carriage. That about sums it up, does it not?"

Again that rich giggle that so intrigued him.

"You are forgetting our most notorious encounter," she said, peeking up at him again.

"No, I think that's all."

"What about the masquerade ball?" she asked, her eyes widening. So he hadn't guessed her identity, and all the horrid things he had said had been just as insulting as she had at first thought they were. He hadn't been motivated by anger over her treatment of him in the park.

"The shepherdess," Felix breathed with dawning horror. Stopping the team, he exclaimed, "Bloody hell! I called you a lightskirt!"

She nodded, but he wasn't finished with his shocked self-recriminations.

"Devil take me, Miss Gillingham, I'm an utter fool! There is no way I can possibly make amends for my insults to you. The other times, perhaps, but not that time. I do beg your pardon, but I have no expectation of receiving it. You must hate me!"

"Certainly not!" she injected tartly.

"But you must, any gently bred female must," he said, unwittingly borrowing the description her godmother had so recently used. "I am sorry. I'll take you home immediately. If I had only realized . . . but I'm such a self-righteous, priggish fool." As Felix continued his diatribe, he whipped up his team, and they quickly found themselves back at her front door.

He escorted her up the steps, still ignoring all her vehement protests, and bowed over her hand.

"I assure you, Miss Gillingham, you will not be subjected to my company anymore. And please, keep the cat. Good day."

"Really, Sir Felix, you mustn't think so ill . . . of yourself," she finished quietly as he drove away.

Her shoulders slumped, Gilly climbed the stairs to her bedchamber, sitting down at the dressing table and staring at her image without really seeing it.

When Betsy entered the room some ten minutes later, she

jumped. "I'm sorry, miss. I thought you were still out with that handsome Sir Felix. Where does the time go?" she asked no one in particular, carefully putting away her mistress's clean linen.

When Gilly still had given no indication that she was aware of the maid's presence, Betsy cleared her throat loudly and asked, "Did you need anything else, miss?"

"What?" said Gilly with a surprised frown. "Oh, I'm sorry, Betsy. I was wool-gathering. Did you need anything?"

"Uh, no, miss, I asked if *you* needed anything."

"No, no, I am fine. Really, just fine," she said, giving the servant a weak smile before falling silent yet again.

The maid hesitated, then left the room.

"Well, you really did it this time," Gilly said, making a face at herself in the glass. "You had to go and kiss the man, and now he thinks you are fast.

"If you'd stayed shy and innocent, none of this would have happened." Tears sprang to her eyes, and she said sternly, "None of that, my girl. You have only yourself to blame."

Gilly rose and went downstairs, out to the garden where the late afternoon sun sent long shadows streaming across the pathway. She sat down on a cold stone bench. Picking up a stick from the ground, she began to trace patterns absentmindedly in the gravel path. After a few minutes, she smiled at the detailed house she had "sketched," just like when she was a little girl, daydreaming about the home she would someday share with her husband.

Then, she and her friends had woven tales of happily-ever-after. Now, she knew it was not so easy to find her Prince Charming. And when she did, she managed to scare him off before she could convince him that she was his Cinders.

Gilly swiped at the tears that dared to trickle down her cheeks. She would not give in, she vowed. She would not allow her timidity to keep her from finding her happily-ever-after. Rising, it was with a determined tread that she reentered the house, set on donning her prettiest gown for the evening's entertainments. She would tell Felix he was forgiven for his imagined transgression, she would tell him . . . that she loved him.

Ten miles outside London, Felix finally pulled into the yard of a posting inn and surrendered his lathered team to a groom.

"Cool them down proper," he said. "I'll check on them later."

So saying, Felix entered the low-ceilinged public room and ordered a pitcher of ale. Searching out a table in the darkest corner of the room, he settled into a chair and proceeded to drink his memories away.

Before total oblivion overtook him, he had beaten himself up many times for all the injustices he had done to poor Gilly. The landlord, refilling his glass, listened to his tales of woe with a sympathetic ear. After all, the gent was paying for it.

"So then I called her a lightskirt!" he mumbled, resting his chin on the lip of his glass.

"And she wasn't?" prompted the wily landlord, accepting the second payment for the same pitcher of ale.

"A lightskirt? Heavens no! She's a lady, a sweet angel with eyes like the summer sky and hair like wheat when it's ripe and ready to be picked."

"Sounds to me like yer oughta go back and marry th' gel."

"She wouldn't have me now. Not knowing what she knows I know," said Felix, frowning. He blinked twice and shoved away from the table. Peering out the window, he noticed for the first time that it had grown quite dark.

"Have you got a room for the night?" he asked. He was not, after all, so cast away that he would risk his prime bloods on the road in the dark.

"I've only got the one left, guvner. It's my best one, so it will cost a little more," said the landlord.

"Lead on, Macduff," said Felix.

"Th' name's Trent, sir. But th' room's this way."

"But Gilly, a lady never visits a gentleman's quarters. And under no circumstances should she pursue him!" exclaimed Rose, throwing herself in front of the door leading from the drawing room the next afternoon.

"Why not? If he is so foolish as to turn away from her on the flimsiest of pretenses, doesn't she have a right to an explanation?"

"Gilly, just wait a moment. I . . . I think I may know why Sir Felix was so distressed. I think I may have told him something to . . ."

Gilly's chin jutted out, and she raised one delicate brow. "What, exactly, did you say to him yesterday?"

"I . . . I merely explained that you had been betrothed before."

"And?" she prompted, for surely there was nothing unusual about that.

"And that your fiancé died two years ago," said the older woman, unable to meet her goddaughter's relentless stare. "I told him you had been in mourning for the past two years because you were so devastated by your fiancé's death."

"You did what? Good heavens, Rose! Do you have any idea what you have done? Felix believes I was so in love with my fiancé that he can't possibly compete, especially when he has planted his foot squarely in his mouth more times than I care to count. It is no wonder he ran away!"

"If he had wanted to offer for you, he would have done so," asserted the older woman, her lips pursed stubbornly.

"Well, I may never know that unless I can see him again. And you are going to help!"

"I refuse to be a party to such a scandalous scheme, Gilly."

"Then I will go to Sir Felix's house by myself, without so much as an abigail."

"Oh, very well. But this is blackmail."

"Call it what you will, Rose, but I don't intend to give up so easily. I will take Blackie with us and return him to Felix's aunt."

"His aunt? Of course. I forgot about her. We will call on her, if he happens to be at home, too, then there is nothing improper about that," said Rose, pleased to allow this rationalization to placate her sense of propriety.

When they were seated in the small carriage with the basket containing the kitten on the seat between them, Rose ventured, "Gilly, I do hope you will not demand to speak to Sir Felix."

"I will ask to," said Gilly, smiling at the thought.

"What has come over you, Gilly? I vow you have changed in the past two weeks since meeting Sir Felix. I hardly know you, the Gilly I know would never be so bold. Why, two weeks ago, I could barely get you to hold a casual conversation with a gentleman."

As they neared their destination, Gilly's smile widened, but she didn't dare voice the thoughts that were dancing through her head. They were private thoughts, too tentative to be spoken out loud yet. She had changed since meeting the darkly handsome Sir Felix. The old Gilly would never have been able to seek him out and force him to . . . to what? To offer for her? To love her?

But again, the thoughts were too fragile for consideration. First, she had to see him again. And if he could be persuaded to take her in his arms and kiss her again, so much the better.

"What are you thinking about now, Gertrude Gillingham?" demanded her scandalized godmother. "I have never seen you blush like that."

With a roguish gurgle of laughter, Gilly shook her head and pointed to the window. "Here we are!"

The house was nothing like she had feared. There was nothing to suggest a witch lived there. On Curzon Street, it was rather larger than the others in the block, but other than that, it appeared quite ordinary. Even the butler who opened the door and took her card was unexceptional.

"You see, Rose, this is just an ordinary household," whispered Gilly as the butler turned to inform his mistress of the visitors.

A door slammed, and the butler was almost bowled over by a servant in a black coat carrying a battered portmanteau.

His tone hysterical, the fleeing servant exclaimed, "Please tell Sir Felix I am sorry, Mr. Winchester, but I cannot remain in this household with that woman another hour!"

"Mr. Waverly, please, don't go. At least wait until Sir Felix comes back," exclaimed the butler, tugging on the valet's sleeve.

"I cannot, I cannot. Do you know what that woman did to me?" he shrieked.

"Gilly, I think we should leave," declared Rose, backing toward the door.

"Nonsense. Obviously there is some misunderstanding here. Excuse me. Mr. Waverly, is it?"

"Yes, I . . . Oh, I am so mortified," he cried upon seeing the two ladies watching the scene. "I do beg your pardon, ladies. I am not . . . Oh, no, not again!" he shouted, covering his eyes with the tail of his coat.

Throwing open the door to the drawing room, Aunt Felicity entered the fray. "There you are, Waverly! What is all this shouting about? It is not at all appropriate for the . . ."

"Me-e-e-o-o-o-w!"

Felix's aunt dropped the wand she was thrusting at the valet and bawled, "Francis! Is that my Francis?"

"It is," said Gilly, opening the basket and allowing the kitten to escape, it bounded to the floor and then hurdled into Aunt Felicity's waiting embrace.

"Oh, Francis, Francis, I have missed you so," she purred,

cuddling the black ball of fur. "I'm glad to see you have finally come to your senses, Miss Gillingham."

Gilly giggled when Blackie looked back at her and winked.

"I don't know that I appreciate your speaking to my god-daughter in that manner," said Rose Pargeter, her face flushed and her nose in the air.

"It's all right, Rose," said Gilly. "I don't mind, and I think there is a problem here that is more important to everyone."

"What's that, my girl?" asked Aunt Felicity.

"Mr. Waverly still appears to be intent on leaving," she said, pointing toward the cringing valet.

"Why is that, Waverly?"

"I will not stay another hour . . ."

"Yes, we heard that, Mr. Waverly. Mr. Winchester, is it?" said Gilly, turning to the butler, who nodded. "Perhaps you would be so good as to show my godmother and Miss Baring to the drawing room while I speak privately to Mr. Waverly."

"Very good, miss," said the relieved butler.

When the reception area was cleared, Gilly smiled at the nervous valet and said, "How do you do, Mr. Waverly? I am Miss Gillingham, a friend of Sir Felix."

"I have heard him speak of you, miss."

"Really?" she said, brightening. "Would you please tell me what caused you to decide to leave today?"

"I hesitate to speak ill of my employer's family; after all, I have served Sir Felix for the past ten years."

"Really? So you were with him in the army?" she said.

"Oh, yes, and proud I was to serve such a fine man."

"And is Sir Felix less fine now that he is no longer in the military?"

"No, of course not, miss. Sir Felix is not the problem." The valet looked toward the drawing room before adding quietly, "It is his aunt, she is constantly putting spells on me. Once, she told me I wasn't dressing Sir Felix properly. Well, I could not let that pass, miss."

"Of course not, Mr. Waverly. May I ask you one question?" When he had nodded, she said, "You appear to be fit and quite normal. Has any of these spells caused you harm?"

"Well, no, miss, but it is most unnerving to have that silver wand poked at one," he said, picking up this weapon from the floor where Aunt Felicity had dropped it.

"Quite, but I feel certain Sir Felix wouldn't penalize you if you were to say as much to his aunt."

"I, uh, suppose not."

"Good. Then that is all you need do the next time she comes after you with this ridiculous silver stick. You must stand up to her." His color changed from red to white, and she continued firmly, "You have already said that her spells cannot harm you, and you know that Sir Felix would only applaud your courage. So you will stay?"

"I suppose so, miss. Thank you. I didn't really want to leave Sir Felix after all this time, you know. But I simply couldn't continue the way things were."

"And Sir Felix didn't know what to do about it," said Gilly.

"He tried, miss, but his aunt is very strong-willed," replied the loyal servant.

"Sometimes the most logical solution to a problem is impossible for those closest to it to discover. Tell me, Waverly, have you seen Sir Felix this afternoon?"

"No, miss, he never came home yesterday. I heard him tell Master Oliver that he was going for a drive with you, and he never came back."

"Thank you, Waverly. Why don't you go get settled again?"

"Thank you, miss. I will," he said, opening the drawing room door for her before retrieving his valise and heading for the stairs again.

"Hello, Gilly, my dear. I have just been having the most extraordinary conversation with Miss Baring. Did you know she can read palms?"

"And tea leaves," said the spinster.

"Indeed, yes. My tea leaves told her that I would marry again. Can you imagine?" said Rose with a girlish giggle.

"Certainly I can. Any man would be lucky to win your hand," said Gilly.

"What about you, my child? Shall I read your palm?" asked Aunt Felicity, patting the sofa.

"No, thank you. I prefer to find out my future as I go along, Miss Baring," said Gilly, sitting down.

"Might as well call me auntie," said Aunt Felicity, winking at the kitten, who was sitting on the sofa by her side.

"Meow," said Blackie.

Just then they heard a commotion in the hall, and Gilly sat forward, watching the door.

It opened, and Felix stepped inside, followed closely by Oliver, who was importuning his brother, dogging his every step.

"But what should I do?" demanded Oliver.

"How the deuce should I know? Do you see any evidence about that labels me a dab hand with the ladies?" snapped Felix.

Turning back toward the room and finding four pairs of eyes glued on him, he groaned.

"I beg your pardon, ladies," he began, his gaze coming to rest on Gilly.

"Aha! Here's someone who'll know," said Oliver, passing Felix. He reached the sofa, picked up Blackie and handed him to his aunt before sitting down and turning to Gilly.

"Tell me, Miss Gillingham, if a gentleman sent you several bouquets of flowers, would you not be ready to fall at his feet?"

"Don't be daft, boy," said his aunt.

"Well, would you?"

"Oliver, Miss Gillingham doesn't want to be pestered by your petty problems," said Felix, easing into the chair closest to the sofa.

"I don't mind, really," said Gilly, smiling shyly at him before turning back to his younger brother.

"I can't answer for every young lady, Mr. Baring, but I think she would be impressed."

"You see, Felix! I told you so! Now, please, can I have an advance on my allowance? Just until quarter day."

Putting his fingers to his temples and massaging them gently, Felix moaned, "Please, Oliver, not so loud."

"Oh, sorry," said Oliver. Leaning closer to Gilly, he whispered, "He's got a sore head from drinking too much, you know. I suspect he has been disappointed in love?" He made this last a question, but Gilly only smiled and blushed.

"Oliver," warned Felix.

"Yes, yes. Well, back to me. So you think I should send the lady in question lots of flowers?"

"I didn't say that, Mr. Baring."

"Might as well call him Oliver," said Aunt Felicity.

"Meow," seconded Blackie.

"See, even Francis agrees," said Aunt Felicity.

"If the lady is taken with you, she wouldn't care how many flowers you did or didn't send her. You could send her one, and it would suffice."

"Ah, I see," said Oliver, nodding sagely and then rising.

"Where are you going, fledgling?" asked Felix.

"I'm going to buy a perfect rose for a perfect young lady. Thank you, Miss Gillingham."

"You're welcome, Oliver," called Gilly.

Rising, Aunt Felicity announced, "Mrs. Pargeter and I are going to have a comfortable coze in my sitting room."

"Oh, I don't think . . ." began Rose.

"I have a box of the most exquisite chocolates," said Aunt Felicity with great cunning.

"How did you know I love chocolates?" asked the amazed Rose.

"I have my ways. Come along, Francis." The kitten and

Rose followed obediently. At the door, she paused and added, "You really should make an offer for her, Felix. She even talked Waverly into staying when I had driven him to leave again."

"Thank you, Aunt. That will be all."

When they were alone, Gilly ducked her head and said softly, "I am sorry you are not feeling well."

"It's not so bad," said Felix, moving to the sofa and taking Gilly's hand. "I have only myself to blame. If only I wasn't such a clunch. I hope you realize I never suspected it was you behind that mask at the ball. I mean, you add that to all the rest, and I can hardly face you."

"You have nothing to apologize for, Felix. Except, perhaps, for having drunk too much last night."

"I have everything to apologize for, my dear Gilly. I have made such a muddle of this courtship from the very beginning."

Her face shining, Gilly looked up and smiled, studying his dear face without a smidge of shyness.

"Courtship?"

Felix grinned down at her. Then, groaning at the throbbing in his head, he slipped off the sofa and knelt on one knee, taking her hands in his.

"Dear Gilly, I will be brief so that I don't manage to make a muddle of this as well. I love you, Miss Gillingham. Will you do me the great honor of becoming my wife?"

"Oh, yes, Felix, yes!" she said, leaning down and taking his face in her hands and kissing him thoroughly.

"Now my head really is spinning," said Felix, moving back onto the sofa.

"I am so sorry, I wouldn't cause you pain for the world, Felix," said Gilly, but she smiled.

"Except with an umbrella," he said dryly.

"That was very unlike me, Felix. But I am glad to know, however, that my kisses don't repulse you."

"Repulse me? What kind of nonsense is that?"

"You know. You did apologize after the last kiss."

"I was afraid you would be insulted by my advances," he said.

"Not at all," breathed Gilly, eyeing his lips once again.

Laughing, Felix winked at her and took her hand, saying, "Don't worry, my love. I'm a warlock, you know. I'll just cast a spell and make the pain go away."

"Just so long as you don't go away, Felix," murmured Gilly as he swept her into his arms for a proper embrace and kiss. From outside the door, Rose, Aunt Felicity, and Francis congratulated each other on the match.

"Say what you will about witches and warlocks, Mrs. Pargeter, I think your goddaughter did a good job of bewitching my nephew. Don't you agree, Francis?"

"Me-e-o-ow," replied the black kitten, his wide green eyes twinkling up at them.

# THE
# BLACK KITTEN

*Catherine Blair*

# ONE

"You're out of your mind, Griffith." Allan Fothering took a sage gulp of brandy and then regarded his friend over the rim of the glass. His expression was comically severe. "She's the scourge of England. Everyone says so. Repelled fourteen suitors in three years." He set down his glass with a bang. "At the very least she's an unbearable harpy." His brows lowered. "And there are some that say she's a witch."

"Nonsense." Jonathan tilted his chair back and smiled placidly. "Provincial nonsense. Besides, she can be as ill-tempered as she likes. I shall have little to do with her once we are wed." He linked his fingers together and leaned his head back on them in a relaxed attitude. "I shall have the collection, and she shall have her solitude. Or her book of spells, or her cauldron of brew, or whatever it is that she wants. It will work out rather well, actually." He grinned. "Better than most matches, despite all the romantic folderol in fashion these days."

Fothering was regarding him with an expression of patent disbelief. "In your bridal dreams of marrying Harrington's Egyptian collection, I believe you are forgetting one small detail," he said.

His friend was right. Jonathan's fingers were itching to examine Harrington's horde of Egyptian artifacts. It was a well-known fact that the man knew nothing of antiquities. He probably had no idea of the real academic value of his amassed collection, shoved away in a remote corner of Cumberland. The man was an avaricious pack rat of the highest order. He bought—some said stole—for the sake of having, not for any love of the pieces he brought back. It was maddening. He realized Fothering was looking at him expectantly. "What?"

"The daughter."

"I believe we'd moved on past the daughter and straight to the point where I was cataloging the collection."

"She won't have you."

"Another drink for Mr. Fothering!" Jonathan called out to the man in charge of drinks at White's. "He is obviously far too sober to appreciate the subtleties of my plan."

Allan leaned on his elbow with a look of resignation. "Fourteen suitors, Griffith. Her father is as rich as Croesus, and she's no ape-leader. Everything a man could ask for, if she wasn't born with the devil's own temper. You may think you're a sly one amongst the ladies, but I can tell you, she won't have you."

"Care to wager on it?"

"Of course." The shoulder that was not propped on the table rose and fell in a shrug. "But you'll lose your blunt as well as your pride. She turned Ashford off last month with a flea in his ear. And he's a duke. Five estates, they say. You're only a viscount with nothing to recommend you but a pile of mud and rocks in Wales."

Jonathan let this jab go by. "She can stay at her own pile of mud and rocks in Cumberland for all I care. As the most amiable of husbands, I shall let my lovely bride do anything she wishes. Here is your drink, Allan. Toast to me and my future wife and prepare to appreciate the genius of my plan to win her."

Fothering grunted.

"I shall traipse up to Wythburn to see the Egyptian collection, and"—he paused for effect—"I shall ignore her."

Fothering regarded him in silence for a long moment. "That is your brilliant plan." His mouth twisted in a sarcastic smile as he nodded slowly. "How much did you say you would wager?"

Jonathan leaned in, suddenly enthusiastic. "Women cannot bear to feel ignored. Especially a beautiful one. Think on it, Allan! She has had fourteen suitors. If I go up there and pay her no mind, she will fling herself at me! I will allow myself to be persuaded to marry her, and we will both have what we want. Let's see, a fortnight, three weeks at most. Yes, by All Hallow's Eve we will be betrothed. She will have a husband who will put up with her wretched temperament, and I shall have the finest private collection of Egyptian antiquities in England."

Fothering failed to look impressed.

"What have I to lose?" Jonathan said with a careless gesture.

"A hundred pounds."

He threw back his head and laughed. "Very well. I'll wager a hundred pounds Miss Harrington will be my betrothed by All Hallow's Eve."

Allan narrowed his eyes and rubbed his chin for a long moment. "You shall come off the loser in any case. I'd rather lose a hundred pounds than end up leg-shackled to a witch."

Jonathan rolled his eyes.

"Ashford swears it!" Fothering protested. "She is called the Witch of Wythburn! He said his skin crawled the whole time he was there. Strange noises and ghostly figures that disappeared when you drew near them." He snapped his fingers. "Gone! Smells of sulfur in the night and odd bonfires out on the hills. Wicked things, Griffith. Miss Harrington put a spell on him, and he came out in a rash."

Jonathan smothered an elaborate yawn behind his hand. "I'm terrified."

"You shouldn't take it so lightly. They're odd people up there. Wild country breeds strange people. There are still druids there who know things decent people should not know. And fairy rings!" Fothering's pale blue eyes were open wide. "Kit Rose went up to woo her, and he wandered into a fairy ring and was lost for days. Near snapped his mind, it did."

Jonathan squinted at the fire through the liquid amber of his brandy. He had heard that Harrington had a papyrus written in demotic. He would happily brave an army of druids for a look at that. Thomas Young was making progress on translating the ancient language. With a few more samples of it, they could surely learn to decipher it, and then the Rosetta stone would reveal its mysteries. The Greek and demotic on it were undoubtedly translations of the hieroglyphics. And once they understood hieroglyphics . . .

"She has a cat. A familiar, like. You know how witches keep a familiar?" Fothering was still harping on about Miss Harrington.

"The notion sounds, er, familiar." He suppressed a mocking smile.

"You laugh, but you shouldn't, Griffith. The cat goes with her everywhere. It is as ill-tempered a creature as she herself. Shredded every single pair of silk stockings Ashford brought. Every pair."

"I must remember to pack pantaloons." He swirled the last of his brandy and finished it off, then stood and carelessly brushed the wrinkles from his sleeves. "Your warnings are well taken, Fothering. I shall bring catmint to woo the feline. Perhaps befriending Miss Harrington's, ah, familiar will endear me to the termagant."

"You'll be lucky to get off merely a hundred pounds the lighter." His friend shook his head.

Jonathan's eyes narrowed, and for the first time he spoke seriously. "You don't know how much I want this collection, Allan. For years I have hoped to see it. I dream about it!" He put both hands on the table and leaned down to speak to Fothering with an intensity that made his friend lean back in surprise. "Harrington cares nothing for it. Rumor has it he has abandoned Egyptian collecting and has moved on to Chinese art. *I* can appreciate it. I won't horde it away. I will make it available to the world's premier Egyptologists. We will understand more about that great civilization than we have ever known before. If it requires marrying the Witch of Wythburn, I will do so."

Fothering looked slightly taken aback at his speech, then turned back to his drink with a shake of his head. "Nothing is worth marrying that harridan. You'll be glad when she's drummed you out of that place."

"No." Jonathan smiled to himself. Harrington was reputed to have hauled home the contents of an entire tomb. That could keep him busy for the rest of his life. He threw down some coins to pay for the drinks. "Harridan, witch or merely a nag, the price will be worth it."

The road was so pocked with ruts and holes that the words to Akerblad's treatise on the Valley of the Kings were bouncing before his eyes. He sighed and put it down on the seat. Drops of rain were beginning to tap at the window, so he took his handkerchief and rubbed away the fog that had formed on the glass.

What a grim part of the country this was. The sky was dense with heavy gray clouds that seemed to hang only a few yards above the landscape. There was a fierce bleakness in the sheer gray rocks that rose up to pierce the gray sky. The wind whistled around the carriage in a mournful howl that made him pity the coachman.

"Fairly miserable time of year to go courting," he grumbled. For the first time since he had conceived the plan, he felt a twinge of misgiving. Harrington had enthusiastically invited him when he had expressed an interest in making the journey, but it might have been better to wait until spring. Surely even Miss Harrington's heart would be more easily melted with the spring thaw. Wooing in the inhospitable month of October would be a challenge anywhere. He looked up at the rocky crags. He certainly would not be able to count on idyllic inspiration from the scenery.

But no, by spring someone else might have claimed her. The thought of Harrington's collection going to someone who cared nothing for it made his skin crawl uncomfortably.

He let down the window and stuck out his head. A few drops of cold rain stung his face. It wouldn't be long before they would be in for a downpour. "Are we nearly there?" he demanded.

The coachman turned around from his hunched position on the box. His face was red and wind-chapped. "There." He pointed toward a craggy fell that looked very like all the others. At the bottom he could barely make out a bedraggled clutch of houses. The little town of Wythburn was hopelessly gray, like everything else around here. Wythburn House was just beyond the town.

Then, in the distance, he saw a patch of blue and orange. It was a long moment before he realized it was someone on horseback. The gray of the horse blended with the landscape to give the unsettling impression that the rider was flying across the stony ridge of the road on nothing at all.

The indistinct colors gradually took the shape of a red-haired woman in a deep blue riding habit. She wore no hat and the brilliant fire of her hair was a strange contrast to the bleak surroundings. Jonathan could hear the sharp spatter of her horse's hooves on the macadam.

She pulled up and regarded him with a haughty expression.

He felt vaguely foolish sitting there gaping with his head out the window of the coach.

She was striking, in an unconventional way. Her hair was far more ginger than auburn and the splash of freckles across her nose and brow would exclude her from any claim to real beauty in most circles. But there was something arresting in her upright carriage that made her an object of notice, if not admiration.

He realized she was still staring down her nose at him.

"Well?" she demanded. "Are you number fifteen?"

# TWO

Beau Brummell sat in the window seat looking particularly smug. Lorna picked up one of the kittens playing hide and seek under her skirt and carefully detached it from the blond lace flounce. Parenthood had made Beau placid. Six weeks ago her cat would never have allowed a stranger to seat himself on her favorite chair in the best drawing room without hackling up her glossy black coat and hissing in protest. As it was, Beau merely blinked her amber eyes and turned her attention to the fat orange furball intent on mountaineering up the drapes.

"You are lucky you found us before the rain began, Lord Griffith," her father was saying in the most cordial of accents as he poured their guest a generous glass of madeira.

"Indeed. Your daughter was kind enough to show me the way," he replied. Lorna half expected him to launch into a litany of praises for her supposed thoughtfulness, but he didn't spare her a glance.

The kitten in her lap was trying to burrow underneath her hand to encourage her to pet it. She frowned and complied. Another suitor thinly disguised as someone interested in her father's collection. Well, she'd see him on his way soon enough. At least this one was handsome. That is, if one had an appreciation for the somewhat weathered look of the Egyptian archaeologist. He was nothing like the pasty, lisping

Browning, who had a passing knowledge of Egypt but had obviously never been there.

This man had undoubtedly spent a good amount of time sifting through the dirt under the Egyptian sun. His long fingers were callused, and though he wore a well-cut coat obviously made by a fashionable London tailor, he seemed somewhat ill at ease in it. He was younger than her father's usual cronies, but she felt the same sense of envious dislike. No doubt he had the same patronizing ideas that no gently bred female could possibly survive anywhere but in the most sedate of drawing rooms.

"I hope it was not an inopportune time for me to take you up on your offer to see the collection," Lord Griffith said politely.

"Which collection?" Her father waved his hand in a flippant gesture.

Lord Griffith's brows drew together over eyes that were a surprising gray in his tanned face. "The Egyptian one." He seemed slightly perplexed.

"Ah. Of course. You see, I have moved on to collecting Chinese antiquities now. In fact, I am planning a journey there in the spring. Depending on the circumstances." He shot Lorna a look impossible to misread. If she were married, he could jaunt around the world as much as he liked without his millstone of a daughter to bring him home.

She regarded him placidly and continued to stroke the head of the black kitten. Its rumbling purr resonated through its whole body. She would not allow herself to be drawn into their eternal argument. Lord Griffith would only think them more provincial.

"Perhaps," her father continued, "you would like to take Lord Griffith to see the Egyptian rooms, Lorna." His brows rose meaningfully.

The man was the most hopelessly ham-fisted matchmaker

in history. Was there no man under fifty he would not throw at her head?

She opened her mouth to coldly reject the plan when Griffith spoke up quickly. "No need for her to put herself out. I would prefer for you to show it to me yourself when you have the time, sir. I would very much like to hear how and where you found the artifacts."

Her father frowned slightly. "Certainly. But I am afraid I am obliged to take care of a few trifling things right now. Perhaps you would enjoy a walk in the gallery. Lorna knows some very interesting stories about her ancestors, do you not, my dear?"

"I think I would rather retire to my room if you do not mind." The man interrupted her reply again. "I have some rather pressing letters to write."

"Then Lorna can—"

She shot her father a quelling look and stood to her feet. "I will show you to your room." The kitten in her arms wiggled in protest at this change in altitude. Beau Brummell had always allowed herself to be carried about with all the regalness of a queen. Her progeny, however, had attained no such dignity.

She struggled to suppress a laugh. It would be difficult to squash this gentleman's pretensions with her usual aloof scowl when the kitten had now managed to turn about in her arms so that his head was shoved into the crook of her elbow and his tail curled back and forth under her chin.

Griffith followed her from the room without seeming to notice. They walked nearly the entire length of the house before the silence began to irritate her.

"You come to us from London, my lord?"

"Yes, most recently. I am originally from Wales."

"Oh." The sound of her shoes was strangely loud along the corridor. "I have never been to Wales." She bit off the comment that she had never been anywhere. It seemed ridiculous to admit that one had never been beyond the confines of one's own parish.

"It's nice enough." He seemed disinclined to continue the conversation.

"You have been to Egypt?" What an incredibly stupid question. Of course he had been to Egypt. She had no idea why she was putting herself out for this man. It should suit her very well if he had no wish to converse with her. It made no sense at all that she would feel the sudden urge to mouth inane pleasantries.

"Yes. I was there since 'thirteen. I have only been back three months."

She did not ask him how he found it, as he would undoubtedly launch into an excruciatingly dull monologue of that exotic place she would never see.

Griffith merely shoved his hands into his trouser pockets and began to whistle. She shot him a glance of reproval at this gaucherie, but he appeared blissfully unaware of her existence.

If he was indeed a suitor, he was not making much of an effort. She was surprised to feel a whiff of disappointment. Certainly he was not as impressively titled as the insipid Lord Ashford, nor as handsome as Mr. Crowley, nor as gratuitously charming as Lord Wendall, but she had hoped for a little challenge from him. She felt a little foolish for her brash comment when they had met. Perhaps he really was here merely to see the collection.

"We have had a good many visitors of late." The words popped out before she could remind herself that she was not interested in maintaining a semblance of conversation with him.

"Unusual for so remote a place," he agreed.

He was looking at her steadily. She dropped her gaze and frowned. The paleness of those eyes gave her a strange, though not wholly unpleasant sensation in the pit of her stomach.

"Very remote," she said, and was surprised to hear the bitterness in her own voice.

"I heard they had hoped to win your hand."

She looked up in surprise, but he was striding along apparently unaware that he had spoken with shocking bluntness.

There was something vaguely insulting about his nonchalance. She cast off the feeling of annoyance and reminded herself that she should be glad he was not making horrid prosy compliments or slyly trying to embrace her in the dimness of the passageway.

He was either unbearably dull-witted or not courting her after all. Fourteen suitors must have made her vain, she chided herself. She should be glad of a visitor who was not out to obtain her like some kind of curiosity.

"Yes, they did hope to marry me," she said, her chin jerking up. "But not because I am charming or beautiful or witty." Her voice was scornful. "Most came because my father is rich. Some came merely because they heard that I do not wish to marry anyone." She shot him a defiant look. "And a man cannot bear to think that there is a woman in the world who does not wish to marry him."

"How perfectly ghastly for you. I apologize on behalf of my gender." He stifled a slight yawn behind his hand. "Dear me. What a very tiring trip it was."

She had obviously been mistaken in the look of intelligence she had seen on his face when she rode up to him on the road. The dull creature would be dashing out of here with his tail between his legs in less than a week. "Papa has given you the blue room," she said as coolly as she could with a kitten tail batting her in the mouth.

"Very nice."

She smiled slowly. "They say the room is haunted, but I am certain you are not fainthearted enough to believe such silly rumors."

Ashford had blanched at those words, but Griffith merely shrugged. "The usual story? Love-crossed suicide? Or was it murder?"

"It was never proven." She tried to draw out the words ominously, but the kitten had turned himself right way round again and was trying to climb inside her bodice. "It was said that old Gregory Harrington, my great-grandfather, poisoned his wife. She died in agony swearing her revenge." She tried subtly to remove the animal. "It is said that her ghost haunts these halls and that no Harrington will have a happy marriage." Her words were rendered somewhat less ominous since the kitten had managed to get its head stuck in the décolleté of her gown.

"Are you having trouble?" Griffith asked helpfully.

She looked up with a mixture of annoyance and embarrassment. "I think I can manage."

The kitten set up a frightened mewing. Lorna turned her back on the man and helped the kitten extract itself from its ridiculous predicament.

"It could have suffocated." His mouth pulled into the faintest of smiles. "And what a terrible way to die."

She looked up in dismay, but her lips trembled with a laugh. She felt a blush burning all the way up to her scalp. "You wretched animal!" she hissed at the kitten while she rubbed the soft fur of its nose. It reached out a velvety paw and touched her chin.

"Well," he said in a cheerful tone, "I shall endeavor not to be visited by specters before dinner, in any case. All Hallow's Eve is on the way. Surely the evil spirits are much too busy with preparations to be bothered haunting someone so entirely unimpressionable as myself."

"I will see you at dinner?" she surprised herself by asking.

"Yes."

He smiled, and she realized that he had rather nice, even teeth. One, his right incisor, was slightly turned. For some reason, she found the imperfection appealing. She felt the blush start again and stanched it with a shrug of supreme indifference.

He paused in the doorway and looked back at her. "And do try to keep that kitten in line. He shows every sign of growing up to be most impertinent."

# THREE

She walked down to dinner several hours later to find that
Lord Griffith was already waiting in the drawing room. It was
somewhat shocking to see Beau Brummell, who had until now
possessed a singular hatred for all males of the human species,
curled up on his lap as though they were the best of friends.
He stood up when he saw her enter the room, and set Beau
on the floor. The mother cat looked up at him with a ludicrously besotted expression, then reluctantly went over to
check on her four kittens.

"Rather crotchety thing, your cat," Griffith said, attempting
to brush the black hairs from his white breeches.

"Yes, but she seems to like you." The faithless creature had
turned into a complete coquette.

"They always seem to be attracted to the people who like
cats least." He grimaced, then looked up with a surprisingly
open smile. There was something about it that made one want
to smile back.

She frowned.

"I take it you are fond of cats?" He indicated Beau, who
was absorbed in foiling her kittens' attempts to escape the
wicker basket where she had incarcerated them.

Lorna sat down and gestured that he should do the same.
How like her father to be late to dinner just to force her to

converse with their guest. "Yes, I am. Beau Brummell was my childhood playmate."

His brows rose. "Beau Brummell?"

"Yes, well, I thought she was a male, you see. And she does look very like Beau Brummell I think."

"Yes, with the white shirtfront and gloves, the resemblance is quite striking. I believe, though, that Brummell himself is generally too well bred to *shed.*" He examined his breeches resignedly.

"Well, I did realize my mistake, but it was too late to re-name her." She watched Beau deposit the black kitten back in the basket. "This is her first litter. I was quite surprised, as she had never shown any inclination to . . . to . . . pro-create." It was not a drawing room word, but she could not think of any other. "But there they are," she finished lamely.

The room seemed rather hot. She wished her father would not insist upon overheating the house to such an uncomfortable degree during the winter months. She got up to move away from the fire and went to close the drapes. The early autumn darkness had sunk over Wythburn. She could see her own reflection in the window. Behind her was the ridiculously comfortable image of Griffith gingerly patting Beau on the head. She pulled the drapes closed with a jerk. If the man was trying to get into her good graces by making up to her cats, she would soon set him straight.

"Have you named them all after famous leaders of fashion?" he asked.

"No. The one that looks like her mother is Imp, the all black one is Mephistopheles, and the one with the splash of white down his nose is Incubus."

"Laudable names for black cats born in a house reputedly haunted," he said cheerfully. "And the sole orange one who is about to pitch out of the basket onto his nose? Beelzebub? Goblin? Devil?"

"Marmalade."

"Oh." He cocked his head to one side. "Well, we can't all have frightful names, I suppose." He reached over and caught the kitten before it launched itself from the basket's rim.

"I couldn't think of any other," she said ruefully. She went to take the animal he was holding out to her with an expression of wary disgust.

Obviously she, herself, was going as soft as Beau, she thought with some annoyance. Lord Griffith would be making himself at home in no time at all. She made a mental promise to put vinegar in his tea in the morning. And perhaps stinging nettles at the bottom of his bed. She had the horrible feeling that right now she was looking up at him with an inane smile.

"Oh, you are both here." Her father entered the room, beaming. "I must apologize profusely for my lateness. Unavoidable, I'm afraid."

Lorna backed away from Griffith, but her father continued to nod and rub his hands together.

"Shall we go in to dinner?"

By the time they had finished the fish course, Lorna was beginning to think that her matchmaking father would be doomed to disappointment even without the help of vinegar, nettles, Beau Brummell, or herself. Lord Griffith had talked of nothing but the Egyptian collection.

"Yes, I have heard that your collection of grave masks is considered one of the finest in the country." He was leaning forward, his slate gray eyes alight with interest.

Her father waved a dismissive hand. "Yes, it was a matter of great trouble and expense to me at the time. You should take a look at them. Lorna can show you. I make no pretense at scholarship, so I would not be able to enlighten you as to much of their meaning. Though I hear Silvestre de Sacy and Akerblad have made some progress on deciphering the Rosetta stone. It would be interesting, I suppose, to know what all the symbols mean."

"You have a papyrus written in demotic, I believe?"

"Yes. Somewhere in that wing I do. I must admit to be much more interested in my Chinese collection at the moment."

Griffith sat back and looked around him as though he had just realized where he was. "Have you gone on many trips with your father, Miss Harrington?"

She was somewhat surprised to be addressed. They both seemed to have forgotten her presence entirely. "No," she said brusquely.

"The places I go are entirely too uncivilized for a lady of breeding."

This was not the time to get into another spat with her father regarding that topic, so she returned her attention to her plate.

"Oh, I am not so certain," Griffith said. "Miss Harrington strikes me as a very resourceful woman."

She was not certain if he meant it as a compliment, but it was somewhat gratifying to hear him say it. Her answer was cut off by her father's guffaw.

"Resourceful! Resourceful in shunning her duty as a daughter." He gave his mutton a vicious jab. "I could be in China right now if it was not for her mulish temper." He remembered himself. "Well, well, Lord Griffith, no need to talk about that, eh? A girl as pretty as Lorna isn't likely to stay single for long, I should say!"

Lorna clenched her teeth and fought back the urge to snap out that she did not appreciate being discussed as though she were a prize-winning pig. She looked up to see that Griffith's eyes were upon her with an expression of sympathy. She scowled at him. He couldn't stay here. There was something about him that made her acutely uncomfortable. There was no point in analyzing those feelings when they could be excised.

Whether he was here as a suitor or not, he would have to be convinced to leave. Perhaps the South American red pepper powder would be a better choice for his sheets than the nettles.

"Well." Griffith cleared his throat with some awkwardness. "Your daughter must know the countryside around Wythburn very well. It is certainly different than any I have ever seen."

"Yes," her father said brightly, "Lorna can show you around the town and the surrounds. Many consider this region the most beautiful in England."

"I must admit that I am far more interested in the Egyptian collection. Though I thank you for your offer."

"And I must collect some bitter milkwort. You know how it helps with the cough, and with winter coming on—"

"Ha ha! Lorna is a little amateur apothecary! She loves to brew up her little mixes. Nothing strange about that! Very sweet hobby really," her father exclaimed brightly.

Their guest failed to look either impressed or anxious. Harrington scowled at them both and returned his attention to his plate.

"What exactly are you hopeful of finding during your trip to China?" Griffith asked, in a clever bid to win back her father's affection.

He obligingly launched into a monologue that promised to last until the covers were removed. Griffith shot her an infuriating grin and then went back to nodding fatuously at her father. Lorna gave him a bland smile in return. Yes, suitor or not, he must be gotten rid of immediately.

# FOUR

Jonathan awoke with a start. There was a weight pressing down on his chest, and he could not breathe. For a moment he felt a panicked disorientation in the pitch-black room. His sleep-paralyzed limbs refused to move. He was stifling, but he could not cry out.

At his feeble strugglings, the weight on his chest shifted and rumbled. He moved again, and it gave a little protesting growl and reluctantly rose to its feet.

"Cat!" he exclaimed, coming fully awake. "You had me convinced I was being pressed to death." He tried to bat her away, but Beau Brummell ignored him. "How did you get here, you little monster?" He was at last obliged to forcibly remove her from his chest. He deposited her onto the floor and she slunk resentfully under the bed.

The brief moment of muzzy-headed alarm had brought him completely awake. He sat up and rubbed a hand across his face. How had that stupid animal gotten in here in any case? He felt certain that Beau had been dozing placidly by the drawing room fire when he had gone upstairs and closed his door for the night. A series of ridiculous apprehensions prickled across his skin. But no, he was being fanciful.

He dropped back on the pillows and tried to sleep, but it was impossible to regain that peaceful state. He had the annoying feeling that he had been in the midst of some fairly pleasant dream when Lorna's cat had decided to make his chest her resting place.

He also had the strangest burning sensation on his feet and ankles.

The rain outside was scratching at the windows and there was a similar faint scratching within the walls of the old house itself. Probably mice, he told himself. Outside, the wind moaned over the fells and rattled the shutters.

He threw off the coverlet in irritation. It was impossible to try to sleep when he felt so awake. He struck the flint by the bed and lit the candle. For an instant he thought he saw the curtain by the window move, but it was most likely Beau Brummell prowling about. He jerked on his dressing gown with a scowl and moved over to the chair by the fire. He might as well continue with Akerblad's treatise.

He was halfway through the chapter on the well-known Harrington collection when he put down the book in disgust. It was ridiculous to be reading about the merits of the collection when he was in the same house with it. Harrington would not likely approve of his houseguest snooping about in that wing; but then, was he likely to ever know?

He thought of the treasures, many of which Harrington had not even bothered to catalogue, lying jumbled in those rooms. The lure was too strong. He looked around for the cat, but it was nowhere to be seen. The wind set the rain pecking at the windows again, but inside the house it was quiet. He picked up his candle and slipped out of the room.

The house was bigger than he had originally thought, but it was laid out in a somewhat logical U fashion, so it should not be difficult to find the East wing. His candle sent yawning shadows stretching across the great gallery of pictures, but he registered the effect only vaguely. His thoughts were entirely on the collection.

He opened several doors filled with disappointingly Chi-

nese-looking artifacts. The life-sized set of terra-cotta soldiers was a somewhat alarming surprise, but he decided to
examine those pieces some other time. It was the Egyptian
horde he was after. At last one of the heavy, oak-paneled
doors revealed what he had been looking for.

Even in the feeble flame from his single candle, the room
reflected back a glow of light. He let out a hissing sigh of
satisfaction and closed the door behind him. Three large
mummy cases leaned up against the wall. Two were merely
painted wood, but the third was bright with gold. The detail
of the expressionless, carved faces of the coffins contrasted
strangely with the unformed bulk of their bodies. All three
cases were covered with thousands of tiny symbols.

Jonathan felt his hands trembling. A near perfect sand-
stone sarcophagus stood in the middle of the room with a
somewhat less well preserved one beside it. The lids of both
were covered with rolls of papyrus, small statues, and pots.
All around the room were shelves holding similar artifacts
and hundreds of clay figures of slaves in the act of grinding
grain, rowing boats, and making offerings. Jars with the
heads of jackals, falcons, and cats were jumbled amongst
carved fragments of panels and glazed amulets. The strange
smell of dust and antiquity in the room was heady.

He lit the sconces on the walls and the lamp that sat on
the head of a squat stone baboon. Oh yes, this was well
worth the trip indeed. It mattered little now that Harrington's
daughter was an ill-tempered shrew or that Harrington himself was incapable of appreciating the stunning beauty of the
collection he himself had amassed. Jonathan ran his hand
along the smooth, polished surface of a crouching sphinx.
It did not even matter if this collection was never his own
through marriage to the red-haired creature. What mattered
now was that he was here. And for the next few weeks he
could plunge himself into this world.

His eye was caught by a green statue of Bastet, the cat

goddess. At first he thought it was made of copper, but on closer examination he realized it was highly glazed ceramic. The animal sat very upright and stared out of its narrow pointy face with glittering rock crystal eyes. A silver amulet in the shape of the eye of Horus hung around its neck and gold rings pierced the ears and nose. Something about the cat's coolly remote expression made him think again of Miss Harrington.

He frowned and turned away. It would be best to go back to bed, now that his initial curiosity was satisfied, but his heart was beating faster, and he knew that he would never be able to sleep. He turned to examine a table littered with gold and bead jewelry.

He did not know how long he had been absorbed in pouring over the artifacts when he felt the hairs raise on the back of his neck. He resisted the urge to check to see if he was alone. There was a soft thump behind him. He whirled. A black kitten had jumped up to sit beside the statue of Bastet.

"What are you doing here?" Miss Harrington said calmly.

He shot a glance at the door but found that it was still closed. How had she gotten in? "I couldn't sleep," he said. He stamped down the sudden, ridiculous notion that Fothering might have been right about her.

She held her dressing gown tight to her throat, and her blazing hair was about her shoulders. She was regarding him with the cold, glittering eyes of the Bastet statue.

"I thought I would come and take a look at the collection," he continued, feeling a little foolish.

"My father would not like to hear that you were grubbing about among his things. Even if you do fancy yourself an expert." She ran a long forefinger along the edge of the sarcophagus and then examined her finger in distaste. "Could you not wait until morning to look at these"—her hand dropped limply to her side—"treasures?" The tone in her voice suggested that she thought the collection little more than baubles.

"No." He turned back to the table and pretended to be absorbed in the bead necklaces. Of course she wasn't a witch. It was merely that his plan was working better than he had anticipated. She had sought him out in the middle of the night to be rude to him. Surely there was no better proof of her interest.

He could feel her gaze on him. "Your father said I could examine the collection whenever I like," he said, not turning toward her. "If I choose unconventional hours, surely it is my concern." He paused for a moment, then shot a glance over his shoulder. "Why are *you* here?"

She flushed slightly. Ah yes, things were going very well indeed. The fourteen previous suitors obviously had absolutely no knowledge of the feminine mind.

"I thought I heard a noise," she stammered at last.

His mouth twisted. "You must have excellent hearing, Miss Harrington, if you heard me all the way from your chambers at the other end of the house."

Her cheeks pinkened even more.

"Or were you following me?"

Her hand tightened at the neck of her wrapper. "Certainly not."

The black kitten, which had been picking its way across the cluttered sarcophagus, rubbed up against his arm. The cat's stubby tail brushed against a top-heavy jar crowned with a jackal's head. The jar teetered.

Jonathan's hand shot out and caught it as it fell. "Cats!" he exclaimed. "Cats everywhere!"

"If you do not like them, you may leave." Her chin went up and her lips curled in a cold smile.

"No. I do not wish to leave." He gave a half-rueful laugh and carefully replaced the jar. He then swept up the kitten and deposited it unceremoniously into her arms. "Cats are generally attributed with gracefulness, but I see that myth has been exposed." He went back to examining a pile of stone plaques carved in high relief with the inscrutable hieroglyphics.

He sensed she was still standing behind him and felt a smug surge of triumph. Beautiful as she was, the vain creature could not stand to be ignored. With patience and cunning, winning her over would be ludicrously simple. "Why do you hate the collection so much?" he asked after a long silence.

He turned back to see her white fingers go still in the kitten's dark fur. "I do hate it." Her voice was so low he had to step closer to hear it. "It is all things from places I have never been. Places I will never go." Her shoulders lifted in a gesture of disdain poorly masking disappointment.

"I would take you wherever you wanted to go," he said in a low voice, wondering if it was too soon to try to kiss her.

She looked up at him with slightly raised brows. Her eyes were the lapis blue so often used in Egyptian arts. "You are impertinent." Her voice was icy.

"I meant"—he retreated behind an apathetic shrug—"if you were my daughter." Perhaps it would not be so easy to win her after all. Very well, he enjoyed a challenge. Furthermore, behind her formidable defenses, he sensed she might be a rather interesting woman. Marriage to her would be no hardship, anyway.

The faintest ghost of a dimple showed in her cheek. "I must say that I am very pleased that I am not your daughter."

"Well, if you were, I wouldn't allow you to have so dashed many cats."

She stepped over to the cat statue and leaned over to examine it carefully. "Yes, you would rather spend all your time with Bastet here."

She looked up, and again he was struck with the same sharp look she and the statue shared. "Certainly," he agreed. "She would never, as a goddess, allow herself to clumsily knock things over, get under one's feet, or"—he could not help adding—"get her head stuck in young ladies' bodices."

Miss Harrington continued to examine Bastet without looking at him. "And if she did," she said tartly, "she would certainly not be so ill bred as to mention it ever again."

He followed her over to the statue. "So you know Bastet. And I thought you hated the collection."

She made a dismissive gesture. "One cannot help picking up a little knowledge of Egypt. I know only that she is one of the most important figures in the Egyptian afterlife." She reached out and stroked Bastet's head as though she were a real animal. "The Egyptian people domesticated cats and revered them, mummified them and hoped to take them with them to the afterlife." She rubbed her thumb across the eye of Horus that hung from the statue's neck and then let her hand drop abruptly to her side. "But that is all I know."

"I believe it is all anyone knows," he said, rather impressed by her knowledge. He was surprised at his body's reaction to her. He had planned to woo her rationally, instead, he found himself struggling with an unexpected stirring of desire.

"Surely *you* know more." The dreaminess in her voice was gone, and she was mocking him again.

"Not really," he admitted. "We've found a good many cats in tombs especially in Bubastis, the city devoted to the cat goddess Bastet, but whether they were there for protection or as a sacrifice to her, no one knows. We can't read the hieroglyphics, you know."

She traced the outline of the figures in a cartouche on the side of the marble sarcophagus. "Yes, I know. I suppose that is why my father lost interest. The experts seem to know all that will ever be known." She gave them one last caress and then looked up at him. "Unless they can decipher the Rosetta stone."

At the moment he did not give a damn about the Rosetta stone. "Ah, yes. We had high hopes for it at first. The demotic does seem to be a direct translation of the Greek, but so little is known of it. Very little of the language survives. It is a bit hard to translate something like the Rosetta stone when you don't know two of the three languages. I hear the collection holds several papyruses written in demotic." Yes, ignoring her had been a stupid plan. Kissing her was a much better one. "But enough about the detested Egyptology." He leaned slightly closer to her. "You must tell me what you do like."

She seemed to come abruptly to herself and drew herself up to her full height. "I like to be left alone," she said regally.

"Ah, so that is why you followed me here?"

"I believe I already explained my reason for being here."

"Oh, yes, you heard noises, I believe. Very understandable."

"I don't care whether you believe me or not."

Something about her indignation made her seem even more beautiful. What an added bonus that she should be both clever and lovely as well as heiress to the collection. It was practically unfair to take Fothering's hundred pounds on top of it all.

"May I ask you a question?" she said suddenly, her eyes narrowing.

Ah, yes, the moment had come. "Certainly," he lowered his voice, "if I may ask you one."

"Are you here to court me?" She was watching him closely with her pale, feline eyes. Though she was still, he sensed that she was coiled to pounce.

He felt a chill pass over him. Instinct told him that the moment had not come after all. "No. I assure you, Miss

Harrington, my only reason for coming to Wythburn was to see the collection." The lie came out smoothly, but he felt the barb of it snag in his conscience. The shadow of an expression crossed her face, but before he could interpret it, it was gone. She looked as coolly detached as Bastet herself. "And now my question," he said, hoping to lead the conversation away from this dangerous territory. "Why do people say you're a witch?"

The question hung in the air for a moment. She wrapped her arms protectively around her waist and scowled. "Because I'm exceptionally bad tempered," she said at last.

He looked at the ceiling for a moment. "Very well. But I suspect there is more."

"Well, the men I refused to marry had to excuse their failure somehow."

He grinned and stepped back from her. "I think that is the more likely reason. And, as you harbor a deep hatred of suitors, you do nothing to dispel the myth. Ashford's haunting was extremely well done, I hear." Perhaps he should go back to his original plan. Seduction could come later.

She looked flustered. "Indeed! I—"

"Oh, you don't have to tell me your secrets," he assured her. "I suspect your knowledge of herbs explains his rash." He considered the matter for a moment. "And my burning feet, come to think of it." He ignored her gurgling protest. Oh, but she was lovely when she was needled. "And I would wager that your mysterious comings and goings without doors are aided by the fact that this house is riddled with priests' holes and passageways."

She looked guiltily indignant. "I never claimed to be a witch!"

"I'm certain you never did. Doubtless your sour face and bad temper alone gave them pause. Oh, don't misunderstand me," he said cheerfully, "the nettles were a good idea too. You can never be too careful when it comes to suitors." His laughter at her expression of fury lasted long after she had swept up the black kitten and banged the door behind her as she left.

# FIVE

Lorna scowled at her reflection in the mirror. "I don't like my hair," she said bluntly.

Meg's fingers stilled. "But this is the way you always wear it, miss." Her mouth slowly curved into a dimpled smile. "Will you let me try something different? I always said that something different would suit you better."

"I don't care about looking better," she snapped. "I'm just tired of wearing it the same way every day." She gave her head an irritated shake. "Carrot orange. And bran-faced as a tenant farmer."

"Your hair's lovely, miss," Meg protested. "Everyone says so."

"I don't care what everyone, or anyone, says." She brushed out the offensive hairstyle with an impatient hand and then threw down the brush. "Do whatever you wish with it. I'm sure it makes no difference to me."

Meg took the silver-backed brush and began her work again. "Your father's visitor seems like a very polite kind of gentleman," she said after a moment.

"I suppose he is," Lorna replied cautiously. "Too much levity, in my opinion."

"Everyone belowstairs says he's a very fine gentleman indeed. And so very handsome."

"Well, doubtless they only praise him because he's been free with his money." She waved a hand. "And I didn't engage you to listen to you prattle on about my father's guests." She sounded as severe as she could, but Meg continued to look pleased with herself. The hairstyle was progressing rather well. She turned her head slightly to admire the effect. "Besides," she said in a tone of supreme aloofness, "I don't think he's handsome at all."

"As you say, miss," Meg replied, prim-faced.

"His chin is too square. And he is as tanned as a sailor. And even if he is well-enough looking, he is unbearably dull. And when he is not being dull, he is being rude."

"As you say, miss."

Lorna stood to her feet and examined her hair critically. The rust-colored curls were much more softly styled than the severe chignon she usually wore. "Well, it will have to do. I look like a ridiculous actress, but there is no time to change it now. I will wear it the old way tomorrow." Ignoring Meg's comical expression of forbearance, she pulled a face at her reflection in the mirror and turned to go downstairs to breakfast.

Her father and Lord Griffith were deep in a discussion of grave goods when she slipped into her seat.

"Oh, Lorna," her father said at last when he reached for the marmalade. "You look different. New gown?"

"No." She felt unaccountably irritated. Griffith did not look up at her.

"Oh. Well, never mind that. Griffith is hoping to see the collection this morning."

"Is he?" She raised her brows at her father's guest, daring him to admit that he had already given the collection a good looking over.

"And he has generously, very generously, offered to catalogue a few things for me."

"How kind," she said dryly. Griffith merely regarded her with an infuriatingly placid smile.

"So you will want to get started right away." Her father was beaming innocently.

Lorna swallowed a bite of toast too quickly. "What have I to do with it?" she demanded.

"I thought you might help Griffith." Mr. Harrington's gray brows wagged expressively. "You have such lovely, clear handwriting, my dear."

She reached for the teapot and poured herself a cup with a calmness she knew would irritate him. "I am sorry, but I already have plans for the day. I have a poultice to prepare for Mrs. Breven's children. They all suffer from the most appalling skin condition."

"Do it this afternoon. This morning you will help Griffith." The sugary sweetness of his tone dissolved into a gruff command.

"It would be a great help," Griffith chimed in unexpectedly.

She looked at him in surprise. His gray eyes were steady on her face. How dare he look so boyishly hopeful when just last night he had insulted her to her face. She looked from her father's face to his. "Only for an hour or two," she said grudgingly.

She went upstairs to gather her writing materials, wishing she had not agreed so readily. But, after all, her father would be working with them on the cataloging, so there would be no need for them to converse directly at all.

"Ah, Miss Harrington." Griffith looked up when she arrived. "I must tell you again how much I appreciate your help. It is good of you to take the time when you have very important caldron stirring to do."

She narrowed her eyes at him and sat down on the high wooden stool without responding.

Her father rubbed his hands together and began sorting through a pile of papyrus rolls. "Symbols, symbols, a rather nice one with a drawing of an ox, symbols, two ladies with black cones on their heads, symbols. . . . In fact, all the rest are symbols. I don't know why I kept them. Can't read the damn things. Might as well just pitch them in the fire and make room for other pieces." He moved toward the hearth.

"No!" Griffith bounded across the room and caught his arm. "You cannot destroy them!"

"Why not? They are mine. And I don't want them."

"But someday we will understand the symbols, and think of what we will learn from them!"

It was strange to see Griffith so impassioned.

"But they probably don't mean anything," her father insisted with an impatient shake of the papers. "The pictures are rather nice. Don't care for the cone-on-the-head fashion, but they're a novelty in any case." He cast a glance over his shoulder at the two illustrated papyrus rolls.

"I don't think you should be the one to decide to destroy them, Papa," Lorna put in. "They might be very interesting later." She exchanged a glance with Griffith, who was still looking somewhat alarmed.

"Very well," her father conceded. He shoved the rolls toward Griffith. "Fourteen dull papyrus rolls. Write that down, Lorna."

Griffith hid his smile, but she saw it. He really did have a rather appealing sense of humor when he was not trying to be charming.

Even if she cared nothing for it, it was interesting to see someone who found the Egyptian pieces so very fascinating. His expression when he looked through the artifacts was so intense, so passionate. She shook off the thought and concentrated on gathering her papers together.

"Any scrolls with demotic?" Griffith asked suddenly.

"What?" Her father looked up from where he was still examining the illustrated papyrus rolls. "I say, Griffith, did you notice these women's gowns are transparent?"

"A language that looks different from hieroglyphics? Have you anything like that?" Lorna could see he was struggling to control his eagerness.

Her father made an impatient gesture. "I don't know. I have hundreds of things I've never laid eyes on."

Griffith exhaled what might have been a sigh and ran a hand through his hair. "Perhaps we should begin with the masks."

"Yes, much better." Harrington proudly held two aloft. "They're quite nice, don't you think? Bought them off a chap in Cairo. The whole lot."

His face fell. "You know nothing about them?"

"Well, the man said they had been in his brother-in-law's family for years, but I fancy the two of them were tomb robbers."

Griffith sat down heavily on a wooden stool and leaned his head against the wall. "They could have come from anywhere."

Her father shrugged. "The beard is interesting on this one, don't you think? It looks as though it is tied on. I have some statues from China with similar beards. Only they are real, of course. Well, not real, but meant to represent real beards rather than to represent fake ones." He set down the mask carelessly. "Would you like to see them?"

Lorna could see that Griffith was restraining himself from going to the mask's rescue.

"I would prefer to focus my efforts on this collection, if you do not mind."

"Suit yourself." Her father shrugged. "But I think you

would find the beard phenomenon fascinating. I shall bring one of the statuettes from the Chinese wing." He trundled off to find it.

"I doubt he'll come back, you know," Lorna said dryly after a moment.

"Most certainly not." Griffith agreed. "Do you mind if we continue the cataloging?"

"Continue? Had we begun?"

He laughed. "Well, let us begin."

She sat waiting while he looked at the masks. "One wooden mask in a primitive style. Most likely of much older origin than the others. While the face wears a masculine headdress, there is no beard. I have seen similar, though more sophisticated masks in Thebes."

He spoke quietly and slowly, then looked up. "Have you got that?"

"Yes."

"Good. Let's go on."

Her pen sped across the paper. Sometimes she had to ask him to wait when he got too interested in what he was examining, but she was surprised at how quickly the page filled with notations.

"Oh, God, I've forgotten myself. You must be very tired," he said at last.

"No, not at all. I'm actually finding it interesting." She was astonished to hear herself admit it.

He looked up, his pale eyes registering an expression of surprise. "Are you? I thought I must be boring you to flinders. You must tell me when I begin to rattle on."

"You can be assured that I will," she said, making an attempt at tartness. She ducked her head and finished what she had been writing.

It was more interesting to hear him talk about the collection than it was to hear her father go on about it. Griffith didn't just brag about how little he had paid for the pieces, or who he had gotten them from. He knew stories about the lives of the people who had used the objects, and he explained how the ancient civilization had changed over the centuries.

Griffith had lapsed into a long silence, so she got up and began wandering about the room. "What is this?" She picked up a brown morocco book that was lying on the window seat. She opened it up. Instead of print, it was filled with neat script. Diagrams and sketches illustrated nearly every page.

Griffith looked up with a distracted expression. "My diary," he replied.

She clapped the book closed. "I'm sorry. I did not realize it was personal."

He smiled and set down the elaborate headdress he had begun cleaning. "It is not very personal. It is more of a record of my travels in Egypt. I don't mind if you look at it."

She paged through it in silence for a few moments. "Do you plan to have it published?" The book fascinated her. With Griffith's words she could feel the heat of the Egyptian sun and the glaring light of the endless sand. She was no longer in the drafty wing of Wythburn House, she was in the tombs of the pharaohs.

"I doubt anyone would be interested."

"I am," she said quickly, with more enthusiasm than she had meant to show. "I would very much like to read it. If you don't mind, of course."

"I'm flattered. I did not think you liked Egypt."

She frowned and carefully put the book down. "It is more interesting than I previously thought it to be," she said cautiously. "But I have amused myself for long enough. We should get back to cataloging."

"You are correct. I had forgotten myself. We must not neglect dearest Bastet." Griffith smiled and crossed over to the regal statue. Imp, sitting next to it, looked comically squat and fluffy.

"Lovely Bastet," he said softly in a voice that for some ridiculous reason made her feel slightly wistful. "She is a ceramic cast glazed with green pigment. Late style rock crystal eyes and gold ear and nose rings." He ran his fingers lightly along the jawline of the cat.

He had the kind of voice an archaeologist should have. Soothing and passionate. She found herself distracted, wondering what the words would sound like murmured close to her ear. His breath would caress the side of her face. She closed her eyes. She could imagine the warmth of his lips as they brushed the edge of her ear—

"I found the statuette I wanted to show you." Her father burst into the room. "I'm sorry I was so long, but I ran across some vases I had forgotten about. I bought the lot of them for a song from an old Chinese woman. She said they came from a temple."

She came out of her reverie with a guilty jump and looked around. Griffith, too, blinked up at her father like someone waking from a sleep.

"Oh. Well, the statuette is quite nice," he said vaguely. "I don't know much about Oriental art, but it really seems . . . quite nice." He was obviously struggling to bring his attention back to the present.

Her father needed no encouragement. "You must come see the vases." He grabbed Griffith by the sleeve and dragged him toward the Chinese wing.

Imp walked over to the end of the table, sat down, and regarded her expectantly.

"You are thinking that I wasn't trying very hard to scare him off," she said with a faint smile. The kitten blinked at her for a moment, then became distracted by the suspicious activity of a foe cunningly disguised as its own tail. "Well, I didn't see the point, honestly. It is obvious he cares for nothing but Egypt." Lorna picked up the kitten and kissed it on the top of the head. "We'll see how he behaves himself and then we will decide if we wish him to stay."


Harrington ushered him into the large room filled with terra-cotta soldiers and closed the door. There was something unsettling about the statues, and Jonathan found himself fighting the urge to press against the wall to get away from them. Harrington seemed entirely unaffected. "So how do you like Lorna?" he asked with an arch smile.

Jonathan masked his laugh with an elaborate cough. The man was worse than the mamas at Almack's. "Your daughter is charming," he said, thinking of her remarkably ferocious scowl.

The man looked slightly stunned. "Is she? Well, yes, of course she is. Charming! Ha ha!" His brows lowered urgently. "You will marry her, won't you?"

Jonathan could not hide the laugh this time. He had not told Harrington that he had any intentions toward his daughter, but of course the man assumed, halfway correctly, that that was his goal. "I—"

"Because I am quite anxious to go to the Orient in the spring. I just thought that if you *were* anxious to marry Lorna, you could keep in mind that a short courtship might be convenient. And"—Harrington's finger waggled triumphantly—"you and Lorna could have the collection! As a wedding present! Yes, it's perfect. I have no interest in it, and you have!" His blue eyes were comically alight. "Lorna hates it, of course, but that's no matter. She hates everything. Yes, it's a perfect plan."

He thought of Miss Harrington and how she had looked, sitting on the wooden stool taking notes in the room full of Egyptian antiquities. Despite her temper last night, today she had been rather pleasant company. A lovely wife, who might end up amiable after all, and of course, the collection. "A perfect plan indeed." He smiled.

# SIX

"What are you doing in here?" her father demanded, striding into the kitchen like an agile thundercloud.

"I am making a mustard plaster," Lorna replied, without looking up. She added the contents of a small bowl to a large saucepan and stirred.

"Always brewing something awful-smelling. Little wonder the villagers are frightened of you." He shook his head. "Why aren't you helping Griffith catalogue the collection?"

Lorna consulted a small, stained book and then added a few more ingredients. "I have been helping him all week," she said when she was done. "I thought I would take the morning to myself."

"Griffith! Come here! I found her."

Lorna cringed. The man would stop at nothing. Surely Lord Griffith didn't want her hanging over his shoulder every moment of the day.

The man appeared in the doorway and stood there, lounging. "Ah, Miss Harrington. Stirring your cauldron, I see. Your father insisted we search you out."

"No doubt he did," she muttered.

Griffith sauntered into the kitchen and examined the contents of the saucepan. "Your witch's brew, eh?" With a taunting smirk he dipped a finger in and then tasted it.

It was very satisfying to watch him sputter and turn red with pain. "Mustard plaster," she said sweetly.

"Well, stop what you are doing, Lorna, and come help him catalogue," her father insisted, as though she would prefer to do nothing else than spend all her days with his insufferable houseguest.

"When I am finished, I intended to collect some herbs by the lake," she replied coolly.

"Ah!" Harrington exclaimed in a tone of great delight. "The lake! Have you seen our lake, Lord Griffith? It is considered one of the most beautiful in the Lake District. Perhaps you would like Lorna to show it to you. Perhaps you could go boating! Surely you cannot waste such fine weather on the collection. After all the rain we have had this summer, you cannot waste a fine fall day."

"It sounds delightful," said Griffith in a slightly strangled voice. His eyes were still streaming.

Lorna shot her father a baleful look. "It is far too cold to go boating," she protested.

"Nonsense!"

"Papa," she hissed, "I'm certain that Lord Griffith is busy. He has come to see the collection and, after all, he can go boating anywhere."

"Nonsense!" her father said again in his jolliest of tones. "We shall all go down to the lake. I will ask Cook to put together a pack lunch. Lord Griffith can go back to working on the collection later today."

There was no point in arguing when he had taken an idea between the teeth. She looked at Griffith, but he was still occupied with pouring ladles of water down his throat from the bucket on the table. She smiled faintly and made no further argument.

It really was a fine day. The sun glittered on the surface of the lake as though it was high summer. Only the fiery colors of the trees told the true story that it was far closer to winter

than anything else. It would certainly be the last boating outing before the frost set in.

Lorna tromped down the path after her father and Lord
Griffith. She was glad of her old woolen pelisse, but for an
inexplicable reason found herself wishing she had allowed her
maid to talk her into having a new one made up. The apple
green material Meg had held up at the modist's shop last week
would surely have flattered her far more than the dull slate
blue she had worn for years. She scowled at the triviality of
her thoughts.

"Here is the boat!" her father called out in a voice that
was far too enthusiastic. "And what a fine day to row to the
other side. Why don't I stay here with the luncheon while you
two take a turn?"

Surely no matchmaking mama could be worse. Lorna
scowled at him as he fluttered about the boat. What provincial
fools Griffith must think them!

"Ah! I have a better idea," her father was twittering. "If
you take Lorna and the luncheon over to the other side, we
will have lunch over there. She can set up the things while
you come back for me."

She had the luncheon basket thrust into her arms and was
forcibly put into the boat.

"There now! Isn't that grand? Off you go!" He flapped his
hand and gave the boat a shove that sent it lurching across
the water.

Lorna watched her father as he stood on the shore grinning
and bobbing and rubbing his hands together. She gave a mental groan. Griffith pulled at the oars, his expression impassive.

"I'm very sorry about all this," she said at last.

"What?"

She shrugged herself deeper into her pelisse. "My father
throwing me at you." She covered her embarrassment with a
scowl. "He is desperate to marry me off, so he treats everyone
as a suitor."

"Well, you're perfectly safe from me," he grinned.

For some reason this did nothing to loosen the peculiar knot that had formed in her stomach. For a while there was no sound but the splash of the oars. It was too cold to be out on such a morning. To be expected to make civil conversation on a freezing morning with a man obviously forced to spend time in her company was too much.

"Well," he said at last, "since we have established that I am no threat to your spinsterhood, perhaps you will tell me why it is so important to you."

"Why what is important to me?" she asked irritably.

"Your spinsterhood."

"That is a highly impertinent question."

"And I am a highly impertinent person. As you take care to remind me on every possible occasion." He spoke with a mocking gravity, but there was a suspicious twinkle in his gray eyes. He gave another pull at the oars. "Shall I tell you what I think?"

"Certainly." She waved her hand in an elaborately airy gesture. "It should be amusing, if nothing else."

He looked at the sky for a few moments as though he was thinking. "You are a deeply romantic person."

"I'm afraid I must contradict you from the outset."

He went on as though he had not heard her. "You see little use in the world for men."

"Besides the obvious need for them for . . . for procreative purposes, no." She sat up straight and regarded him severely.

"Because they have always disappointed you."

"You make me out to be a tragic heroine of a gothic romance." The idea made her laugh.

"You think all men are like your father—self-absorbed and with little thought for your own feelings."

Her laughter evaporated. "How dare you criticize my father!"

"As you told me yourself, your suitors have pursued you for

a variety of reasons: your money, your looks, the challenge of it. . . ." He leaned closer. "None for the important reason—you, yourself."

She made a noise of scorn. "You are possessed with a highly fanciful and romantic nature I had not heretofore seen to credit you with."

"I believe I am more perceptive than you have heretofore seen fit to credit me." He smiled beatifically at her. "I think you have a great deal more sensibility than one would think."

"I have not!"

"It is well hidden under that crusty exterior."

"Crusty!"

"I speak metaphorically, of course."

She merely narrowed her eyes at him.

"You are lonely up here in the wilds of Cumberland, Miss Harrington. But someday a suitor will come along who will pull off your layers one by one and discover the treasure beneath your defenses."

"You seem to have mistaken me for one of your mummies," she snapped. "I neither wish nor need to have my psyche unwrapped. Contrary to what your masculine mind can comprehend, I am perfectly happy with my life the way it is."

He leaned back at the oars, squinting into the sun. "Well," he said placidly at last, "I could be wrong."

The fittingly cutting retort she was attempting to formulate was cut short by a plaintive mew.

Her eyes met his. "Did you hear that?"

"It was a bird."

"No, it was a kitten." She looked under her seat. The cry continued. "The hamper!" She opened the luncheon hamper at her feet and a small black head popped out. "Imp!"

"Cats everywhere!" Griffith shook his head with an expression between amusement and disgust.

"Imp likes to hide in places," she said, somewhat unnecessarily. She turned the animal to face her. "Naughty creature.

What are we going to do with you? It should serve you right if you are lost."

"Shall I take the animal back? I suppose the suggestion that we drown it would not be met with approval."

"No, I shall keep him with me while you go back for Papa," she said with all the aloofness she could muster.

"Say it."

She looked at him with raised brows.

"You want to say 'The cat will be better company than you,' in an extremely condescending tone."

She bit her lip to keep from giving him the satisfaction of seeing her laugh. "Well, at least Imp will keep quiet," she muttered.

Griffith jumped out and pulled the boat ashore. He handed her out, put the luncheon basket into her arms, and then shoved off again with no ceremony.

"What a horrid man," she said to Imp, as soon as she was certain that Griffith was out of hearing. "I shall be very glad when he is gone and our life can get back to normal." She sat down and began disinterestedly looking through the luncheon basket, determined not to watch him as he rowed away. He would, of course, be wearing that horrid, self-satisfied smirk.

Imp leapt out of her lap and began stalking a fallen leaf. Her short black tail whipped back and forth.

"The impertinence of presuming to think that he understands me!"

The kitten pounced on her quarry and gave the terror-stricken leaf a shake.

Lorna sighed and scowled at the horizon. Perhaps that was the boat coming back now.

"I'm certainly glad he has no pretensions as a suitor. I would set him aright on that head soon enough." She pressed her lower lip between her teeth. It was highly inconsiderate to be so slow about the rowing when she had nothing to do but sit here on the bank freezing to death.

She was suddenly aware of the sound of voices and laughter coming from the trees. She got to her feet, conscious of the fact that she was no longer on Harrington land. But she had never known the owners of the neighboring land to be at home before.

A woman and two men came out of the woods, laughing uproariously. They were expensively and fashionably dressed, obviously straight up from London.

"Oh!" The woman saw her and stopped. Her hand flew to her mouth. "It's her!"

All three of them stared at her with unabashed curiosity. She felt herself retreating behind a cold frown.

The woman shook herself out of her stupor and approached her. "You must be Miss Harrington. I recognize you on account of your hair. Everyone has always said that it was a remarkable red, and now I see that they are correct. I am Kathleen MacAlister and this is my brother Allan, and my husband Roland. Our estate borders yours, I believe."

Lorna gravely shook hands with all of them, uncomfortably aware that Mrs. MacAlister's brother was staring hard at her.

"Is this your kitten?" The woman gingerly detached Imp from the bottom of her cloak.

"Yes, she stowed away in the basket without our knowledge. She is not very manageable, I'm afraid. Did she snag your cloak?"

Of course these people had heard of her. She was well aware that the whole county regarded her as a kind of oddity. People here did not quickly forget the strange stories of her family and the reputed curse of Wythburn House. And up to now, she had rather enjoyed their silly whisperings of witchcraft. At least it had served her well in ridding her of suitors. But now she merely felt self-conscious.

"No, no, of course not. He is a perfectly adorable creature," Mrs. MacAlister said.

## We'd Like to Invite You to Subscribe to Zebra's Regency Romance Book Club and Give You a Gift of 4 Free Books as Your Introduction! (Worth $19.96!)

If you're a Regency lover, imagine the joy of getting **4 FREE Zebra Regency Romances** and then the chance to have these lovely stories delivered to your home each month at the lowest prices available! Well, that's our offer to you and here's how you benefit by becoming a Regency Romance subscriber:

- **4 FREE Introductory Regency Romances are delivered to your doorst**
- **4 BRAND NEW Regencies are then delivered each month (usually befor they're available in bookstores)**
- **Subscribers save almost $4.00 every month**
- **Home delivery is always FREE**
- **You also receive a FREE monthly newsletter, which features author profiles, discounts, subscriber benefits, book previews and more**
- **No risks or obligations...in other words, you can cancel whenever you wish with no questions asked**

Join the thousands of readers who enjoy the savings and convenience offered to Regency Romance subscribers. After your initial introductory shipment, you receive 4 brand-new Zebra Regency Romances each month to examine for 10 days. Then, if you decide to keep the books, you'll pay the preferred subscriber's price of just $4.00 per title. That's only $16.00 for all 4 books and there's never an extra charge for shipping and handling.

### It's a no-lose proposition, so return the FREE BOOK CERTIFICATE today!

# Say Yes to 4 Free Books!
## Complete and return the order card to receive this
## $19.96 value, ABSOLUTELY FREE!

If the certificate is missing below, write to:
Zebra Home Subscription Service, Inc.,
P.O. Box 5214, Clifton, New Jersey 07015-5214
or call TOLL-FREE 1-888-345-BOOK

Visit our website at www.kensingtonbooks.com.

## FREE BOOK CERTIFICATE

**YES!** Please rush me 4 Zebra Regency Romances without cost or obligation. I understand that each month thereafter I will be able to preview 4 brand-new Regency Romances FREE for 10 days. Then, if I should decide to keep them, I will pay the money-saving preferred subscriber's price of just $16.00 for all 4...that's a savings of almost $4 off the publisher's price with no additional charge for shipping and handling. I may return any shipment within 10 days and owe nothing, and I may cancel this subscription at any time. My 4 FREE books will be mine to keep in any case.

Name _____

Address _____ Apt. _____

City _____ State _____ Zip _____

Telephone ( ) _____

Signature _____
(If under 18, parent or guardian must sign.)                    RN090A

Terms and prices subject to change. Orders subject to acceptance by Zebra Home Subscription Service, Inc. Offer valid in U.S. only.

"Having a picnic, are you?" Mrs. MacAlister's brother asked suddenly. "Surely not alone. Where are your friends?" His brows flew up with a sudden thought. "Are they here with us?" His eyes darted around, obviously expecting to be set upon any moment by hordes of picnicking specters.

She fought back her laughter. "They are rowing over now. Though I suppose we ought not have planned to have had our outing on your side of the lake."

"Who is with you?" he demanded.

"Really, my dear! Why are you asking such impertinent questions? Of course Miss Harrington is welcome to spend as much time as she wishes on our estate. Is that not right, Roland?"

MacAlister was the perfect foil for his wife. Whereas she was small, plump, and pretty, he seemed to be made up entirely of joints. His tall, angular body was topped by a nose of remarkable proportions. "Of course," he replied, disinterested in the entire exchange. He nodded toward the bank. "Here comes a boat."

She had hoped to be rid of them before Griffith and her father arrived. Now there would be more gossip for the rumor mill. No doubt in a few days the whole country would be laying bets on whether suitor number fifteen would win the prize. No one would believe that he was merely here to see the collection. She felt a rush of pity toward poor Lord Griffith. But that was replaced with surprise when she saw that he was alone in the rowboat.

"Where is my father?" she demanded as soon as he was within hearing.

Griffith made a face of annoyance. "Your father," he said dryly, "found that he was obliged to return to the house on emergent business and cannot join us." He stepped out of the boat and pulled it up onto the bank. "But I see that you have found other company."

"Lord Griffith is our houseguest," Lorna began miserably.

"He is here seeing my father's collection of Egyptian antiquities. Lord Griffith, this is—"

"Hello, Fothering," Griffith interrupted. "What a very pleasant surprise to see you here." There was a strange sound in his voice that suggested he was neither surprised nor pleased.

"Surely you remembered my sister had married MacAlister." Fothering's grin had something mischievous to it.

"No, indeed I had not."

"A remarkable coincidence that we would end up here at the same time, isn't it?"

"Yes," Griffith said grimly, "remarkable."

# SEVEN

"It was excessively generous of you to share your luncheon with us," Kathleen MacAlister said, gazing wistfully at the last slice of apple tart. "We were just commenting on how dull everything was and how nice it would have been if we had invited some other friends up from Town. But now it shall be very jolly. You will come over to the All Hallow's Eve bonfire next week, won't you? Roland has a collection of ghost stories he has written that he is planning on reading aloud to us. It is the perfect thing for All Hallow's Eve, don't you think? I shall be scared out of my wits!" She shivered. "And I do so love that feeling."

"I suppose I do fancy myself a bit of a gothic scribbler." MacAlister's bony shoulders rose and fell in an exaggerated shrug. "In one of my stories a man is haunted by a ghost." He leaned forward, his voice dropping mysteriously. "But no one else can see it!"

"Isn't that a simply terrifying idea?" his wife squealed.

"Terrifying." She wished that Griffith and Mrs. MacAlister's brother would rejoin the conversation. They had been talking together in hushed voices for a very long time.

"Talking of ghost stories, are you?" Allan Fothering leaned over at last. "Is MacAlister going on about the one with the ghost that only one man can see? I don't know why he thinks it is frightening. Pretty dull stuff. What is gruesome about a ghost that no one can see? What you need is a story with a human head that rolls about on its own. Or a beautiful woman with no eyeballs or some such thing."

"Don't be disgusting, Allan," his sister chided.

"Miss Harrington's home is haunted," Lord Griffith volunteered suddenly.

"Really?" Mrs. MacAlister's eyes were open wide.

Lorna could cheerfully strangle Griffith. Just when she was making friends for the first time in her life, they would think she was as odd as the villagers did. "It is a terribly disappointing story. Just the usual scenario, I'm afraid."

"You are obliged to tell the story anyway, as Fothering is considered the expert." Griffith smiled at her, and she felt the peculiar sensation in her stomach again.

"My great-grandfather was a horribly unpleasant old man," she began reluctantly. "But he was very rich. Everyone here knew of his temper, and there was not a man in Cumberland who would be so cruel as to marry his daughter off to him, no matter what his fortune. He finally was forced to go to London and buy himself a wife."

Griffith had stretched his legs out in front of him and leaned back on his hands. In changing his position, his fingers brushed against hers. She was ridiculously aware of his nearness, and at the same time terrified that he would move away. He did not.

"Buy?" Mrs. MacAlister repeated indignantly.

"Certainly. It was very common. It is still very common." Lord Griffith spoke up. "What else do you call it when a rich, ill-tempered old man makes a very good settlement on a young, pretty, and poor woman?"

Was it her imagination or did he move his finger in a light caress? She cleared her throat, which was showing the most alarming signs of closing up entirely. "Well, in any case, he acquired a wife. He brought her back to Wythburn House, and she bore him a son. But it was not long before old Harrington fell in love with a young widow in town. The poor widow was at least five-and-twenty years younger than he, and she, of course, was terrified of him, but he was determined to have her." She traced her finger around the rim of a half-full glass of wine in front of her. The crystal rim sang out beneath her finger in a clear, sad note.

"Old Harrington began to slowly poison his wife. At least, that is what is said. In any case, she quickly became unwell. Harrington did not allow the doctors to see her. She became delusional, screaming that he was trying to kill her. It is said she put a curse on him that neither he nor any Harrington would ever have a happy marriage."

"Did she go completely off her nut?" Allan asked eagerly.

Lorna laughed. "I suppose she did. In any case, she died a terrible, agonizing death. Harrington married the widow two months later." Perhaps Griffith had mistaken her fingers for merely a lump in the tablecloth, or even someone else's fingers.

Mrs. MacAlister shuddered. "Not even out of deep mourning, the wicked man!"

"Not many months later, the second wife was found drowned in the lake."

"This lake?" Mrs. MacAlister looked repulsed.

"Yes. It was never clear if it was an accident or suicide. Of course, there are fanciful people who claim that it was the ghost of the first wife who pushed her in."

"Not a family I would want to marry into," Fothering said, with a sideways glance at Griffith.

"I suspect we can all boast of characters like old Harrington in our family's lineage," he said mildly, sitting up and removing his hand. Lorna stayed very still, just to show she hadn't noticed. Her hand felt very cold now.

"You would think the ghost would have had the sense to push old Harrington into the lake, not the second wife," he continued. "But one never knows. Ghosts are such capricious creatures."

"Have you had any dealings with the ghost at Wythburn House?" Fothering prodded. "Rashes? Ruined stockings?"

"Certainly not. I'm afraid it has been quite a pleasant stay."

Lorna watched Griffith twitch a long blade of grass in front of Imp. The kitten was dancing back and forth, alternately frightened and aggressive. There was some subtext between Fothering and Griffith that she did not understand. And she did not like it.

"I think it is a frightful story," Mrs. MacAlister announced. "Not nearly as good as Roland's." She gave in and took the last piece of tart. "Do you think we will see her ghost this All Hallow's Eve?"

"Are you worried?" her brother taunted. "What if she, jealous of your happily married state, takes you by the neck and throws you in the lake!"

Mrs. MacAlister let out a bloodcurdling shriek as Fothering laid a cold spoon to the back of her neck. "You monstrous creature!" She slapped him away. "How dare you do that! You have given me an attack of the nerves I am likely to never recover from! Roland! Where is my vinaigrette? Really Allan, you're quite impossible."

"Perhaps you would like to go home now, my dear?" her husband asked, still looking slightly sulky at the eclipse of his own ghost story.

"No, I wish to walk about for a few minutes to calm my nerves. Perhaps I can persuade you to accompany me, Miss Harrington?"

"Certainly." She got to her feet and picked up Imp, who was obviously irritated to be removed just when she was getting the upper hand of the blade of grass.

"Isn't this lovely?" Mrs. MacAlister linked arms with her and drew her down the path by the lake. "I must say, it is a good deal colder here than I expected. But I daresay that will make the bonfire that much better, don't you think?"

"Yes," she agreed, since there was nothing else to say.

"How fortunate that we happened upon you! It was really the most charming thing imaginable. Now we shall have everyone who is anyone at the bonfire. But I suppose you were rather annoyed to have us interrupting your courting."

"We were not courting," she replied coolly.

The woman's brows rose very high on her forehead. "You are not?" She held her hand over her mouth in an even more exaggerated gesture of surprise. "Well, I thought for certain that you were. Well, well, well!"

"Griffith is merely a guest of my father's. Papa was to come with us today but was unexpectedly detained." She felt like a complete fool, having to explain her behavior. Trust her father to leave her in a situation where her reputation could be shredded.

Mrs. MacAlister simpered. "Well I must say that that is good news indeed. He is very handsome, Griffith, and quite the catch, they say. If you have no objections, I would simply adore to have him come to the bonfire."

"Why could I possibly object?"

The woman gave her a sly look. "My sister from Leeds is coming, and I must confess, we have high hopes for her. She would be the perfect wife for Griffith."

Lorna felt suddenly as though someone had stuck her in the ribs with something sharp. "Of course," she heard herself say faintly.

"He is ever so handsome, don't you think? Not so much as Roland of course, but very handsome indeed."

Lorna cast a doubtful glance at Mr. MacAlister. To her, he was very nearly ugly. It made her feel odd to think that one's opinion of handsomeness depended so heavily on one's feelings for someone. Griffith, however, was undoubtedly handsome. In the classic sense, of course. Anyone would think so.

Mrs. MacAlister sighed. "Well, of course she will have to put up with all those dreadful Egyptian things." She shuddered. "It is well known that Griffith is enamorate of them. And of course no one knows better than you, my dear, how perfectly abhorrent they are to a woman of sensibility. Heathen tombs! It makes my skin crawl!"

"Perhaps she will gain an appreciation for them." Lorna squinted across the lake, where she could see the roof of Wythburn House in the distance.

"I suppose she might. Though it would be an odd thing indeed if Arabella turned bookish all of a sudden."

Arabella. What an insipid name. She would doubtless be pretty, petite, and entirely freckle-less.

"And of course the All Hallow's Eve bonfire will be a prime opportunity for courtship, don't you think? And we all know that Griffith, just come back from Egypt, is hanging out for a wife. And why should it not be Arabella!" Mrs. MacAlister looked quite pleased with her logic.

"Griffith does not want a wife," Lorna protested. It felt strange talking about him when he was not present. She could feel her cheeks grow warm, and it irritated her. "He is entirely devoted to his work."

Mrs. MacAlister's look was skeptical. "Of course he wishes for a wife. He just may not know it yet. Arabella will entice him."

Lorna realized she had been petting Imp in the wrong direction. She smoothed the animal's ruffled fur. "Tell me about the bonfire," she said, forcing a smile.

"We used to have one every year in Leeds. It was grand fun. Dancing and mulled wine by the light of the fire. We always stayed out ever so late. Obviously it was quite proper," she amended quickly. "You will come, won't you? Everyone in the neighborhood is coming. I wanted to invite you, but I was a little afraid. Everyone says you are a—don't like parties." She cut herself off and looked guiltily embarrassed.

Lorna didn't know if she liked parties or not. She had never been invited to one. "I would very much enjoy the bonfire, I am sure."

Mrs. MacAlister gave a little skip. "Marvelous! Won't everyone be surprised that I have managed to entice you to come? It will be quite a coup. And then, when it is seen that Griffith greatly favors Arabella, I will be considered a great matchmaker as well as a great hostess."

Lorna wished she could retract her improvident acceptance. The idea of watching Griffith make a fool of himself over Mrs. MacAlister's sister was slightly repugnant. The poor man was doubtlessly naive when it came to women. He would be quite ensnared before he knew what he was about.

# EIGHT

They turned to walk back toward the men, who were laughing uproariously over some joke. Griffith looked up and smiled when he saw her. She wished again that she had not accepted the invitation to the All Hallow's Eve bonfire.

But it was not long before she was swept up in Griffith's amusing stories about Egypt and the ridiculousness of fashionable life in London. Mr. MacAlister chimed in with vastly less amusing stories, but even these made her smile when Griffith and Fothering were constantly interrupting him with silly questions. For the first time in her life, she realized how pleasant it was to be amongst friends, or at least people who might someday be friends. It threw the loneliness of her upbringing into sharp relief.

"Are you ready to go, my dear?" MacAlister said, getting to his feet at last.

"Yes, perhaps we'd better. It is getting late, and we had not planned to stay for luncheon."

Fothering stood, still laughing. "Well, we have doubtlessly worn out our welcome. Perhaps we'll see you again, eh, Griffith? And until then, best of luck." He winked broadly and then set off again into peals of laughter.

Lorna waited until the party had gathered up their things and disappeared along the path into the woods before she confronted Griffith. "You know Fothering from before, don't you?"

"Fothering? Certainly. He's a friend of mine from London. At least, I suppose one would call him that."

"I don't like him."

Griffith paused in putting the plates back into the hamper, then shrugged. "Then you are lucky indeed that he is not *your* friend."

"He kept staring at me."

"You are uncommonly beautiful."

She felt her face go hot in a blush. She had been told so by fourteen men previously, but strangely this was the first time she found the pronouncement pleasing. "I don't think that was why he was staring," she mumbled.

Griffith got to his feet and carried the hamper to the boat. "Fothering is a fool. You should pay him no mind."

She picked up Imp and followed him. "Well, I can't say that I am sorry that we met them. I had a rather nice afternoon. I've never been to a picnic before. At least not a real one. I used to have tea parties with my dolls when I was a child, but I never had a real outing like this. It was just like in a book, with everyone talking and laughing." She knew she was making a fool of herself with such ebullient, nonsensical talk, but she didn't care. "It would be lovely to have outings like this all the time."

"Why don't you?" he asked, handing her into the boat.

She settled herself carefully into the back and then reached out to take Imp from him. "I don't know. Papa never cared to have anyone to the house but his own friends. Egyptologists during that phase, and now scholars who study the Orient. Orientologists?" She had the uncontrollable urge to giggle. "Well, anyway, today was just marvelous." She wrapped her arms around herself and sighed. "I hope they were sincere when they asked me to come over next week. Though I must say MacAlister's ghost stories sound dreadfully dull."

Griffith was staring at her with a strange expression. "I have never seen you like this before," he said, puzzled.

She laughed. "You must think I am very pathetic to be so happy at the notion of having neighbors. Neighbors who one could actually visit. Who might actually become one's friends."

He turned and looked at her for a moment. "I don't think you are pathetic." His gray eyes were unsettling in their cool assessment. "I think I have discovered the root of your shrewishness."

"My what?" The ebullience drained from her.

"Shrewishness," he repeated pleasantly. "I thought at first it was because you were spoiled, but now I see that it is merely shyness."

"I am not shy!"

Griffith continued to pull at the oars. He seemed completely unaware that he had insulted her. "Well, if not shy, then merely socially inept."

"You are the rudest person I have ever had the misfortune to meet!" It made her more angry to realize that she cared what he thought of her.

"I am not known for my social graces myself. And it is little wonder, as you have been trapped here all your life with no friends and no one who cares about you, and I have spent most of my life abroad."

She set her jaw and stared hard at the hills in the distance. For some reason her eyes were beginning to sting.

"It was rather nice to see you talking and laughing with the MacAlisters today rather than sitting about with that sour look on your face." He seemed to think that she would take this as a great compliment. "It would do you a great deal of good to spend more time in the company of clever, pleasant people."

"Well, I am certainly in neither clever nor pleasant company now." She resolutely ignored the pain in her chest.

"You are piqued because you know that it is true. If your father had seen past the end of his nose and had taken you to London, or better, to Paris, you would really have shone. Instead he has left you here with your infernal cats."

"I don't know why you think you have a right to comment on the way I have chosen to live my life. You have known me no longer than a week or two and you seem to think that you know everything about me. I can't imagine—oh!" Her rant was cut short as Imp, who had been perched on the gunwale watching the green water slip under the boat, reached out toward a floating leaf. Before Lorna could grab her, the kitten lost her balance and was over the side with a splash.

Griffith dropped the oars and flung himself to his knees in the bottom of the boat. "Don't move." He pushed her back with one hand. "You'll capsize us. I'll get it."

Lorna held her breath while he reached over the side of the boat. There was a rather frenzied splashing, a frightened mew, and then he pulled the bedraggled ball of fur back into the boat.

"Imp!" She took the kitten from him and wrapped it in the bottom of her pelisse. The poor thing seemed so much smaller with its wet hair plastered to its tiny body. She could feel its whole body shaking.

Griffith pulled himself into the seat beside her. "Is it alive?"

She peered into the little cocoon she had made for the animal. "Yes. She's just miserable."

He examined his sleeve, wet to the shoulder, and the multitude of scratches up his hand and wrist. "Why did the ridiculous animal do something so addlepated?" he muttered. But he reached inside the bundle she had made and stroked the kitten's nose with a gesture that was almost tender.

"Thank you," she said stiffly. She had been too frightened for Imp to be angry at him, but she still felt an awkwardness between them. She said nothing, but continued to watch the animal. Griffith was sitting far too close, but he seemed intent on assessing Imp's welfare.

"Are you hurt?" She touched the scratches on his wrist.

"No."

He was very close to her indeed. He turned his hand over and brushed her own, then let it go.

"I hurt your feelings, didn't I?" he asked quietly.

She looked up. He was watching her intently. "I suppose you did." She lifted her shoulders. "But only because you are right. I have become rather ill-tempered and willful in my solitude."

His mouth quirked to one side. "I didn't mean it to sound like that. Obviously it is I who have no social graces." He nudged her with his shoulder with a kind of schoolboy gesture of placation. "I only meant that I liked seeing you laughing with other people today. I liked seeing you let down your defenses." He looked rather sheepish. "I didn't mean to sound . . ." His voice drifted off.

"Like an arrogant prat?" she supplied.

"Yes." He laughed softly.

"Judgmental?"

"Yes."

"Critical?"

"Very sorry." He ducked his head in a comical expression of contrition.

"Completely ignorant in assuming that you could possibly understand my circumstances?" Now she was laughing too.

"An all-around unbearable person." He leaned in to peer at Imp, who had recovered enough from her ducking that she was struggling to escape her swaddles.

Griffith really shouldn't be sitting so close. She should insist that he take his place at the front of the boat and row them home instead of sitting pressed against her while they drifted unguided across the smooth surface of the lake. "I don't think you are *entirely* unbearable." She meant to say it normally, but somehow it came out almost a whisper.

"No?" He looked up at her with an expression that was almost hopeful.

He smiled, and she had the unexpected urge to touch his one slightly turned tooth. "Not entirely."

He took her face between his hands. One was cold from its plunge in the water and the other was warm. She realized she was shaking, but that it had nothing to do with the weather. His face was very close to hers.

Ashford had kissed her once when he had caught her alone in the passageway after dinner. It has been unpleasantly wet and squashed. She had slapped him so hard that the red imprint of her fingers had remained on his face for hours.

This was different. This time she wanted it more than anything. She drew a quick breath and closed the gap between them.

His arms went around her instantly. She was vaguely aware of his fingers in her hair and the warmth of his mouth. Her heart was pounding very hard in her ears, and she felt as though her breath could not quite keep up with her body. It was nothing like she had imagined it. It was something that seemed to take on a life of its own and wrest her self-control from her grasp.

A faint, distressed mewing dragged her back into reality.

"Kitten!" Griffith sighed in a voice of fond irritation.

Imp struggled out of the pelisse and began picking her way toward the luncheon hamper. Her dainty progress across the murky puddle that had collected at the bottom of the boat was impeded by the need to shake each little white paw after every step. Her damp fur stuck comically out in all directions. She reached the hamper at last, gave a baleful glare at the world that had treated her so thoughtlessly, and climbed in.

The moment was gone. Lorna suddenly realized that she was cold and that her feet were wet. She struggled out of

Griffith's arms. What had come over her? Miss Lorna Harrington was not the kind of woman who was hurt because a man thought badly of her. And she was certainly not the kind of woman who fell apart after one kiss. No, she was not the kind of woman who needed anyone. "Well, I suppose we had better be going home," she said coldly.

Griffith looked stung. "Lorna, I—"

"I don't think I want to discuss it."

"But you don't understand. I—"

She looked at him with unblinking eyes and then said with a steadiness she did not feel, "Lord Griffith, I believe it would be best if we acted as though this regrettable moment never happened."

# NINE

Jonathan stared at the tablet with unseeing eyes. Was there a pattern in the symbols? A common element with the dozens of other scrolls that littered the Egyptian rooms in the west wing? He sighed and pressed his fingers to his tightly closed eyes. He didn't really care. For the first time since he had set foot in Harrington's spectacular collection, he found that he could not feel any interest in it.

He stood and walked around the crowded room. There was so much more cataloging to do, but he couldn't seem to keep his mind on it. His toe caught on the leg of the stool set at the other side of the sarcophagus. How stupid of him to have hoped that Lorna would join him as she used to. He gave the stool a savage kick and watched in satisfaction when it skidded across the floor with an irritated squawk.

The day on the lake had been disastrous. After he had been so cork-brained as to have allowed himself to kiss her, she had closed up like a book. The trip back to shore had been long, cold, and silent. How Fothering would laugh when he found out. He had been so close to winning her, and then he had ruined it through his own unaccountable attraction to her.

He ran his hand through his hair and continued his circuit of the room. The collection was everything he had hoped it would be. Perhaps even more so. But Lorna had not spoken to him since the day on the lake, and that had been nearly a week ago. She had been off to the MacAlisters every day. They had provided a slew of autumnal amusements that would certainly keep her from ever feeling lonely. He realized now that her isolation, her loneliness had been the only thing he had had in his favor when he had started his suit.

He leaned up against the window frame. The bound volume of his Egyptian travels lay on the window seat where Lorna had left it. Every day when he had gone to meet her to start cataloging the collection, he had found her reading it. Her expression when she read it was one of dreamy absorption.

He would take her to Egypt one day. She would love it there. The idea of traveling with her as his wife gave him a strange thrill he did not expect. If he was patient, he could win her over. He picked up the book with a feeling of resolution. Yes, there was no other option. She must be convinced. He thought of her passionate response to his kiss. It had been a brief moment, but it had been so very real. She could not be completely indifferent.

Out the window, he saw her walking in the grove of trees that bordered the lawn. As he watched, she stooped to pick up a brilliantly colored leaf. She twirled it between her fingers and then let it fall again. Before he even realized he had made a decision, he had thrown down his pen and gone to get his coat.

She looked up in surprise when she saw him crossing the lawn toward her. For a moment he thought he saw something like fear in her eyes. But then there was nothing but the cold mask of civility.

"I thought you had gone to the MacAlisters to help collect wood for the All Hallow's Eve bonfire," he said, striding up to her.

"I decided not to go."

Her eyes were very blue in her pale face. He was surprised by his body's mutinous urge to kiss her again. Had he learned nothing from the first time? "What are you doing?" he asked, feeling excruciatingly like a schoolboy infatuated with an elegant lady. So much for his grand plan to ignore her until she fell in love with him. He couldn't stay away from her if he tried. How Fothering would laugh.

"Walking."

"I will accompany you."

"If you feel that you must."

He tried to laugh. "I see that you have brought your requisite kitten with you."

"Yes."

She wasn't going to make this easier for him. "How has Imp survived her ducking?"

"Very well. But this is not Imp." He thought he saw her smile, but before he could be sure, she leaned down to pick up a leaf. She had quite a collection now, like a brilliantly colored bouquet. "It is Incubus."

"Incubus, Imp, whatever. They look exactly alike!"

"To you, perhaps," she said, as though one would have to be a complete dolt to mistake one black cat for another.

They walked along in silence for a moment. Miss Harrington collected a few more bright leaves.

"I am having a bit of trouble with the cataloging," he said at last, after searching around for something witty to say.

"How unfortunate." Her voice was cool.

"Can I interest you in helping me?"

"I don't believe that I have the time." She plucked a leaf from her collection, looked at it carefully, and then cast it away.

"What about you, Incubus?" he addressed the cat in her arms. "Are you going to reject me as well? I don't blame you if you do. After all, I rudely mistook you for one of your brothers."

"Sisters," Miss Harrington corrected.

"But I was very much hoping that I could convince you to come up and sit with Bastet as you used to do."

"That was Imp."

Jonathan repressed the urge to laugh. "Perhaps, then, you could convey the invitation to Imp. I would very much like him—"

"Her."

"—her to return to her former habit of keeping me company while I work. Her absence is very distracting."

Miss Harrington's expression was hidden by the edge of her bonnet, but he thought he saw her lips curve into a smile. "I believe that Imp has other engagements."

"I realize that a kitten's schedule can become unduly crowded with social engagements, but I hope that you, Incubus, will convey to her my most sincere application for her company."

Incubus struggled to get out of her arms, so Lorna set him on the narrow walk. Jonathan stopped and crouched down to the animal. "Why is Miss Harrington so cross with me?" he asked in a dramatically loud whisper.

The cat just stared at him, but he could hear Lorna make a contemptuous noise behind him.

"I had thought that we were well on our way to being friends."

"Friends do not—" She made a strange noise in her throat. "Friends do not kiss in rowboats."

"You are right," he said to the cat. "They do not. But I faithfully promise I will never, ever, ever kiss Miss Harrington in a rowboat again."

"Or say that she is shrewish, though she undoubtedly is," she prompted.

"Exactly." He reached out and smoothed the fur on the kitten's head. It closed its amber eyes and looked well pleased. He stood to his feet and brushed the wrinkles out of his trousers. He looked up at Lorna with an expression of exaggerated surprise. "Oh! You're still here!"

She rolled her eyes.

"What are you doing? Collecting leaves? For another terrible brew to poison me?"

"No." He could see a smile pulling at the corners of her mouth.

"Dare I ask why? Or will you pounce upon me and tear me to shreds?"

"I will let you survive for now," she said dryly. "Mrs. MacAlister asked me to bring them. She is making garlands for the bonfire. It's tonight, you know. Will you go?"

"Do you want me to?"

He saw her cheeks go slightly pink. "Well, I'm certain I don't care." She appeared to conceive a deep interest in the leaves she carried. "I'm sure the MacAlisters would be terribly disappointed if you did not attend. They were talking about you the other day."

"What did they say?" he demanded, suddenly suspicious that Fothering had spouted some nonsense.

She looked up, her pale brows drawn slightly together. "Only that they wished you to come." She stooped to pick up another leaf, and he could not see her face. "I did not know you knew Fothering so well. I got the impression from you that you were only passing acquaintances."

He stilled. "I did not mention it, perhaps."

"Well, he certainly spoke a great deal about you."

"Indeed." He braced himself. There was no way Allan would have remained discreet. He would enjoy the joke too much.

"I can't say that I am overly impressed with him," she went on. "He always wears a sly look, as though he is making fun of me. I told him we had worked on the cataloging, and he gave me a very odd look indeed."

"Pay him no mind," he said firmly. A puff of wind blew down the walk. He could see it coming toward them in a torrent of leaves.

"How is your work going?"

He realized a silence had fallen between them. He cleared his throat, thinking rather sheepishly of the amount of time he had spent aimlessly pacing the rooms upstairs. "Quite well."

The wind had found them. The treetops above them shuddered with it and a spill of leaves rained down around them. He suddenly wished very much that he had not promised not to kiss her again.

"Still puzzling over the hieroglyphics?" She smiled.

It was difficult at that moment to give a damn about anything but that smile. "The work is going slowly," he admitted.

"I thought of going to see your progress. . . ." She turned to watch Incubus take a running start at the trunk of a tree, skitter several feet up, pause, and then drop to the ground.

"Why didn't you?"

Her shoulders heaved in an expression he couldn't interpret.

"Rowboat," he said, suddenly aware of her thoughts. He wondered if the memory of that kiss affected her the same way. He gave a short laugh. "I understand you have conceived a deep aversion to them, but I assure you, there are none in the Egyptian collection."

The wind had caught up a lock of her hair that had escaped from her bonnet, and it was leaping about as though it was alive. He restrained himself from touching the burnished coil.

Incubus made another race at the tree. He nearly reached one of the lower branches but, alarmed at his success, he gave a shrill mew and jumped to the ground again.

"It will not be long now before you understand its secrets."

"What?" He didn't remember what they had been talking about. "Oh, hieroglyphics. I hope not."

A leaf had caught in the collar of her pelisse. He reached out to brush it away but stopped himself.

"Well—" She turned away, and he realized once again that a silence had fallen and that he had been staring at her like a besotted fool. "I suppose I shall go in. It is getting rather cold."

"Certainly. I think I will walk on for a bit." Yes. He needed to clear his thoughts. A little time alone and he could refocus his energy on the collection. It was ironic—he had come to this godforsaken place to win her and now, when he should make the final push, he found himself unable to do it.

He cleared his throat. "I brought you something." He shoved the diary toward her with no ceremony.

She accepted it with an expression of bewilderment. "But this is yours."

He drew a quick breath. "No, it is yours. I want you to have it."

"Why?" Her fingers moved gently across its brown morocco cover.

"Because you liked it." He smiled weakly. "Because it is the only thing I have that is really mine to give you." The leaf caught in her collar touched her neck. She brushed it away with an impatient motion, and it spiraled slowly to the ground.

Her mouth trembled slightly at the corners. "I don't know what to say. I've never been given anything that . . . that meant so much to me."

He did not realize until that moment that he had been holding his breath. "Then you like it?"

Her voice was barely above a whisper. "Yes."

"Miss Harrington," he said urgently, afraid the moment would slip away, "I don't want to distress you, but there is something I wanted to ask you."

"Yes?" She did not look up.

"I was thinking—I was hoping—That is—" He was making a hash of it. How had he ever been so arrogant as to think that he could charm her? The idea of spending the rest of his life with the woman before him was a dizzying prospect indeed. He realized at that moment that nothing in the world mattered more. He charged ahead again. "I was hoping—"

She looked up at the sound of a small, shrill cry.

"Where is Incubus?" she asked quickly. The kitten was nowhere to be seen. "He was just there, trying to get up that tree."

Only the wind stirred the leaves banked against the pale trunk. The moment was lost. Jonathan wanted to catch her arm and blurt out his offer, graceless as it would undoubtedly be. He needed to know now that she was his.

"Incubus?" she called, as though the creature would have the wits to answer. She walked over to the tree and peered up into the branches. "There you are!"

He followed her over to the tree. "Where?" She pointed up to a branch far above their heads where a bit of black fur was ruffling in the breeze. "How did it manage that? Two minutes ago she couldn't get up more than a foot!"

"He," Lorna corrected him in a distracted tone.

Incubus looked down at them. His mouth opened in a mew, but the wind carried the sound away.

"He can't get down."

Jonathan crossed his arms. "Of course he can. Kittens have been climbing trees since the world began. They always get down. Miss Harrington, there is something very important I must speak with you about." His urgency was lost on her as she stood with her face to the sky.

"Look at him, he's terrified!" She gestured at the kitten, who was indeed looking somewhat uncomfortable in its perch.

"He'll figure it out. If kittens were innately unable to do so, don't you think the trees would be simply filled with them?"

She looked at him with dismay. "He will get tired and fall out. He'll be hurt."

He stripped off his jacket and swung himself onto a limb. The tree branched often, and it wasn't a particularly difficult climb, but the kitten seemed to have gotten itself rather higher up than he had originally thought. Below him, he could see

Lorna's white face staring up at him. No doubt he would fall and be killed for the sake of her ridiculous kitten.

"Jonathan! Do be careful!" she called out in alarm.

He suddenly wished she had three or four kittens stuck in trees. The feeling of heroism was rather heady.

Ignoring the violent protests of his body, he snatched the kitten from its perch. It immediately adhered to his shirtsleeve with all its needlelike claws. He was now posed with the problem of climbing down with one hand. After a moment the problem was solved, rather painfully, by allowing the tiny animal to cling to his cravat. He arrived on the ground wearing the kitten somewhat like a large, furry medal on his chest.

"Why did you do that?" she chided. "You could have been killed!" She collected the kitten in her arms. "I shouldn't have let you do it. I'm perfectly capable of taking care of things on my own." Her nose was buried in the kitten's fur, but her eyes were bright.

"I know," he said quietly, acutely aware of her closeness. "But I wanted to do it for you."

For an instant he saw an expression of vulnerability pass over her face. She raised her chin and laughed it off. "But you don't like cats, Lord Griffith."

He reached out and gently touched the kitten's head. She held the animal close to her cheek and his fingertip brushed against her as he caressed the animal's warm fur. "But I like you," he said softly.

He saw her knuckles whiten on the spine of the book she held in her other hand. "You do?"

"Yes." He wondered if, since he had specified that he would not kiss her again in a rowboat, if kissing her right now would be considered a breach of contract. He leaned in closer. "Lorna, I—"

"Griffith!" A hail came from across the lawn. "I suspected I should find you together!" Fothering strode over wearing his most irritating smirk. "When am I to wish you happy?"

Lorna turned away from them both with a scowl.

"What do you want, Fothering?" he growled. He crossed his arms, suddenly aware of the cold.

"I've come to take you lovebirds to the bonfire. Are you going to save it until then to make your interesting announcement?" In the awkward silence, a slow light dawned in Fothering's face. "Oh, I say, I'm a bit premature, am I? Well, you can't blame me! An honest mistake. The way you two were looking at each other. Well! Anyone would have thought—"

Jonathan put his coat back on, fighting a feeling of impending doom. Lorna was too clever to believe any excuse he might invent, and her trust was too fragile to accept the truth: He had come here with a rational plan to marry her and had ended up falling irrationally, passionately, wholly in love with her.

He saw her expression of suspicion and felt like his heart was being pulled to bits. She would drag the story out of Fothering in two minutes.

"Well, anyway, are you coming to the bonfire?" Fothering was saying, blithely unaware that he had just destroyed his friend's chances of happiness.

"I'm afraid I have a good deal of work to do," he said gruffly. Unable to meet Lorna's eyes, he strode off toward the house.

Lorna watched him go. He had left so suddenly and with such a miserable expression. She felt her stomach tighten with anxiety.

"Ignoring you, is he?" Fothering said with an odd laugh.

She frowned at him. She did not like the way he continued to smile at her, but he fell into step beside her in the most companionable way.

"Well, don't mind him," he continued cheerfully.

"I don't." The lie came out fairly convincingly.

"It is getting late. He has not made an offer?" Fothering seemed genuinely surprised.

"I cannot see that it is any of your concern." She turned from him and primly clasped her hands together. A movement caught her eye. In the upstairs window, a room she knew was part of the Egyptian collection, she could see Griffith looking down at her. But the instant he saw her he moved away.

Fothering kicked through a pile of fallen leaves. "Well, I saw how you looked at each other. I've lost anyway. He'll make you an offer tonight."

Her head jerked around. "What do you know of such matters?" she demanded.

His face grew flushed. "Nothing," he said quickly.

If he had continued to tease her, she would have thought nothing of his comment, but now she was suspicious. "What is going on, Mr. Fothering?"

"Nothing!"

"Did Lord Griffith indicate that he . . . he wished to propose to me?" The words stuck awkwardly in her throat.

"Well . . . that is . . . in London. . . ." His face was going a guilty red.

"London?" She felt a strange frisson of alarm.

"Well, it is an arrangement that would suit the both of you," he said helplessly.

"He said to you in London that he wished to marry me?" She put her hand on one of the gnarled trees for support. She felt as though she could not catch her breath.

"Well, surely you must admit you like him better than your previous suitors."

She shot him a look that she hoped indicated her utter loathing of both him and his friend on no uncertain terms.

"But do me a favor, won't you?" Fothering caught her arm and lowered his voice conspiratorially. "Don't accept him until after the All Hallow's Eve bonfire. I've a hundred pounds riding on it." His dull blue eyes were alight with interest.

"What?" The faint warmth she had felt on hearing that Griffith wished to marry her evaporated entirely. "Are you saying that Griffith came up here with the intention of marrying me"—she heard her voice go shrill—"and that you wagered money on it?" She looked up at the window, but the drapes were closed. An unholy fury was rising within her.

"Listen, just don't accept him until after All Hallow's Eve." Fothering still wore an expression of hopeful conspiracy. "I'll give you ten pounds."

"What?"

"I'll give you twenty, then. Now look, don't get in a ruffle. He'll have the collection and you'll be respectably married."

"I do not wish to be respectably married," she said coldly.

Fothering looked bemused. "Of course you do. Can't see what you should object to about Griffith. Fine sort of man. If you don't mind playing second fiddle to a bunch of dead Egyptians wrapped in bandages!" He threw back his head and laughed.

He seemed to grasp after a long moment that she was not amused. "Ah, go on. I saw how you looked at him. You're as in love with him as he is with you. Now be a good girl and don't say yes until after the bonfire. Fifty pounds. I'll give you half the money if you wait. That would be nice pin money for you, wouldn't it? And it would be such a laugh to see Griffith thwarted."

"I don't want your fifty pounds, Mr. Fothering," she said regally through clenched teeth. "But I think I can safely promise you that it will be a long, long time after All Hallow's Eve that I agree to marry Jonathan Griffith."

# TEN

The door of the room holding the Egyptian collection banged hard against the wall when she flung it open. Griffith looked up. His expression was grim.

"You wagered I would marry you before All Hallow's Eve," she said quietly. She clenched her hand on the doorknob to keep it from shaking. How could he do such a thing? After all the pleasant afternoons they had spent together? She looked around the room in disgust. All so that he could have this collection.

"No."

"No?" She tried to curb the hope that shot through her.

"I did not wager that you would be married to me by then. I wagered that you would be betrothed to me by then." He gave her a weak smile.

Her fingers itched to slap him. "Then there is a very great difference indeed. You are *not* the biggest liar I have ever met. You have *not* abused both my trust and friendship, and I am *not* going to ask you to leave this house immediately."

"Good." He pretended to be absorbed in his writing, but she could see the tight muscle in his jaw.

There was a silence while she struggled to control her temper. "Get out."

"So you *do* mean to ask me to leave the house immediately?"

"Enough! I never want to see you or speak to you again. You deliberately set out to seduce me."

"Not seduce—marry," he corrected her calmly.

"For money. For a wager!"

"It was merely a hundred pounds, my dearest. I hope your offense does not stem from the fact that the wager was relatively small. I wanted the collection."

She could see his anguish beneath the flippant words, but she did not care. "The collection." Her voice was derisive.

"You must not repeat everything I say. It's a very bad habit, my dear."

She resisted the urge to scream. "You villainous man. You would like nothing better than to have my father dead and be married to a woman who despises you. All for the collection."

He placidly dipped his quill in the inkpot. "I rather like your father, actually. I was hoping he could be persuaded to cling to life for a few more decades at least."

She wanted to throw something. She looked down and saw with a vague sense of surprise that she still held his Egyptian diary. The memory of the look on his face when he had given it to her now made her feel physically ill.

"Well, I am so sorry to have lost you the collection as well as the one hundred pounds," she said acidly. "But I shall return this to you. The one thing that was ever really yours." Her voice was mocking. "It is fitting you should have it back, as neither the collection nor myself ever will be yours." She slammed the book down on the table and left the room.

Imp had been dozing at her usual place at Bastet's feet. She jumped at the sound of the book hitting the table and leapt to the floor. Jonathan saw too late that the animal had managed to unbalance the statue. It rocked for a slow moment, and then, just as he reached out in a futile attempt to catch it, it fell to the floor with a crash.

He stared at the pieces in horror. A more symbolic incident could not possibly have occurred. Bastet was smashed to pieces. Lorna was gone. The collection would never be his.

"Devil take the collection," he growled, taking bitter satisfaction when Imp skittered under Lorna's wooden stool at his words.

It was Lorna he cared about. Her face had so transparently shown her pain. He raked his fingers through his hair. No, the collection didn't seem very important at all.

He squatted over the shattered body of the cat. It had broken in three large pieces and the head was still intact. Then his heart stopped beating. The entire inner surface of the statue was covered with writing. Demotic. The lost language that might lead to the deciphering of hieroglyphics at last. It was doubtless the largest complete example of the language ever found. Someone, thousands of years ago, had painstakingly written the tiny, even characters that covered the inside surface. Then the two halves of the cast had been sealed together.

"Lorna!" He stumbled to his feet and ran down the hall. His heart was hammering hard by the time he reached her room.

"Go away," she said calmly from inside.

"Lorna, It's demotic. The missing language. We found it!"

"Go away!"

"Inside Bastet! The inside is covered with demotic."

There was a pause. The door opened a crack and one sky blue eye appeared. "Inside Bastet?"

He wanted to push the door open, but he refrained. "The statue fell. Imp knocked it over. The inside is covered in demotic writing."

"What's all this about?" Harrington demanded, striding down the hall. "All this shouting! I was just starting to go through my collection of Chinese coins when this infernal smashing and bashing and shouting begins."

Jonathan felt a guilty knot form in his stomach. "Sir, I

must apologize profusely. While under my care, the large statue of Bastet came to be broken."

"He didn't do it, Papa. It was one of the kittens."

He shot her a grateful glance, but Lorna stood with her arms crossed and an expression that left no doubt that her feelings were anything but tender.

"Bastet?" Harrington said blankly.

"The cat statue," she explained with an impatient toss of her head.

"Oh, that. A pity. It was rather fine. Nothing to be done, though, I suppose."

"Papa, Lord Griffith was just telling me that the inside of the statue is hollow and is covered with demotic."

"With what? Is this some witchcraft the villagers are always talking about? I must say, it is very dangerous to give them food for gossip, my dear. The herbal remedies are quite bad enough. You may find it amusing that they think you are a witch, but I assure you, it will ruin your marriage prospects for certain."

"It is a language, Papa. Used in Egypt." Her foot tapped impatiently.

"I'm terribly sorry that the statue came to be broken," Jonathan put in. "But the finding of this example of demotic could be most important. It could lead to the understanding of hieroglyphics."

"Really?" Harrington seemed interested for the first time. "Well, what does it say?"

"I don't know yet, sir." He was not certain he wanted to admit he had run for Lorna the moment he knew it was demotic. It occurred to him now that it was odd that his first wish was not to examine it, but to share the momentous news with her. How could he explain to her that even though his objective when he arrived had been the collection, things had changed entirely.

"Well, when will you know?" Harrington was saying. "That

collection will be a damn sight more interesting when we know what the symbols mean."

"Not until after a good deal of study, I should say."

"And unfortunately, Lord Griffith has informed me that he must go back to London. Immediately." Her words were like a dash of cold water.

"Yes." There was nothing else he could say. If she wanted him gone, he would go.

"Oh, dear! Most unfortunate! Just when things were getting interesting. Are you certain you must go? Right away?"

"Yes," he said grimly, knowing that if he looked, he would see the hatred in Lorna's eyes.

"Well, then, take the statue with you. I've no use for it now that it is broken. Actually, I had no use for it before it was broken either!" He laughed heartily. "Take it, study it, and then if it ever yields up something interesting, you can mention my name when you write up the treatise or whatever it is that you call them damn dull things. No chance of changing the name of the language to Harrington, I suppose. No, I thought not. Oh, well, call it the Harrington cat statue. Bassinet, or whatever the name was."

"Bastet," Jonathan said in unison with Lorna.

"Right. Harrington's Bastet statue." He thought for a moment. "The Harrington Bastet. No, I don't like that. Couldn't we just call it the Harrington Cat? I rather like that. Well, anyway, I'm off back to the coins. You will let me know if anything comes of it, won't you?" He wandered off down the hall, still trying various combinations of names for the statue.

Jonathan was left standing alone in the corridor with Lorna. She drew a quick breath, several unreadable emotions crossing her face at once, and then turned to go back into her room.

"Wait."

She paused, her hand on the door. But she did not turn around.

"I would like to ask a favor of you."

She looked up at him, her blue eyes cold. "I do not think you are in a position to ask for any favors at all."

"I know. But this would mean a great deal to me." When she did not say anything, he went on. "I would like to take Imp back to London with me."

"Imp? But you hate cats."

He shoved his hands into his trouser pockets in a school-boyish gesture he thought he had long conquered. "I've grown rather fond of her, I suppose."

"You wouldn't know the first thing about taking care of a cat." She wore the same scowl she had when she first met him. But now he found it made him very much want to kiss her.

He caught up her hands in a desperate gesture of pleading. "I will learn. Please let me have her, Lorna."

Her hands clenched into fists, but she did not pull away. "Why?"

"She . . . she will remind me of you." He choked out the words, aware that Lorna was bound to think him trying to wriggle his way back into her confidence.

She removed her hands from his. Her expression was as blank and unreadable as Bastet's had been. "I do not believe Imp would wish to be separated from the rest of the litter."

He looked at her for a moment in silence, trying to memorize every detail of her face. "Very well. I understand. I will leave in the morning." He turned to go, but then turned back to her. "Miss Harrington, I know you can never believe me, but I must say it anyway. I came here with the intention of marrying you merely to have the collection. But in the time we spent together, I grew to love you more than I ever thought it was possible to love something. I know you don't believe it now, and perhaps you never will, but I do hope that someday you will be able to look back at the time we spent together and know that once I knew you, I cared for nothing else in this world."

He saw her throat move as she swallowed. Then she dropped her gaze to the floor and stepped back into her room. The door clicked shut in the silence. Jonathan sighed and turned to go pack his belongings.

# ELEVEN

"My dearest, dearest Miss Harrington!" Mrs. MacAlister flew over to her and embraced her. "I'm so delighted you are here. We are about to light the bonfire, and it is such a marvelous night for it, don't you agree?" She linked her arm with Lorna's and pulled her over to where a crowd had gathered around an enormous pile of wood. "But where is Lord Griffith? Surely he came with you."

"I'm afraid he cannot attend," she said through the odd lump that had formed in her throat.

"Cannot attend? Why not? Is he ill?"

"No, ma'am, not ill. He is leaving tomorrow to go back to London."

"Leaving?" Mrs. MacAlister's voice was shrill. "Tomorrow? He cannot! Not when Arabella has just arrived. I won't allow it. Roland!"

Her lanky husband looked up where he was reading over his manuscript of ghost stories in a nervous mutter.

"Roland, come here. You must ride over to Wythburn House and fetch Lord Griffith at once. I will not have Arabella come all the way from Leeds if Griffith is not to see her."

"Oh, no," Lorna caught his arm as he reluctantly lay down his sheaf of stories with a sigh. "I beg you won't. He is very busy packing." But the excuse sounded ridiculous, even to her own ears. There were plenty of servants at Wythburn House to pack up his belongings, and it seemed positively churlish to announce that Griffith should not be fetched because she did not wish to see him.

In any case, her feeble excuses were run over roughshod by Mrs. MacAlister's orders that her husband ride off and not return until he had Griffith in tow.

"Very good. Now that's settled!" she said briskly. "What a fright you gave me. Not coming indeed! Here"—she pulled Lorna over to a knot of men clustered around a petite dark beauty—"Miss Harrington, this is my sister Arabella Stead. Arabella, Miss Harrington of Wythburn. Lord Griffith is a houseguest of Miss Harrington's father," Mrs. MacAlister prompted.

The news seemed to make Arabella a good deal more pleased. "Oh! It is a pleasure and an honor to meet you, Miss Harrington," she gushed. "Do you find Lord Griffith a pleasant man?"

"Well yes, I suppose. His manners are all that they should be." Except for the fact that he was a deceitful liar of the highest degree.

"And so very clever!" Mrs. MacAlister added.

"Indeed. Quite clever." She wished now that she had not given in to weakness and written Griffith the note. She had thought at the time that she would never see him again. But now . . .

"And you cannot deny that he is the handsomest man to come this way in many a year."

Lorna was becoming very uncomfortable with this conversation. But both Arabella and Mrs. MacAlister were hanging on her every word. "Indeed, he is considered quite well favored," she admitted begrudgingly. Enough that he thought he could have anything he wanted, the arrogant creature. "But I must say, he cares for nothing but Egypt. A woman can never hope to hold a place in his heart that is not far inferior to all of Egypt." It gave her physical pain to say the words.

Arabella's shoulders rose and fell in a gusty sigh. "I think that is so very romantic. I like a man to be passionate about his hobby. In fact, I could help him. Perhaps we could travel to Egypt together." She clasped her hands and looked rapturously into the distance.

Lorna made a noise in her throat. It was going to be a very long evening indeed.

For a while she was able to forget herself. The musicians the MacAlisters had engaged were very good, and she found that she was not lacking for partners once it was plain she was not averse to dancing. Then, quite in the midst of a most enjoyable country dance, she heard Mrs. MacAlister set up a delighted squawking.

"Lord Griffith, you have arrived at last! I heard you were resigned not to come, you naughty thing. As though we could have a party in the neighborhood and not insist that you come."

"Mr. MacAlister was very persuasive," she heard Griffith say calmly. She was surprised to find her arms prickle with gooseflesh at the sound of his voice.

"I merely told him that you said I was not to come back until I brought him, my dear," Mr. MacAlister chortled.

Lorna smiled at her partner and wished desperately that it was their turn to dance down the row together.

"You must allow me to introduce you to my dearest sister, Miss Arabella Stead. She is here from Leeds. Do you know Leeds, my lord?"

"Not well."

Lorna continued grinning like a death head at her partner and tapped her foot. Perhaps after this dance she could plead the headache and go home. At last it was their turn, and she was spared having to hear Miss Stead simper breathy praise to Griffith.

"I must say, Miss Harrington, I'm delighted you have joined us tonight. I don't believe you have ever attended one of our local assemblies. What a pity, as you are a fine dancer indeed," her partner, Mr. Bowlings, exclaimed rapturously.

"I doubt I will attend another one," she said. "I find it does not suit my constitution."

He looked somewhat dismayed, so she softened her comment with a smile. "It is very hot here. The bonfire gives off such a great quantity of heat, I am likely to be singed. Perhaps we could walk over to the fountain?" The monstrous creation, sprouting all manner of cherubs and flora, was farthest away from where the MacAlisters stood conversing with Griffith.

She made halfhearted conversation with Mr. Bowlings while she watched them. Arabella certainly knew how to make good use of her fan. There was not a moment when it was still. She playfully slapped it on Griffith's sleeve with a mocking pout. She spread it open to laugh behind it. She lay it against her cheek with an expression of arch coquetry. Very well, let the girl catch him. It would serve Griffith right to be leg-shackled to a girl without a wit in her head. Griffith himself looked rather impassive.

As she watched, a footman came up to the group and bowed. He seemed somewhat disturbed and then deposited something in Griffith's hands. The entire group reacted with alarm.

"Mr. Bowlings, I declare I have grown quite cold now. May we walk back toward the fire?" She stood up and pulled the bewildered man after her.

"You say that the cat hid itself in your greatcoat pocket and that you did not notice it?" Mrs. MacAlister was shrilling.

"I daresay she was asleep in there. And she always was fond of stowing away." Griffith rubbed his knuckles across Imp's tiny head, and the kitten butted against his hand appreciatively.

"But my lord! I must insist that you have it taken back to Wythburn House immediately. You cannot have a cat at a ball. Arabella is violently allergic!" Indeed, the girl's eyes were already puffy and streaming.

"I am going home. I will take Imp with me," Lorna said calmly, then realized she had made it obvious she was listening in on their conversation.

"Oh, no." Griffith turned to her. "I will not part with the creature." His long fingers ran down the kitten's fur. She could hear the comically loud rumble of its purr.

"How very eccentric to be sure," Mrs. MacAlister said disapprovingly.

"But you do not understand, madame. The animal was a gift to me. A gift made more precious by the fact that the friend who gave it to me cared very deeply for it."

Lorna felt her heart constrict in her chest. Then Griffith must know what heartache it had cost her to write the letter saying that he might take Imp with him to London.

Griffith's voice was low when he continued. "And I cared very deeply for the one who gave it to me."

"Well! How very touching to be sure," Mrs. MacAlister said stiffly. "Arabella! Do stop sneezing! It isn't at all lady-like!"

"I do apologize." Griffith bowed. "I'm certain Miss Stead will recover when I remove the animal from her presence." He started to move away, then looked over his shoulder. "Miss Lorna, your father charged me with a message for you. Perhaps, if you wish for a cup of mulled wine, I could give you his missive."

"No, I . . . That is . . . I . . . well, all right," she conceded gracelessly.

She followed Griffith over to the punch bowl, and after an interminable time spent pouring out the mulled wine and thanking the attendant, he put the warm cup into her hands.

"I know you are not pleased to see me here," he said abruptly.

"No." His closeness made her heart beat faster, and she hated it.

"But I did not see how I could refuse so pointed an invitation."

She could not take her eyes off his hand, slowly moving down the length of Imp's back. "I understand." She cleared her throat. "What message do you have from my father?"

"Well," He turned to receive his own cup of mulled wine, "it was nothing urgent."

"What was it?"

Griffith's face was impassive in the flickering golden light cast by the bonfire's flames. "He said not to be missish, and that you'd better try to catch me tonight, because you weren't likely to have any suitor this winter, and he would like to go to China in the spring."

"Oh." She felt her cheeks grow warm. How like her father to charge Griffith with something sure to embarrass them both. She turned toward the fire and took a sip of wine.

"But the message is of little moment. I wanted to get you alone so I could thank you." He looked down at the little black bundle in his arms. "I have come to be very fond of Imp, and it means a great deal to me that you would let me keep her."

She frowned and shrugged her shoulders. She had no idea why she had decided to give him the kitten. Especially when she had told Griffith earlier that she did not wish Imp to be taken away. But the animal looked well pleased to be in his arms.

Griffith transferred Imp to one hand and offered her his other arm. She reluctantly took it and walked beside him.

"Are you taking Bastet with you?" she asked to fill the silence.

"Yes. But I do not wish to talk of Bastet. I do not wish to talk of anything but you."

"I'm afraid I have nothing to say."

"I don't expect you to say anything. I just want to look at you." She could see the reflection of the flames in his eyes.

"I know I have no right to ask to do that either. But you must show some pity on a man, who through his own vanity and arrogance, has managed to destroy his only chance at happiness."

She said nothing, but she could still feel him watching her. "When were you planning to propose to me? Tonight at the eleventh hour? Just to make Fothering sweat?" She tried to summon up the requisite amount of vitriol.

"No." He smiled faintly. "I would not have done so until I was well assured of your affection. After the setdown in the rowboat, my courage might have failed me entirely."

"You would have lost the wager."

He stopped and turned to her. "I credit you with no little intelligence. Why is it that you find it impossible to believe that once I knew you, the ridiculous wager meant nothing to me. The collection meant nothing to me." His gray eyes looked intently into hers. "You were the only thing that mattered."

"I came here intending to marry you, not fall in love with you, Lorna. But somehow it happened. And I do not believe that you could tell me truthfully that you do not care for me. If we are so stupid that we would throw away happiness with both hands, because of arrogance on my part and because of pride on yours, then we do not deserve it in the first place." He caught her chin in his hand. "Love, Lorna. It does not happen very often."

She stood in silence for a long moment. Every bone in her body ached. She felt on the precipice of an enormous decision. "I don't know," she admitted at last. "I don't know if I love you. I have never been in love before."

He smiled, but there was sadness in it. "There is no hurry. I will go back to London and leave you in peace. Contrary to your father's warning, there will be plenty of other suitors." There was a peculiar wistfulness in his smile. "But if you should discover at some point that you are consumed with the desire to accept my offer, I do hope you will let me know."

They lapsed into an awkward silence again. She watched the play of light across his face. He seemed absorbed in his own thoughts.

"Is it feeling acutely miserable in thinking I will never see you again?" she asked at last.

"What?" He turned to her, looking slightly confused.

"Being in love."

He smiled faintly. "Perhaps."

"Is it wishing very much that I could work with you to study the demotic hidden inside Bastet?" Her voice was low.

"I suppose it might be."

"Is it that really rather uncomfortable feeling I had when I knew you would care for Imp because you cared for me?"

He reached out and touched her cheek. "I have not previously been known to be overfond of cats."

She felt her face grow warm. "And the feeling I had when you kissed me?"

His grin was mischievous. "That I cannot vouch for. Perhaps we should see if you feel it again." He leaned down and kissed her.

"I believe I did." She laughed breathlessly against his shoulder when he let her go at last.

He caressed her cheek. "I am beginning to think that you are indeed a witch, Lorna Harrington. An enchantress. How else could a self-centered, arrogant man who cared for nothing but his work be turned into a cat-loving, simpleminded, besotted fool."

"I have one last spell to cast," she said pertly, twining her arms around his neck. "The one that will break old Harrington's curse and will ensure you will win your All Hallow's Eve wager after all."

# A CAT BY ANY
# OTHER NAME

*Joy Reed*

# ONE

"Some people," said Sylvia, "think Lizzie Bragg is a witch."

Miranda laughed scornfully. "What people would be silly enough to think that?" she asked.

"Maddie Jordan does. She says her sister Betsy bought a love charm from Lizzie—and that it worked, too. Betsy's engaged to be married now, this coming June."

"And she really believes Lizzie's charm was responsible? I knew the Jordan girls were silly, but I never realized they were as silly as that."

"I suppose it is silly," admitted Sylvia. "But the Jordans aren't the only ones who think Lizzie's a witch. When Polly was packing this basket for us to take to Lizzie today, she told me to be sure to speak respectfully to her while we're there or she might put the evil eye on us. She says all the villagers are very careful not to anger Lizzie for fear she'll make their cows go dry or their crops fail."

"Yes, well, Polly's a serving girl. It's natural that she should believe such superstitious nonsense, along with the rest of the village. But surely you don't believe it, Sylvia? After all, if Lizzie really had some kind of magic powers, I can't believe she'd be living in a tumbledown hut and wearing rags. Why, that dress she was wearing when we saw her in the village last week was hardly decent, it had so many holes in it."

"Yes, it was very bad," agreed Sylvia.

"Well, then!" said Miranda triumphantly. "That just proves my point. If Lizzie was any kind of witch at all, she could conjure up new dresses and a mansion to live in and anything else she might desire. Instead of which she dresses in rags and lives in the oldest, most dilapidated cottage in the neighborhood, with only a lot of cats for company. Why, that alone ought to prove she's not a witch! Only a goose would believe in the effectiveness of Lizzie's love charms when she herself is a spinster!"

Sylvia laughed. "I must say, that circumstance does tend to throw doubt upon her witchly powers," she agreed.

"Of course it does," said Miranda. Having won her sister to her point of view, she felt she could afford to be magnanimous. Her voice softened as she went on. "But I suppose it's not surprising people tell such tales about poor old Lizzie. She really is the most eccentric-looking creature. When I saw her last week, striding through the village in that ragged old purple dress and a man's overcoat that looked as though she stole it off a scarecrow, I could hardly keep my countenance. At the same time, though, I felt we ought to do something about it. You know, the Strong family have always made themselves responsible for the poor and needy hereabouts. Of course, it really ought to be Cousin Benedict who dispenses the charity nowadays, seeing that he is the one living at The Vineyard. But there's no use hoping *he* will ever recognize his responsibilities!"

"No," agreed Sylvia with a sigh. "Oh, Miranda, I know it's been years since Papa died, but I still can't help feeling it the unfairest thing that Benedict should have got The Vineyard instead of us. I know the property was entailed, but still it was *our home!* We lived there all our lives, and to see someone else living there now—especially someone as thoughtless and irresponsible as Cousin Benedict—cannot but be very painful."

Miranda said nothing, but inwardly she acknowledged the truth of this statement. It could not but be very painful to be turned out of one's childhood home immediately after the death of one's father. It was even more painful to see that same father's place taken by a rackety individual like Cousin Benedict. The Vineyard was by no means a large or luxurious house, but it had been in the Strong family for centuries, and to see it running slowly to ruin under its present owner was a peculiarly painful spectacle.

So Miranda reflected, but she did not voice her reflections aloud. Even after three years, her sister had a tendency to grow despondent whenever the subject of their diminished fortunes was discussed. Of course there were moments when she, too, felt despondent, but unlike her sister she could not afford to indulge herself in such an emotion. Someone in the family had to be strong in nature as well as in name, and as the eldest sister that role fell naturally to her. It was a role Miranda had been playing for the greater part of her life.

Her mother had died when she was only eleven, and Sylvia a mere child of two. Their father, disabled by his own grief, had had little time or attention to spare for either of his daughters, and certainly not for a demanding two-year-old who persisted in crying for her mama and would not be put off by pious talk about Long Journeys and Better Places.

Miranda's own grief in the loss of her mother had not been negligible, but Sylvia's had been so much worse that she had put aside her sorrow and devoted herself to comforting her little sister. Sylvia had responded by becoming passionately attached to her. And as they grew, the attachment had continued, with Miranda assuming more and more a maternal role in their relationship, until it was quite natural for her to act as arbiter and instructor to the younger and less experienced Sylvia.

Accordingly, she sought to turn the conversation to a safer topic. "I do hope Lizzie won't be offended at us for bringing her these things. One never knows with persons of her type. If she was a common beggar, there would be no difficulty about assisting her—but then, one would be less inclined to assist her in the first place! I daresay she has a great deal of pride. These country people often do, and I think the better of them for it, but it makes it very difficult to help them in any way. You had better let me do the talking, Sylvia."

Sylvia meekly assented to this proposition. "I do hope we can get her to accept the clothes, even if she won't take the food," she said, peeping into a hamper that contained a stuff dress, a warm woolen cloak, and a red flannel petticoat that she herself had edged with a dainty trimming of crochet work. "It's getting to be spring now, of course, but there's sure to be chilly days ahead, and I hate to think of her going about in nothing but that ragged old coat and dress."

"Yes, it would be gratifying if she would accept the things. I am glad we are still able to aid a worthy object now and then, even if we are reduced to living in a drafty cottage with a pocket handkerchief-sized garden!"

Sylvia sighed. "Yes, and we used to have such lovely gardens at The Vineyard. I drove by there with Henry last week, and I promise you, Miranda, you couldn't see the flowers for the weeds. I felt quite blue all the rest of the day, remembering how things used to be."

"They might be worse," said Miranda firmly. "We have a roof over our heads, enough income to keep us in a decent style, and even a little left over to assist people like Lizzie Bragg. Think how dreadful it would be to be actually poor, like her! Why, we are wealthy enough to keep two maids and a manservant, not to mention our own carriage. Such a luxurious carriage, too! I am sure Lord Longworth himself might envy it."

Sylvia giggled at this, for the "carriage" in which they were riding was a simple gig, driven by Miranda herself and drawn by a sedate chestnut mare. "I doubt it," she said. "Lord Longworth probably affects something a bit more dashing in the way of carriages. I wonder if it's true that he means to come to Longworth Hall soon? There's a rumor going about that he plans to spend the summer there."

"There've been rumors like that any time these dozen years," scoffed Miranda. "I'll believe it when I see it."

"But wouldn't it be exciting, Miranda? If he comes to the Hall, perhaps he would hold a party there—perhaps even a ball. They say the balls of Longworth Hall used to be famous."

"I wouldn't know about that," said Miranda. "There haven't been any held there as long as I can remember."

"But wouldn't it be exciting? A real ball!"

"Oh, it would be exciting enough," allowed Miranda. "And I'll confess that if it were up to me, I'd as soon Lord Longworth came here as not. For a nobleman he seems quite a respectable person, not one of these idle creatures who does nothing but drink and debauch and dissipate the fortune his father left him. There was a speech of his published in the *Times* last week against the Corn Laws that was quite the best thing I've ever read on the subject."

Sylvia, who had no interest in Corn Laws, dismissed this subject to return to the subject of a possible ball. "I've never been to a real ball," she said wistfully. "Just a dancing party now and then, and the assemblies at the village rooms. Speaking of those, did I tell you Henry has invited me to accompany him to next week's assembly?"

"No, but I might have guessed," said Miranda dryly. "I don't think Henry's missed inviting you to a village assembly for the past year and a half."

Sylvia colored prettily. "No, I don't think he has," she said. She hesitated a moment, then went on with shy eagerness. "Upon my word, Miranda, I have sometimes thought lately—it has seemed to me he is growing very particular in his attentions. Almost as though he really meant something by them, you know. What do you think?"

Miranda did not immediately reply to this question. In truth, there were several things she thought about Mr. Henry Ellis's courtship of her sister, and none of them was very complimentary.

It was not that Henry himself was objectionable. He was a good-looking young man in his mid-twenties, possessing a moderate fortune and a very respectable pedigree. No more than Lord Longworth was he a low, drunken, dissipated wretch. Moreover, he really seemed to care for Sylvia, and it was clear that Sylvia returned his regard. It was in every way a most suitable match. Miranda acknowledged as much to herself, but this did not prevent her from resenting Henry's courtship with an intensity all the greater for being sternly repressed.

She knew such resentment was selfish. It was natural that at some point in her life, Sylvia should want a home and family of her own. But now that Henry Ellis had appeared on the horizon and the time for such things appeared imminent, it seemed to Miranda that her sister was far too young to think of marrying. Yet Sylvia was twenty now, and younger girls than she were married every day. And though Sylvia had not that strong and decided character that Miranda had tried for years to instill in her, still she did, in her own gentle way, appear to know her own mind. There was, in fact, no reason why she might not marry Henry if she chose—except for the simple and selfish reason that Miranda did not want her to.

"And it is selfish," she owned to herself. She had lived with Sylvia so long that life without her now would be perfectly unimaginable. What would it be like to come home from a day's shopping and find no Sylvia there to admire her purchases?—to sit in the evenings with her book or needlework and have no companion to exchange quiet gossip or confidences with?—to eat all her meals alone and fall into bed at night without even anyone to say good night to her?

And though these things, by themselves, were reason enough to dread Sylvia's departure, there were other reasons that Miranda hesitated to acknowledge even to herself—reasons that were quite as pressing and infinitely more sordid. The fact was that Sylvia's leaving would injure her in a very material way. Their present standard of living was funded on the income from both their "portions," those monies that had come to them from their deceased mother. Without Sylvia's income, Miranda would be forced to abandon their present home, small and inconvenient as it was, and seek one still smaller and less convenient. She would have to sacrifice one and perhaps two of their servants. She would no longer even be able to keep her "carriage" and the bay mare.

It was useless to imagine that Henry Ellis might allow her the use of Sylvia's portion after their marriage. He was a kind-hearted and not ungenerous young man, but his wife's income would doubtless be very welcome to him—and he would be quite within his rights to demand it. Miranda felt she would rather starve than make any such unreasonable request of him. But the picture of her future without Sylvia was a bleak one indeed, and it was not surprising that she hesitated before answering Sylvia's question.

"What do I think?" she repeated. "Why, I think that Henry admires you very much, dear sister. Indeed, I should think so much would be clear to even the most casual observer."

She spoke lightly, but Sylvia merely looked at her with clear blue eyes that were remarkably penetrating for all their apparent mildness. "You don't like Henry, do you, Miranda?" she said.

There was a note of hurt in her voice that cut Miranda to the heart. "Why, yes, certainly I like him, Sylvia," she said quickly. "He seems a very well-mannered, worthy young man. If I sound less than enthusiastic about him, it is only because

I don't think he's good enough for you. But then, nobody could be."

She smiled as she spoke. Sylvia smiled back, her eyes aglow with soft emotion. "Oh, but you would not say that if you knew Henry better, Miranda," she said. "Only wait till you do. Then I am sure you will value him at his proper estimation."

Miranda felt she already did value him at his proper estimation, but she kept such cynical reflections to herself. She was glad when they arrived at Lizzie Bragg's cottage a moment later, eliminating the need for further conversation.

The cottage was a tiny, thatched, wattle-and-daub structure, picturesque-looking from a distance but appallingly dilapidated when seen up close. Sylvia shivered as she regarded its unglazed windows, dangling shutters, and drunkenly leaning chimney. "It really does look like a witch's house," she whispered to Miranda.

Miranda said nothing, but inwardly she could not help agreeing with her sister. There was something eerie about those blank-eyed windows, which seemed to watch her and Sylvia with a knowing leer as they got down from the gig and hauled out the hampers of food and clothing. As they approached the cottage door, a large black cat emerged from some nearby shrubbery. It paused to stare at them, then whisked noiselessly through the open cottage door.

Something about this incident unnerved Miranda. Half-remembered tales of witches' familiars and devils' imps flitted through her mind, but she refused to give way to such nonsense. "Come on," she told Sylvia. "Let's see if Lizzie's home."

Lizzie proved to be home, and the warmth of her welcome quite astounded Miranda, who had feared they and their errand of charity might be summarily rejected. "Come in, my dears, come in," bade the old woman, grinning wide to show her few remaining teeth and throwing open the door of her cottage. "Come in and sit ye down. I've just put on a pot of tea, and I'd be glad of a bit of company."

Thus urged, Miranda and Sylvia stepped across the cottage threshold and stood looking about them. The single room was small and poorly furnished, but they were relieved to see it was tolerably clean. It was also very full of cats. Cats reclined on the low couch that served as Lizzie's bed and perched atop the rude table where an earthenware pot of tea stood brewing. A litter of kittens romped in front of the hearth in an exuberant game of toss and tumble.

Lizzie shooed a few of the cats off the couch, then made a gesture indicating that Miranda and Sylvia were to seat themselves there. Her manner was that of a queen welcoming guests to her palace. She must have noticed the hampers the sisters were carrying, but she made no reference to them. With some embarrassment, they deposited their burden on the floor before gingerly perching themselves atop the tangle of dilapidated bedding.

" 'Tis a lovely day," said Lizzie, serving forth the tea into a pair of cracked mugs. Miranda and Sylvia politely agreed that it was. They watched with apprehension as Lizzie finished preparing the tea and presented it to her guests with a flourish. "Go on and drink it up," she ordered. They did not dare disobey, though Miranda had doubts about the cleanliness of her cup and had personally witnessed one of the cats thrusting its head into the milk pitcher a moment before.

"Is your tea strong enough for ye?" inquired Lizzie soliciously. The two sisters said hastily that it was quite strong enough, and the old woman beamed. "Ah, 'tis me best India tea. I knew in me bones I'd be having company to tea today, and so I brewed me a potful." She drooped one eyelid in a sly wink. "I've the second sight, ye know. I saw the two of ye setting out from home and told myself, 'Ah, Lizzie, there's the Strong ladies meaning to come and pay ye a friendly call. Ye'd best be putting the kettle on.' "

Sylvia looked awed and a little scared, but Miranda kept her face impassive. Lizzie might or might not possess second sight, but that did not affect the purpose of her call. "Yes, my sister and I decided to drop by and see how you were, Miss Bragg," she said. "I hope we find you well?"

"Aye, pretty well—pretty well, all things considered. Of course I'm getting up in years and not so spry as I once was. And then the rheumatism do be troubling me something awful at times. I've an ointment that charms it away in a trice, but last week I was so stiff I couldn't even get out of bed to fetch me ointment! I was in a bad way, and no mistake."

This was just the opening Miranda had been looking for. "Yes, my sister and I heard you were not well," she said. "That is why we called today—and why we ventured to bring with us a few things we thought might be useful." She indicated the hampers at her and Sylvia's feet. "Since you were laid up with the rheumatism, we thought you might find it difficult to get out shopping—and of course, it's a long walk to the village from your cottage. I hope you'll excuse our presumption."

Stumbling through this speech with Lizzie's shrewd dark eyes fixed upon her, Miranda felt all at once that it *was* presumption. She felt very awkward and young and foolish, and it was clear from Sylvia's face that she felt the same. But Lizzie seemed conscious of no awkwardness. She arose with interest and came over to look into the hampers.

"Ah, 'tis very kind of ye ladies to think of me! What have we here—a roast chicken, by all that's wonderful. Well, and we'll dine well tonight, won't we, my loves?" She leaned down to caress a couple of her cats, who had joined her in inspecting the hamper's contents. "And here's a fine meat pie—and a loaf of fair bread—and a deal of garden stuff, forsooth! 'Tis a most bounteous feast, and I'm sure I'm much obliged to ye ladies."

Miranda and Sylvia smiled stiffly and sat watching with

mingled interest and embarrassment as Lizzie went on to inspect the hamper of clothes. Fortunately, this was as well received as the food. Lizzie exclaimed over the dress, expressed vociferous approval of the cloak, and rubbed the fabric of the petticoat between her fingers with an appreciative air. " 'Tis fine stuff and no mistake. Very smart, too, with this handsome trimming." Touching the crocheted border, she looked at Sylvia. " 'Tis your work, if I mistake not, miss?"

"Why, yes, it is," said Sylvia, regarding Lizzie with awed blue eyes. "But how did you know?"

Lizzie looked mysterious. "Ah, 'tis me second sight again! The minute I touched the cloth I could feel it, miss—just as I can feel 'tis your sister's hands that made this handsome cloak." She threw Miranda a challenging look.

Miranda, who had indeed made the cloak, was secretly impressed by this prescience but determined not to show it. "Well, I hope the things will be of use to you, Miss Bragg," she said, rising to her feet. "It is time my sister and I were going. Thank you very much for the tea."

Lizzie also rose to her feet, looking very solemn. "Ah, but you know I can't take these things without making ye some return for them, miss," she said. "It's never been my way to accept charity. Fair is fair, and fair payment for fair goods is what I always say."

"Indeed, Miss Bragg, we want no payment," protested Miranda, but Lizzie ignored her. Turning to a battered cupboard that stood against the wall, she opened it and produced a small vial.

"Ah, 'tis the very thing! That's for ye, miss." She presented the vial to Sylvia with an impressive air. " 'Tis a charm guaranteed to bring your young man to the point. Ye've a sweetheart, haven't ye?"

Sylvia's face turned bright red. "No—that's to say—not a sweetheart exactly," she said with confusion.

Lizzie smiled knowingly. "Ah, ye needn't be telling me,

miss! Such a pretty girl as ye is bound to have a sweetheart. Well, just ye put a drop or two of that in his cup some night, and within a day or so ye'll have him at your feet right enough, and begging ye to name the day. Only mind ye don't use too much. 'Tis a very powerful charm, and I can't be responsible if ye use more than I tell ye to."

Sylvia began to stammer out some rejoinder about not wanting or needing the potion, but Lizzie ignored her and turned to Miranda. "Now for ye, miss. What shall it be, eh? What shall it be? Not the love potion for ye, I think—no, not that, to be sure. Ye'll be needing something very different if I'm not mistook."

Miranda frowned. She certainly did not want any of the love potion, which was an evil-looking dark fluid that looked more as if it might be poison than any love philter. But neither did she like the implication that she had no need of such things. "I don't think—" she began.

Just then, one of the kittens that had been romping with its fellows in front of the hearth detached itself from the group and came racing over to Miranda. It stopped short just before her and stood looking up at her, a small coal-black creature with inquisitive golden eyes.

Lizzie swooped down on it with a cry of delight. "Ah, the very thing! Ye'll be needing a cat, I've no doubt. And though I do say so myself, there's none so fine as me own cats." She stroked the kitten affectionately. "Only look at the tail of him, and the fine large ears! This fellow here's a tom, of course, and in the general way your toms aren't so good as mousers as your she-cats. But ye'll be after knowing all my cats are good mousers, toms and queens alike."

Miranda did not want a cat, and she was in any case greatly incensed by Lizzie's assumption that such a gift would be more welcome to her than a love potion. Almost it seemed to put her on a level with Lizzie herself, an old maid forced to resort to feline companionship in lieu of any other. "I don't think—" she began in her haughtiest voice.

Lizzie went on, unheeding. "I'll just pop him in your hamper here, and ye can take him home with ye that way." Suiting action to word, she deposited the kitten in the empty clothing hamper. He at once began to howl indignantly. "Nay, nay, my darling, ye mustn't be making all that noise," she told him. " 'Tis a good home you're going to, and ye'll be taken care of proper by your new mistress."

These words did not seem to console the kitten. He continued to yowl indignantly. Miranda glanced at Sylvia and saw she was biting her lip, trying not to smile. "It's very kind of you, Miss Bragg, to offer me one of your kittens," she said. "But you see, I don't want him."

"Ah, but he wants ye, miss," said Lizzie firmly. "He's chosen ye, he has, and when a cat's chosen ye, ye've no choice but to go along in the matter. I've had dozens of cats in my time, and I know."

Sylvia, who seemed regrettably inclined to take the whole business as a joke, threw Miranda a look of mischief. "Yes, Sister, it's plain he's chosen you," she said. "One can easily see how happy he is to have you as his mistress!" More seriously, she added, "Indeed, Miranda, you might just as well take him as not. If he's as good a mouser as Miss Bragg says, then we could really use him at the Cottage. You know you were complaining just the other day about the mice."

"That's true enough," admitted Miranda. She looked at the yowling hamper with distaste. "Though if I must have a cat, I would rather have a female."

"Oh, well, then you'd have to worry about kittens," said Sylvia consolingly. "With a tomcat, you don't." Looking at Lizzie, she asked, "What is the cat's name?"

Lizzie shook her head mysteriously. "Ah, that's for him to

decide, miss. Cats generally name themselves, ye know. They're by way of being uncanny creatures."

Miranda was already annoyed with Lizzie and her unwanted cat. This pretense of mysticism annoyed her even more. Picking up the hamper, she said shortly, "That may be, but I'll be satisfied if he does nothing more uncanny than rid the Cottage of mice. Good day, Miss Bragg, and I hope you have no more difficulties with rheumatism."

Miranda was in a bad mood as she and Sylvia drove back to the village. Part of this was undoubtedly due to the presence of the kitten. He continued to complain about the injustice of his imprisonment with a volume and loquacity that caused passersby to regard them with grins of amusement. Miranda disliked being made conspicuous, and this behavior made her resent her unwanted pet even more. But most of her resentment was reserved for the unwarrantable behavior of Lizzie Bragg.

Sylvia unwittingly threw fuel upon the fire by alluding to Lizzie's love charm. "I declare, she quite frightened me by cautioning me so earnestly about using only a drop or two of it," she said, turning the vial over in her hand. "I wonder what it really is?"

"Probably poison," said Miranda shortly. "I wouldn't meddle with anything that ignorant old woman gave you, Sylvia. You'd much better throw the bottle into the ditch and be done with it."

Sylvia agreed that this would probably be the safest course, but Miranda observed that she did not throw the potion away. Instead she tucked it most carefully into her reticule and snapped the clasp shut upon it.

This incident made Miranda feel worse. For Lizzie to give Sylvia a love potion and her a cat was to emphasize a difference between them that she had been trying for several years to ignore. They were both the Misses Strong; they both lived at the Cottage and were acknowledged to be young women of gentle birth and good character. But there the resemblance ended. Sylvia was a pretty young lady whose future almost certainly included marriage and a family of her own. She, Miranda, was a not-so-young lady—a not-so-young lady who had never been really pretty and whose time for marriage was now almost certainly past.

There had been a time when she, like Sylvia, had confidently expected a future that included love and marriage. Though not pretty, she was generally conceded to be a handsome girl, and she had her admirers. Most notable of these had been one Lieutenant Carrington, who had passed a summer in the neighborhood the year she had been twenty-two. In her heart, Miranda believed that if Lieutenant Carrington had lived, he would have asked her to marry him. But he had been killed in the Spanish Peninsula, and those admirers who had come after him had either been less than serious in their intentions or had been men whom Miranda would never have considered marrying.

And now it appeared that her blossom time was past. Miranda felt the bitterness of this admission, but she told herself it was time she faced the facts. She had felt the shadow of old-maidhood hanging over her for some time. Lizzie's gifts had merely served to show her that others beside herself were aware of it, too. For Sylvia there had been a love potion, for her there had been only a cat—traditional symbol of a frustrated and lonely spinsterhood. Again Miranda looked with distaste at the hamper sitting on the seat between her and Sylvia. She felt she could have cheerfully hurled it and its feline occupant into a passing duck pond.

But her own sense of justice obliged her to admit that it wasn't the cat's fault. It wasn't really anybody's fault. It was merely a fact that she, Miranda Strong, had to face, and the sooner she faced it, the better for all concerned. Turning to her sister, she spoke in a calm, matter-of-fact voice. "Sylvia, do you mind if I stop at Mrs. Blackwell's millinery shop before we return home? I think it is time I was buying my caps."

# TWO

Miranda had bought her caps, and from that time on had insisted on wearing them despite her sister's assurances that she was far too young to set up as an old maid. By the time she had been wearing them for three or four months, however, her decision had been tacitly accepted, not only by her own household but by the whole village of Upton Charnhurst, where she and Sylvia resided. No one thought anything about it when the eldest Miss Strong appeared in public with a neat frill of cambric and lace beneath the brim of her bonnet, or was glimpsed through the Cottage windows reading or sewing with a dainty confection of lace and tulle atop her dark head. It was an accepted fact that she had put on her caps and resigned herself to a life of spinsterhood. And likewise, it was an accepted fact that she was fondly—even foolishly—devoted to the kitten that had been given to her by Lizzie Bragg.

This fondness had stolen upon Miranda by degrees. On first bringing the kitten home, she had earnestly sought to banish him to the kitchens. But the kitten had had other ideas. He had cried so piteously that first night that Miranda had finally got out of bed and gone to the pantry, where he had been shut up in hopes that his presence might do something to discourage the mice that had been playing havoc there among the flour and other dry goods.

As soon as Miranda opened the pantry door, the kitten had

come rushing out. He had twined himself around her ankles, gazing up at her with adoring golden eyes and uttering little cries of feline gratitude and thanksgiving.

"You are a dreadful nuisance," Miranda told the kitten severely. "Where do you expect to sleep if the pantry's not good enough for you?"

The kitten had answered this question by following her back to her own room and attempting to get in bed with her. When Miranda had summarily ejected him from her room and shut the door against him, he had remained outside in the hall wailing, until Miranda, in an access of sleepy irritation, had got up and let him in again. He had promptly got into her bed once more, and this time Miranda made no objection. He slept peacefully beside her all the rest of the night, and the first thing that met her eyes when she awakened the next morning was his small, furry form lying black against the white counterpane.

"And getting fleas in my bed, too, I don't doubt," said Miranda crossly. "What a fool I was to take you—a kitten that cries all night and doesn't have the first idea how to catch a mouse. Indeed, you're a worse nuisance than ever the mice were!"

The kitten raised his head, looked at her a moment, then got to his feet with an air of sleepy resignation. Miranda always maintained that he must have understood her charges against his character, for in less than an hour he had vindicated himself by catching and killing not one but two mice and leaving them in the hall outside her door. This pleased Miranda so much that when he indicated his desire to sleep in her bed again that night, she let him with no more than a grumbling complaint against cat hair and fleas. "My mother used to say that cats in one's bedchamber are very unsanitary," she told him severely. "I hope you know what an indulgence I am granting you."

The kitten indicated that he did know and appreciated it

very much. Miranda, mollified, ventured to run a hand along his black silken back. Thereafter it became an understood thing that the kitten spent every night in her room, and though Miranda continued to grumble publicly about this intrusion, inwardly she was becoming quite reconciled to her pet. He might be only a kitten, but it was surprising what a degree of companionship a mere kitten could provide. And though she had never much cared for cats, there was something very flattering in being chosen like this, to the exclusion of all other humanity. When Sylvia called him "nice pussy" and tried to entice him onto her lap, he merely regarded her with contempt. Visitors to the house might call and coax in vain for his attention. And though he condescended to accept milk and an occasional dish of liver from the cookmaid, it was evident that he felt this a mere business arrangement not to be considered in the same category with his attachment to Miranda.

"Really, he is a very discerning cat," Miranda told Sylvia. "When that old harpy Mrs. Lattimer was here the other day, he went and hid under my bed and didn't come out until after she was gone. I wish I could have done the same thing myself!"

"I suppose he's well enough—for a cat," was Sylvia's lukewarm response.

"Well enough! Sylvia, do you realize he's caught more than three dozen mice in the time he's been here? Polly says she never knew a tomcat that was such a good mouser."

"You have got fond of him, haven't you?" Sylvia regarded her sister with amusement. "I'm sure I never would have expected it, considering the way you talked about him that first day or two."

"I'm not fond of him," said Miranda with dignity. "I merely respect him for doing his duty."

"Which is why you're always kissing and coddling him and slipping him all the best bits out of your dinner, no doubt!

No, Sister, it's perfectly obvious that you've got attached to the beast. And that being the case, you might as well go ahead and name him. Or has he already told you his name? You know Lizzie said cats generally name themselves, and I supposed, as you two were so close, he might have whispered the secret to you some night when you were alone together."

Miranda, resenting this speech, told her sister not to be silly. "If he needs a name, then we can call him Tom," she said coldly. "Seeing that he is a tomcat, that will do as well as anything. I'm sure it doesn't matter to *me* what he's called."

Notwithstanding these assertions, she became more and more fond of Tom as time went on. His kittenish antics enlivened her days, and even his presence on her bed at night came to be more a comfort than a grievance. When he made a cat's cradle of the yarns in her workbasket, he was let off with an indulgent smile. When he was discovered helping himself to a piece of cod the cookmaid had been saving for dinner, he got away with no more than a mild scolding. Miranda began to wonder how she had endured the tedium of life without him. And though the presence of a mere cat could not wholly reconcile her to the prospect of losing Sylvia, it at least made that prospect more bearable.

For the moment, the prospect seemed still a distant one. Henry Ellis continued to call regularly and to escort Sylvia to all the local parties and diversions. But it was clear that he had not yet broached the subject of marriage. Sylvia, to all appearances, was perfectly content with this state of affairs; but once, when Miranda was returning a pair of newly darned stockings to her sister's chest of drawers, she had discovered the vial Lizzie Bragg had given her, carefully tucked away beneath a stack of chemises. Miranda, thinning her lips, had shut the drawer with a bang.

By the time late September had rolled around, Sylvia was still unproposed-to, and Tom was a sleek half-grown cat with fur as black as coal and an attitude of insolent superiority toward all around him. A village cat might still occasionally set foot in the Cottage garden, but the same cat was guaranteed never to do so more than once. The butcher's dog had learned to give him a wide and respectful berth. And if there were still mice in the Cottage, their numbers were at least smaller and less obtrusive than they had been before.

Miranda was reflecting on these matters with satisfaction as she sat sewing on the cottage porch one evening. She had been invited that day to make one of a party to a local beauty spot, with a picnic lunch and various other jollifications thrown in to make the invitation more tempting. But since the day was a very warm one and Miranda did not care greatly for picnics, she had excused herself from the proposed expedition. Since donning her caps she had felt a greater freedom in declining such engagements; it was one of the compensations of old age and spinsterhood, she supposed. Sylvia had gone on the expedition, however, and so had Henry Ellis. Miranda had watched them drive off together with only a very mild sensation of envy. She had spent a busy, quiet, not unprofitable day, and now that dusk was falling she was expecting her sister back at any moment.

Surely enough, even as Miranda was folding up her needlework to go inside, Henry's curricle drew up before the cottage gate. Miranda stood up and prepared to make him welcome in her best elder sister fashion. But on this occasion, it appeared that Sylvia had not invited her beau inside for a cup of tea and a slice of cake, as was her usual custom. Her farewell to Henry was a very short one, and her usually sweet face wore a disconsolate look as she came up the cottage walk alone.

"Your sense of timing is impeccable, Sister," Miranda greeted her. "I was just going inside to make the tea. How did you enjoy the picnic?"

"Not at all," said Sylvia flatly. "You were wise not to go, Miranda. It was a most ill-managed affair from start to finish.

I didn't enjoy it in the least." Following Miranda into the house, she sank down on the sofa with a sigh. Her muslin dress, fresh and crisp that morning when she had put it on, was now crumpled and grass-stained, and her pretty tip-tilted nose was slightly sunburned. She took off her bonnet and ran her fingers ruefully through her blond curls. "I have a dreadful headache coming on—the heat, I suppose. Indeed, I could use some tea. Mrs. Granger forgot to pack any for the luncheon, and the lemonade was too sour to drink."

"You shall have your tea," promised Miranda, and set about preparing it as her sister reclined silently on the sofa. "I was surprised you did not invite Henry to come in and drink a cup with us," she remarked as she set out cups and measured tea from the tea caddy. "But there, I suppose he wanted to get home before dark."

Again Sylvia sighed. "It wasn't that, Miranda. I didn't want to invite him in—and I don't suppose he would have come in even if I had invited him. The plain fact is that we have quarreled. I don't expect he will ever want to see me again."

Miranda was ashamed of the selfish surge of joy that welled up in her heart at these words. "Oh, Sylvia, I am very sorry to hear that," she said. "What happened?—or would you rather not talk about it?"

"I don't mind talking about it, but really, I hardly know what happened. It was so beastly hot the whole day—and I had a headache—and Henry accused me of flirting with Mr. Alton, when I was only being polite. The whole thing was a muddle, and I wish I had stayed home with you."

Sylvia was not exactly crying as she spoke these words, but she looked and sounded as though she was close to it. Miranda felt sorry for her and more ashamed than ever of her own selfish preoccupations. Setting a steaming cup in front of her sister, she gave her a hug. "Never mind, Sylvia. I'm sure you and Henry will soon make up your quarrel. Drink up your tea now, and if your headache doesn't get better I'll have Polly brew you a tisane."

Sylvia did not seem much encouraged by this cheerful prophecy, but she drank her tea and presently announced that her headache was better. "I think I'll go to bed," she said, getting to her feet. "I know it's early, but I feel quite worn out after this dreadful day."

"I think I will go to bed early, too," said Miranda. "Let me just call Tom, and I'll lock up the house for the night."

Stepping out to the porch, she cupped her hands and called, "Tom! Tom! Here, Tom." Such was her usual evening ritual, and never before had her words failed to bring Tomcat running from whatever quarter he might be lurking in. Tonight, however, her call brought no response. Miranda repeated it twice and then stepped out into the garden to repeat it once more. But no tomcat was to be seen within the garden's neatly fenced boundaries.

Reentering the cottage, Miranda went upstairs to her sister's room, where Sylvia was brushing out her hair before the glass. "Sylvia, I can't find Tomcat," she said. "I called four times, but he didn't come."

Sylvia did not look up from her brushing. "It's early yet," she said. "I daresay he'll show up sometime."

"But he always comes when I call! I wonder if something has happened to him?"

Sylvia threw her a look of amusement mingled with exasperation. "Oh, for heaven's sake, Miranda! He's a tomcat, that's all. It's natural for tomcats to prowl."

Miranda thought this a very cold, unfeeling attitude. But she reminded herself that Sylvia had suffered a disappointment that day and could not be expected to show her usual tact and sympathy. She therefore quietly withdrew from Sylvia's room and went to her own, where she began to make her own preparations for bed.

Much as she deplored Sylvia's tactless words, she was

obliged to admit that there was some truth in them. Tom was more a cat than a kitten now, and everybody knew tomcats had a propensity for nocturnal wanderings. "But I still can't help worrying," Miranda told herself. "What if he went out of the garden and got lost? What if he is lying injured somewhere and in need of assistance?"

This thought so much unnerved her that she determined to make a further search for her missing pet before going to bed. She had already taken down her hair for the night, but fortunately she had not yet undressed. Throwing a shawl over her head, she went downstairs, lighted a lantern, and quietly stepped back out into the garden. "Tom?" she called softly. "Tom, are you there?"

It was quite dark by this time. A waxing moon cast a silvery light over the familiar landscape of the garden, turning it into something at once mysterious and beautiful. Miranda was too worried to notice its beauty, however. She went through it systematically, shining her lantern beneath shrubs and up into trees, until she had satisfied herself that her pet could not possibly be there.

Having made a final, fruitless search beneath the cottage porch (where Tom had been known to take refuge on hot days), Miranda rose and went to the garden gate. Beyond lay the village common, with the village itself ranged along three sides of it. The fourth side was bordered by a paling, enclosing the home woods of Longworth Hall. Miranda looked long at that shadowy wilderness of trees and tangled underbrush. Was it possible that Tom had gone there? Little as Miranda liked the idea of venturing into Lord Longworth's woods at night, she had to admit it seemed more likely to hold attractions for a cat than the prosaic village. Unlatching the gate, she began to make her way toward the paling, calling softly as she went. "Tom? Tom?"

At the paling, she stopped to reconnoiter. The paling was a tall iron fence topped with a decorative frieze, intended to keep people out and deer in. It was no kind of a barrier for a half-grown kitten, however. Miranda, peering through the bars, could distinguish a rough path winding in and out amid the trees, but little else. If Tom was there, he might be anywhere.

"Tom?" she called. The night seemed alive with noises: crickets chirping in the underbrush; the rustle of the wind among the trees; the distant lowing of cattle. But it seemed to her that somewhere, not too far off, she heard an answering mew. Encouraged, Miranda raised her voice and lantern higher. "Tom! Tom!" she called, her voice vibrant with hope and expectation.

What happened next was the last thing Miranda expected. There was a slight rustling in the underbrush, and then a man stepped out of the shadows.

Like Miranda, the man was carrying a lantern in his hand, but his lantern was not lit. It hung uselessly in his hand as he stood regarding Miranda from the other side of the paling. His eyes were wide and startled, and it seemed to Miranda that they grew wider as he looked at her. He spoke no word, but merely stood gazing at her speechlessly.

Miranda was a good deal startled herself. "Oh!" she said, taking a quick step backwards.

The man said nothing, but only went on looking at her earnestly. Miranda was discomposed by his stare. She supposed the man must be an employee on Lord Longworth's estate—his gamekeeper, perhaps. It was an embarrassing situation, made more embarrassing by the recollection that her hair was loose and tumbling about her shoulders. But loose hair or not, she was still Miranda Strong, and she was not about to let a mere gamekeeper stare her out of countenance. "What are you doing in there?" she said sharply. "You startled me."

"I'm sorry," said the man. Miranda was startled anew by his voice, which was unmistakably well-bred and educated. It was certainly not the voice of a gamekeeper. It was, in fact, the voice of a gentleman; and when Miranda looked at him more closely, she saw that his dress, too, was that of a gentleman. "I'm sorry," said the gentleman again. "But you know you startled me, too."

"I daresay," said Miranda. She spoke shortly, eager to put an end to the interview. Even if the man were a gentleman rather than a gamekeeper, it was still embarrassing to be seen like this with her hair in disarray. Indeed, she was not entirely certain that it wasn't more embarrassing. She turned away, but the gentleman spoke again quickly, almost eagerly.

"Was it—you weren't the one who was calling me just now, by any chance? I thought I heard someone calling my name, and so I came over to investigate."

Miranda, startled, turned back to face him. "No, indeed! I wasn't calling you, I assure you." Suddenly enlightenment broke over her. "Unless you mean—oh, I believe I know what it is. Your name isn't Tom, by any chance?"

"Yes, it is," said the gentleman, looking at her very hard. *"Were* you calling me?"

"No, but I was calling my cat, and his name is Tom, too. Oh, and here he is!" Triumphantly, Miranda stooped to pick up Tomcat, who had appeared suddenly at her feet. "Oh, you naughty cat! What a ridiculous misunderstanding you have caused!" To the gentleman, she added, "You see how it happened, sir, I am sure. I was calling for Tom the cat—and I didn't realize there might be another Tom within hearing distance!"

"A very natural misunderstanding," agreed the gentleman. He hesitated a moment, then went on with a diffident smile. "I must say, however, that I cannot help being disappointed. You must know that when I first heard your voice, ma'am, it seemed to me to have almost a siren quality. I wasn't sure but what it might be some fair Titania, bent on enticing me into her woodland lair. And when I saw you through the palings just now, I was sure of it!"

Miranda laughed, a little embarrassed. "No, nothing like that, I'm afraid. Please accept my excuses for troubling you."

"It was no trouble," said the gentleman earnestly. "No trouble at all." He went on standing there, looking at Miranda.

"I'm glad, then," said Miranda. She thought the gentleman seemed curiously reluctant to put an end to the interview—and, in fact, she was conscious herself of a similar reluctance. He seemed a polite, well-bred sort of man—and the light of her lantern showed her that he was an attractive man, too. Not handsome, precisely, but he had strong, well-cut features, fair hair cropped short in the Brutus style, and a pair of intelligent blue eyes. His smile, too, was attractive. But of course, it was hardly the thing to be holding nighttime *tête-à-têtes* with a perfectly strange gentleman, even with a sturdy set of park palings between to play propriety. Gathering Tomcat closer to her chest, Miranda made the gentleman a dignified curtsy. "I had better be taking this errant feline of mine back home, now that I have found him. Good evening, sir, and my apologies again for disturbing you."

"Where is your home?" asked the gentleman. Miranda felt this question bordered on the impertinent. He seemed to feel it himself, for he went on quickly, in an apologetic voice. "Forgive me for asking, but I would like to call on you, if I may, and—and improve my acquaintance with your cat. He seems an exceptionally fine cat, you know." The gentleman's eyes smiled hopefully at her through the palings. "If I were to find some mutual friend who could introduce us, do you think it might be permissible for me to call?"

"Under those circumstances, I think it might be permissible," said Miranda primly. "Good evening, sir." Hugging Tomcat against her chest, she turned and hurried away.

It was only when she was halfway back to the cottage that she recalled that she had never told the gentleman where she lived. But she told herself it was probably just as well. He was an attractive person, but he was also a perfect stranger. She knew nothing about him apart from the fact that he appeared a gentleman. And everybody knew that appearances could be deceiving. He might really be some quite undesirable person. And even if he was not, it was probable that he would think lightly of a woman whom he had met in such a fashion, especially if she gave him too much encouragement at the start.

"Besides, if he really wants to call on me, he can find out where I live easily enough," Miranda told herself. "Anyone in the village could tell him. I'll wait and see what happens, and in the meantime, perhaps I can find out who he is and where he is staying. That will tell me if he is really someone I want calling on me."

# THREE

The next morning, Miranda set about making inquiries concerning her new acquaintance. "Sylvia, have you heard anything of a strange gentleman who is staying in the neighborhood?" she asked as she poured out her sister's breakfast tea. "A tall man, fair and rather good-looking, with a distinguished manner about him?"

Sylvia considered. "I did hear that Richard Clark had a party of gentlemen staying with him," she suggested. "Some friends of his from Oxford, I think."

"No, this gentleman was too old to be a university student. I thought perhaps he might be something to do with Lord Longworth's estate—his steward, perhaps. He was certainly on Lord Longworth's property when I met him, and he didn't strike me as the sort of man who would go about trespassing."

Sylvia shook her head. "I hadn't heard that Lord Longworth had changed his steward from old Mr. Templeton, but it might be so, I suppose." She looked curiously at her sister. "What were *you* doing on Lord Longworth's property, Miranda? I trust you were not trying to eke out our Sunday dinner with an illicit haunch of venison?"

Miranda greeted this jest with a dry smile. "Hardly! As a matter of fact I was never even on Lord Longworth's property. It was a most peculiar situation." She described how she had gone out to look for Tomcat, and the events that had led to her encounter with the strange gentleman at the boundary of the Longworth Hall woods.

Sylvia was much amused by her story but had as little idea as Miranda who the gentleman might be. "At any rate, we do know his first name!" she said, laughing. "It ought not to be difficult to find out who he is. I'll ask Henry when we go out driving this afternoon. Oh, I forgot." Her face clouded. "I don't suppose Henry will want to go out driving with me today, after everything that happened yesterday."

Miranda tried to comfort her, guiltily conscious that she was acting the hypocrite all the while. But as it happened, both her guilt and her comforting proved needless. At two o'clock that afternoon, Miranda, responding to a knock on the door, opened it to find Henry Ellis standing on the porch. "Er—I just called to see if Sylvia was here," he said, looking rather sheepish. "We had an engagement to go out driving, don't you know."

Miranda was conscious of some mixed emotions as she ushered Henry into the parlor. Overall, however, her predominant emotion was one of relief. She might wish to keep her sister with her, but even more did she wish to see her happy. And the sight of Sylvia moping over the loss of her lover had been very painful to her.

"In fact, I would rather see her happy with Henry than unhappy without him," she told herself with an air of wonder. "I'm not so selfish as I thought." The discovery pleased her, and she was smiling as she tapped on her sister's door. "Sylvia, Henry's downstairs. He said you had an engagement to go out driving."

The effect of these words was miraculous. Sylvia at once sprang to her feet, her face transfigured by a beatific smile. "Oh, Miranda, you're joking! Oh, you're not joking! Oh, Miranda, I'm so happy." She embraced Miranda, then rushed off joyously to receive her penitent swain.

Miranda, feeling that three would be a crowd during such

an interview, thoughtfully took herself off to the kitchen, where she spent the rest of the afternoon helping the cookmaid preserve plums. About five o'clock, Sylvia came dancing in, the smile on her face clearly signifying that the interview had been a satisfactory one.

"Oh, Miranda, it's all settled. He apologized, and I apologized, and we both agreed we had been very silly. And we're never going to go on any more picnic expeditions again!"

Miranda approved this sensible resolution, and Sylvia rattled on for some minutes more, describing all that Henry had said and done and implied. Miranda, listening in some amusement, reached the not unnatural conclusion that she and Henry had had no time to talk or even think of anything other than their own all-absorbing affairs. But after Sylvia had been talking for half an hour or so, she brought up of her own volition the subject of the strange gentleman Miranda had seen the night before.

"I told Henry all about him, and how you met him on Lord Longworth's property last night when you were looking for Tomcat. And he knew right away who he must be. Miranda, it seems that Lord Longworth is actually down here—that he came down to Longworth Hall a few days ago and brought another gentleman with him, a Mr. Phelps. Henry thinks it must be Mr. Phelps you met last night. He says he dropped in at the Stag the other night when he and his friends were having their weekly whist game, and that Mr. Phelps looked exactly the way you described him. 'Tall, fair, and rather good looking'—only Henry didn't think he was particularly good looking. However, I rather gathered from one or two things Henry let drop that Mr. Phelps was a bit patronizing to him and the others—putting on London manners, Henry said, and pretending to be above his company. So that might account for it."

"I suppose it might," said Miranda doubtfully. Her own impression of Mr. Phelps had been of a pleasant, easygoing gentleman with an engaging air of modesty. It was difficult to imagine him being patronizing to Henry Ellis or anyone else. But she reminded herself that she had only spoken to Mr. Phelps for a few minutes, and that he might have many traits of character she knew nothing about.

"Besides, there's no saying but that he might have been justified in his behavior," she told herself. "Some of Henry Ellis's whist cronies are not as genteel in their manners as they might be. They might have inadvertently offended Mr. Phelps, and then been offended themselves when he gave them a set-down. I daresay that was the way of it. Mr. Phelps might be a Londoner, but I saw no sign of his putting on airs last night."

In such a manner did Miranda make excuses for her new acquaintance. It did not occur to her what she was doing, or she might have felt it her duty to explore the motives that led her to defend Mr. Phelps so stoutly. As it was, however, she merely dismissed Henry's account of his ill-behavior and looked forward rather impatiently to see if he would make his promised call at the Cottage.

He did not come the following day, but Miranda caught a glimpse of him nonetheless. She and Sylvia had gone for a walk and were returning home in the late afternoon when she heard the sound of a carriage in the distance. A moment later it came into view, bowling down the lane toward them at a rapid pace.

"Whoever can that be?" said Sylvia. "They seem to be in a dreadful hurry, whoever they are. Four horses—but I don't recognize them, or the carriage, either. What a curious-looking phaeton! I've never seen one like it."

"It's a high-perch phaeton," said Miranda, watching the phaeton's approach with interest. "Now who in Upton Charnhurst would have such a sporting vehicle? Can it be that Mr. Clark has got a new carriage?"

"No, I'm sure he has not, or Henry would have mentioned

it. Oh!" Sylvia gripped Miranda's sleeve in sudden excitement. "I know, Miranda! It must be Lord Longworth. You know this lane leads to Longworth Hall."

"So it does," agreed Miranda. A strange excitement was gripping her heart. The phaeton was near enough now that she could see its occupants, a pair of gentlemen in sporting dress. And though the gentleman driving the phaeton was a stranger to her, she was almost sure the gentleman sitting beside him was her new acquaintance, Mr. Phelps.

The phaeton slowed its pace a little as it drew opposite the two ladies, and Miranda was able to see that the gentleman on the right was indeed Mr. Phelps. It was obvious that he recognized her, too. His face lit up, and he raised his hat, executing a smiling half-bow from the waist. There was no time for Miranda to do more than smile in return before the phaeton had passed them and continued on its way toward Longworth Hall.

"He bowed to you!" said Sylvia, wide-eyed. "Do you know him, Miranda?"

"Yes, it's Mr. Phelps, the gentleman I met the other night," said Miranda, trying not to blush.

"Well, he looks a very nice, well-mannered gentleman. I suppose the other gentleman must be Lord Longworth. I'm afraid I can't say as much for his manners as Mr. Phelps's. Did you see how he stared at us?"

"Yes, I saw," said Miranda. She had been so busy looking at Mr. Phelps that she had spared only a glance for his companion, but that glance had been enough. Lord Longworth had a long, lean, supercilious face, bold, ogling eyes, and a dandified air that contrasted strongly with Mr. Phelps's quiet, gentlemanly appearance. "Why, *he* looks more like a lord than that foppish creature," Miranda told herself with scorn. "I daresay Lord Longworth wears a corset and puts his hair in curling papers every night!"

But she wasted little time scorning Lord Longworth's cherubic brown curls. Seeing Mr. Phelps again had reinforced her first impression of him as an attractive, agreeable, well-mannered gentleman. She began to think she would be very sorry if he did not call upon her. But would he? As a stranger to the neighborhood, it might be some time before he could find out who she was and contrive the necessary formal introduction that must take place before he could call at the Cottage with propriety. For the rest of that day and into the night, Miranda wracked her brain, trying to think of a way she might assist him in this endeavor. And when, on the following day, Sylvia reported hearing a rumor that Lord Longworth meant to attend the village assembly that evening, Miranda thought she had found the solution she was looking for.

"If you do not mind, Sylvia, I think I will come to the assembly tonight along with you and Henry," she remarked casually. "Not that I care about seeing Lord Longworth, but I could use a little diversion. It will be interesting to see all the village toadies falling over themselves, trying to get his attention!"

Sylvia laughed. "Yes, Mrs. Jordan has already announced she intends to have a new cap for the occasion. As you say, it ought to be interesting. Besides, Mr. Phelps might be there, too, and even if you do not care about Lord Longworth, I am sure you would not mind seeing *him* again."

In a reserved manner, Miranda agreed that she would not, and went upstairs to look over her stock of evening dresses. She decided on her *eau-de-nil* crepe with the square neck and corded trimming. But it was her headdress that chiefly concerned her. She had been wearing caps for some months now, and to suddenly leave them off would be to attract undesirable attention. Such critics as old Miss Lattimer would whisper that she had done so because she wished to attract the notice of Lord Longworth and his friend. Miranda winced at the thought of such vulgarity. Yet there was no denying she looked better without a cap. She tried both ways, each time coming to the same conclusion.

"But I simply can't bear to have it said I am setting my cap for Lord Longworth," she told her reflection. Her reflection looked back at her—a dark-haired woman, not exactly young or pretty, but with a distinguished appearance overall, she thought. A cap—even a small, elegant cap—quenched that appearance as surely as a snuffer quenched a candle's flame. But there was no hope for it. Pinning a trifle of lace and net atop her head, Miranda turned away from the glass with a sigh, feeling that all the delight had gone out of the evening.

She had reckoned without Sylvia, however. "No, you shall not, Miranda!" Sylvia cried, as soon as Miranda came into the parlor. "It's bad enough that you must wear those dreadful caps during the day, but there's no reason at all for you to wear one tonight. Is there, Henry? I am sure she would look much better without her cap."

Henry, who was sitting in the parlor along with Sylvia, turned a judicial eye upon Miranda. "I'd say so," he agreed. "But you know I don't know much about ladies' gear, Sylvia."

"Well, I do, and I say she shan't be made to look a guy tonight." Snatching the cap from atop her sister's head, Sylvia ran across the room and held the cap over the fireplace grate. "Indeed, you shall not, Miranda," she said, her eyes bright with laughing defiance. "I'll throw it in if you won't promise to go without it just this one evening!"

"That threat would impress me more if there was actually a fire in the fireplace," said Miranda, smiling in spite of herself. "But as you seem to feel so strongly about it, Sylvia, I'll go without my cap just this once. Would a scarf be in order, or must I go quite bareheaded?"

"I have something better than a scarf. It's really a birthday gift, but since your birthday is only a few days away, I'll give it to you now." Sylvia ran out of the room and reappeared a moment later carrying a small package in her hand. "Open it, Miranda. I got it when I was in Salisbury last month."

The package proved to contain a gold foil bandeau. "Sylvia, how pretty," said Miranda, surveying it with pleasure. "Only— only don't you think it's rather too fine for me to wear on such an occasion as this?"

"Not a bit too fine. Lots of ladies wear them to the assemblies nowadays. Mrs. John Cook was wearing a silver one just like it at last week's assembly, and you know she is generally held to have excellent taste."

The undisputed excellence of Mrs. John Cook's taste was enough to quiet any qualms Miranda might still feel over making herself fine in such a manner. She docilely allowed Sylvia to redress her hair, and the result was infinitely more satisfying to her eyes than her former prim appearance. "You look beautiful," said Sylvia, regarding her with pride and affection.

"I fear you are partial, Sister," said Miranda, but she was pleased by the compliment nonetheless. As she accompanied her sister and Henry out to the latter's carriage, she had the happy consciousness of being stylishly dressed and in her best looks.

Of course, her toilette must appear a modest affair by London standards. It would have been better if she could have draped her shoulders with an India shawl rather than one of domestic manufacture and flaunted real jewels on her bosom instead of a simple gold locket. Still, to dress too finely would have been inappropriate to the occasion. She was likely to arouse enough comment as it was in her capless condition, but Miranda was resolved to brave the comment just this once. The fact that her bandeau was a birthday gift from Sylvia made a good excuse for wearing it, and if she was a trifle finer than usual in honor of the newcomers from London, then so too would be many others.

The accuracy of this prediction was immediately apparent on entering the village assembly rooms. The rooms themselves were just as usual: salmon-colored walls ornamented with designs in white plasterwork and a few rather tarnished gilt-framed mirrors. But the company within were considerably more elegant—or at least, more showy—than was usually the case at the Upton Charnhurst assemblies.

Mrs. Jordan had got her new cap, which bloomed forth in a startling array of pansies and pinks atop her grizzled head. Her daughters both had new dresses, contrived goodness knows how, given the shortness of the notice and the notorious smallness of the Jordans' means. The uncharitable whispered that Miss Madeline's tunic bore a suspicious resemblance to a certain gown that her elder sister had been wont to wear in years past. Miss Lattimer was in her usual severe black, but she had pinned a garnet brooch to her bosom and added a tuft of cock feathers to her famous purple turban to give it a more modish look. Her sister-in-law Mrs. Granger had achieved something like real splendor by appearing in a diamond tiara. In consequence, she was giving herself the most terrific airs, though it was agreed by every other lady present that said tiara was of an antiquated style and badly in need of cleaning.

Miranda barely noticed the unaccustomed finery of her friends and neighbors, however. She was busy looking around the rooms to see if Mr. Phelps was there. She had just made up her mind that he was not, when a little bustle near the door caught her attention. She looked around, and there he was, just entering the room with Lord Longworth.

There could be no doubt that of the two men, Lord Longworth was the more eye-catching. His blue evening coat was padded in the shoulders, peaked in the lapels, and ornamented with very large buttons whose pearly hue exactly matched his stockinette pantaloons. His brown hair was as hectically curly as before, and his neckcloth a monstrous erection of starched linen. A quizzing glass hung from his neck, through which he surveyed the company with a supercilious smile.

In contrast, Mr. Phelps's appearance was one of sober elegance. His black evening coat and pantaloons were neatly tailored to his tall figure but possessed no extravagances of style to draw the eye as did Lord Longworth's. His neckcloth was so plainly knotted as to be entirely unobtrusive, his fair hair was smoothly brushed, and his manner as he looked around the crowded rooms was one of a man willing to please and be pleased. Once again Miranda reflected that he looked a hundred times more gentlemanly than his foppish friend.

Of course she was not the only one to notice the two gentlemen's entrance. There was a great deal of murmuring and whispering, and a certain amount of maneuvering among the bolder souls in the room in order to place themselves where the strangers must notice them. Mrs. Granger cast them a languishing smile; Mrs. Jordan and her daughters began to talk in a highly animated and artificial manner, laughing shrilly at everything that was said while keeping a weather eye on their quarry.

It did not seem to Miranda that the two men were aware of these feminine strategems. They were occupied in greeting Colonel Comstock, an elderly gentleman who was a fixture at all village gatherings and who seemed to be known to them. "Henry, you ought to go over there and say good evening to them, too," said Sylvia, who along with Miranda had been watching the strangers' entrance. "You and Mr. Phelps are acquainted, after all, and it would only be polite."

"Polite or not, I'd as soon have nothing to do with that fellow again," grumbled Henry. Just the same, he went without any noticeable reluctance, leading Miranda to suspect he was not ill-pleased to claim an acquaintance with one of the newcomers.

To her surprise, it was to Lord Longworth that he addressed himself rather than Mr. Phelps. Sylvia was surprised, too. "I did not know Henry had been introduced to Lord Longworth!"

she whispered to Miranda. "He only spoke of meeting Mr. Phelps. Imagine his being such a ninny as not to mention it!"

Miranda nodded, but in truth she was puzzled by Henry's conduct. Her puzzlement grew deeper as she continued to watch. Lord Longworth had acknowledged Henry's greeting with a condescending bow. Now he was saying something to Mr. Phelps beside him, and Mr. Phelps was bowing, too. For several minutes the three of them stood talking together; then Henry glanced toward Sylvia and Miranda and appeared to ask some question of the two other gentlemen. Both of them followed his gaze, Lord Longworth even going so far as to put his quizzing glass to his eye in order to survey them in greater detail. Mr. Phelps, however, no more than caught sight of Miranda than a look of surprise and pleasure lit up his face. He nodded vigorously, and though Lord Longworth made what appeared to be some sort of expostulation, it seemed to have no effect on his friend. Mr. Phelps began to move purposefully toward Miranda, and Lord Longworth, with a smile of resignation, trailed after him.

Miranda, conscious of the eyes of her neighbors all around her, prepared to receive the two gentlemen in a manner that would do credit to the name of Strong. But she very nearly lost her composure when Henry, with a low bow, introduced the gentleman she had come to know as Mr. Phelps. "Miss Strong, Sylvia, allow me to introduce to you Lord Longworth. This is Mr. Phelps," he added perfunctorily, with a nod toward the foppish gentleman in the blue coat. "Lord Longworth, Mr. Phelps, this is Miss Miranda Strong and Miss Sylvia Strong."

Miranda curtsied automatically, but her mind was whirling with surprise and wonderment. Could it be that her acquaintance of the park palings was actually *Lord Longworth?* No, such a thing was ridiculous. She must simply have misunderstood Henry's introduction. Sylvia, less reserved, blurted out the same thought. "Oh, but Henry, you must have made a mistake. Surely I did not understand you to say this gentleman is Lord Longworth?"

She looked at the fair gentleman. Henry looked at him, too, surprise and bewilderment on his face. "Aye, he's Lord Longworth right enough," he said. "Why shouldn't he be?"

"No reason at all," said Sylvia, and collapsed into giggles.

Miranda, while officially disapproving this conduct, felt a strong desire to imitate it. She turned to the gentleman who was revealed to be Lord Longworth and who was regarding her and Sylvia with the uncomprehending smile of one who fails to understand a joke under discussion. "Forgive my sister's amusement, my lord. I assure you that she and I are both pleased to make your acquaintance. If our manner seems a little odd—well, it is only because we have been laboring under a misapprehension."

Lord Longworth's bafflement gave way to a smile of understanding. "I see," he said. "There seem to have been misapprehensions aplenty in our acquaintance thus far. May I hope you will stand up with me for the first set, Miss Strong, and help me thrash them out once and for all?"

Miranda was staggered by this request. Never in her life had she led off the dancing at a village assembly, and to do so in company with Lord Longworth was more glory than she had ever hoped for. "Yes—yes, I should be very pleased to dance with you, my lord," she said faintly.

He smiled and bowed. "The pleasure is all mine, Miss Strong," he said. Turning to Sylvia, he added, "Miss Sylvia, I hope you, too, will condescend to dance with me. Are you engaged for the second set?"

Henry frowned at this, but Sylvia said she was not and would be happy to dance with him. Listening to this exchange, Miranda began to calm down and to recover those powers of rational thinking that had been lost in the first excitement of Lord Longworth's invitation.

"Of course it's really Sylvia he wants to dance with," she

reasoned to herself. "He merely asked me first because I am eldest. Well, that was very polite of him, and I'm sure I couldn't blame him for wishing to dance with Sylvia. She looks very lovely this evening—the prettiest girl in the room."

With a mixture of pride and something oddly like pain, Miranda regarded her sister. Sylvia's golden hair hung in clusters of ringlets on either side of her face, and her dress of cerulean blue gauze heightened the color of her eyes while setting off the grace and elegance of her figure. There could be no doubt that she looked very lovely. She, Miranda, had never been half so lovely, not even when she was as young as Sylvia. For a moment, Miranda felt a maudlin desire to weep for her lost youth. She repressed it immediately, however. It was unthinkable that she should cry at a party, and in fact there was no reason to cry. She ought rather to be rejoicing at the honor that had fallen to her and her sister.

"And who knows but that honor might lead to something else?" she told herself practically. "If Lord Longworth comes to know Sylvia, it's possible he might fall in love with her. Stranger things have happened, after all. Imagine what it would be to see Sylvia a baroness and living at Longworth Hall! And even if it never comes to that, at least Lord Longworth might give her thoughts a different direction and cure her of her infatuation for Henry Ellis. I'm sure no woman in her senses would look at Henry Ellis while Lord Longworth was around!"

She felt this more strongly than ever as Lord Longworth led her out for the first dance. He smiled down at her as they executed the opening figure and prepared to go down the line of other couples.

"You cannot know how pleased I was to see you this evening, Miss Strong," he said. "Ever since our meeting the other night, I have been trying without success to find out who you were and where you lived. Almost I had reached the conclusion that you were, after all, a will o' the wisp instead of a flesh-and-blood woman!"

As the figures of the dance separated them just then, Miranda contented herself with giving him a shy smile in return to this speech. "I must say, however, that I was puzzled by you and your sister's reaction when we were introduced," he continued, as soon as they were reunited. "You seemed surprised to learn my name."

An involuntary laugh broke from Miranda's lips. "Oh, yes! Indeed we were surprised, my lord, for we thought you had been Mr. Phelps." Smiling, she explained how the misunderstanding had come about. "Although I cannot think how Mr. Ellis could make such a mistake, my lord. You and Mr. Phelps are not at all alike."

He laughed ruefully. "No, Gus is generally accounted very much better-looking than I am! But I am pleased to learn your sister's amusement stemmed from such a source." He smiled at Miranda. "You must know that after the awkward way I behaved the other night, I was half afraid she was laughing at the idea of such a Yahoo pretending to be a gentleman!"

"Oh, no, it was nothing like that, my lord," Miranda assured him. As she spoke, it occurred to her that here was a fine opportunity to further her sister's cause. Lord Longworth had obviously been struck by Sylvia, or he would not have brought her name into the conversation. It was up to her, as Sylvia's elder sister, to encourage his prepossession. "Perhaps you wondered at Sylvia's laughing as she did, but that was only because she was taken off guard. Her sense of humor does not run away with her in the usual way. Indeed, I would say that her manners in general are very nice."

"I'm sure they are," said Lord Longworth. "Please don't think I begrudge your sister her amusement at my expense, Miss Strong. It's a poor man who cannot laugh at himself now and then."

"If you say so, my lord," said Miranda uncertainly. "I only did not want you to take offense."

He smiled down at her. "No fear of that, Miss Strong. If I take offense at anything, it is to your addressing me as 'my lord' when we are already on a Christian-name basis!"

Miranda looked at him doubtfully. "But you know I can hardly call you by your Christian name, my lord!" she protested. "We have only just been introduced."

"No, we were introduced the other night, don't you remember? Your cat performed the introductions. I, for one, regard an introduction from a cat as being quite as legitimate as a human one. Perhaps even more so!"

Miranda laughed. "Now you are quizzing me, my lord! I felt very foolish that night, I assure you, and even more foolish this evening when I found out who you were."

He looked down at her meditatively. "I never would have guessed it. You carried off the situation with as much composure as though you had been a cat yourself. And now I think of it, I'm not altogether sure you're not. Those eyes of yours certainly have a feline look to them. I couldn't tell the other night what color they were, but I see now they're green, not gray."

Miranda gave an embarrassed laugh. "To speak truth, they really are more gray than green, my lord. It's only my dress that makes them look green."

To her confusion, he took this remark as an invitation to scrutinize her dress as well as various more personal attributes. "I wish my eyes were like my sister's, my lord," gabbled Miranda, desperate to distract him. "She has the loveliest blue eyes, just like a summer sky."

"Has she? I didn't notice," he said absently.

"Oh, yes, mine are not worth a second look beside them. Sylvia is definitely the beauty of our family. I often wished we could have afforded to give her a Season in London. Such a pretty girl as she is deserves a chance to be seen in a wider circle than the one we presently move in."

This statement, she was relieved to see, served to distract Lord Longworth's attention from her person. He glanced at Sylvia, who was dancing nearby with Henry Ellis. "Yes, your sister is a very pretty girl," he agreed. "But I rather question whether a Season in London would have added materially to her happiness. You know, the only reason most girls come to London is to find a husband—and though it may sound cynical and ill-natured, I should say myself that Miss Sylvia was more likely to find a husband who would make her happy here than there. Indeed, to judge by the behavior of the young man she is dancing with right now, I should be tempted to say she has found one already."

He gave Miranda a quizzical smile. She smiled back at him uncertainly. Was it possible he was asking her if Sylvia's affections were already engaged? Of course they were, technically speaking, but Henry had not yet proposed to her. Miranda decided it was in her sister's interests to play down her relationship with Henry as much as possible. Lord Longworth was, after all, a much more worthy man, and a much more charming one, too. To whistle him down the wind for such a man as Henry Ellis was an idea that struck Miranda as very nearly criminal.

So she said lightly, "You mean Mr. Ellis? To be sure, he has been one of my sister's most devoted beaux, but by no means the only one. She has a great many admirers."

"I am sure she has," said Lord Longworth. He smiled at Miranda. "And I doubt not her sister has her share, too!"

Miranda opened her mouth to dispel this idea, then closed it again. It could do no harm if Lord Longworth supposed her to have as many beaux as Sylvia. Besides, as she reflected cynically, there would no doubt be plenty of people anxious to dispel the notion for her, without her troubling to do so herself. So she merely smiled and said, "You are too kind, my lord," which seemed appropriately noncommittal.

He gazed back at her a long moment without saying anything. At last he sighed and shook his head. "I wish I could say the same for you, Miss Strong. But I am afraid that you are, on the contrary, very cruel. Here you are, still my-lording me, when I want nothing so much as to hear my name on your lips once more. Cannot you bring yourself to call me Tom even once?"

It crossed Miranda's mind that if Lord Longworth had a fault, it was a tendency toward flirtatiousness. Normally she would have censured such conduct, but tonight, to her surprise, she found herself responding in kind. "Perhaps, my lord," she said, and smiled at him provokingly. Again he shook his head, an answering smile on his lips.

"Ah, you *are* cruel! But I will continue to hope you will soften toward me by and by. And in the meantime, at least I have the pleasure of hearing your voice, even if it doesn't address me quite as I would like. You do have a lovely voice, Miss Strong. It quite haunted me the other night as I was going through the woods—and I'm not sure it doesn't haunt me still."

If he had hoped by this means to hear more of Miranda's voice, he was destined to disappointment. Miranda was naturally gratified by his compliment; it was something to be told one had a lovely voice, and even more gratifying when that compliment came from a gentleman like Lord Longworth, who might be expected to be a judge of such matters. But she was so little used to receiving compliments of any kind that for the rest of the dance she was rendered quite dumb with self-consciousness. Lord Longworth did not seem to mind, however, or else he merely took it as another instance of cruelty on her part. "Thank you for standing up with me, Miss Strong," he said, at the dance's conclusion. "Would it

be too much to hope you might dance with me again later
this evening, if you have time?"

His voice was as humble as though he was requesting an
honor rather than bestowing one. His eyes, too, were humble—or if not humble, at least very blue and beseeching. Miranda, looking into those eyes, thought again how attractive
he was. It struck her, indeed, that she was in danger of having
her head turned. "Perhaps," she said ambiguously, and sank
back into her seat quite overcome by all that had befallen her.

# FOUR

Although leading off the dance with Lord Longworth had been a social triumph for Miranda, she was soon made to feel that her triumph was not without cost. Upton Charnhurst society expected its members to conform to certain rigid and well-established precedents. Young girls not yet out were to be seen but not heard when they went out in public. Once the young girls had become young ladies, they were permitted to be heard as well as seen, but only if they behaved modestly and addressed their elders in a suitably respectful fashion. And once a young lady had publicly resigned all matrimonial hopes by donning her caps, it was only at her own peril that she renounced them again, as Miranda very speedily learned.

"My dear, I could not help noticing your—ahem—*head-dress*." This remark, addressed to Miranda in a whisper by Miss Lattimer, an elderly spinster, could not have held more disapproval if Miranda had appeared publicly in her chemise. "Do you really think it wise, my dear, to make yourself so conspicuous? I know the younger girls wear such ornaments, but frankly, given your age and position, I would have thought a plain cap more appropriate."

Miranda was nettled, but determined not to show it. "Are you speaking of my bandeau, ma'am? It was a birthday gift from my sister. I must confess I hesitated to wear it tonight, knowing how critical people can be, but my regard for Sylvia

222 *Joy Reed*

is greater than my regard for any amount of impertinent criticism."

Miss Lattimer, misliking to ally herself on the side of impertinence, tacitly resigned the subject of the bandeau and proceeded to her next issue. "I was quite surprised to see you opening the dancing with Lord Longworth, Miss Strong," she said, flashing her yellowed teeth at Miranda. "However did you manage such a thing? I am sure our local belles must be gnashing their teeth with jealousy."

Miranda shrugged her shoulders. "I don't see why. Lord Longworth was kind enough to engage me for the first dance, but I have no monopoly on his attentions. He is dancing with my sister right now, you know."

"Yes, but he asked you *first,* Miss Strong. He must have had *some* reason." Miss Lattimer's eyes scanned Miranda's face, looking for some sign of guilt or confusion. "You were not previously acquainted, were you?"

"Why, how could we be?" countered Miranda, opening her eyes very wide. "Lord Longworth has only just come to stay at Longworth Hall, has he not?"

Miss Lattimer acknowledged this grudgingly. "I daresay Lord Longworth invited me to stand up with him first merely because I was the first lady he was introduced to," continued Miranda in a calm voice. "Mr. Ellis was previously acquainted with his friend Mr. Phelps, you know, and so it was natural that he should make us acquainted also."

"Is that so?" Balked of satisfaction in one direction, Miss Lattimer determined to take her revenge in another. "Mr. Ellis had better watch what he is about, then," she went on, flashing another venomous smile. "He'll find he's set himself up a rival if he isn't careful. Your sister's a pretty girl, and though it's not likely Lord Longworth would look for a wife so far beneath him, there's no saying but that he might make trouble all the same."

In making such an attack, however, she had exposed her

own flank. The Lattimers were an old and well-connected family, but Miss Lattimer's mother had been a mere shopkeeper's daughter before her marriage. "I don't suppose Lord Longworth has serious intentions toward Sylvia," said Miranda with deceptive gentleness. "But if he does, he might do much worse for a wife. Sylvia is a very superior girl, and her birth is perfectly genteel. It's not as though any of her ancestors have ever been in trade, or anything of that sort."

Miss Lattimer had nothing to say to this remark and took herself off with a loud sniff. Miranda was pleased by her victory, but it proved only the first of many similar skirmishes. There were plenty of ladies besides Miss Lattimer to comment on the absence of her cap; to wonder why Lord Longworth had chosen to single her out as he had done; and to predict that he would never so choose again.

"You do look rather well this evening, Miss Strong, and of course if Lord Longworth was making his choice based on precedence alone, you merit such an honor as much as anybody," remarked one matron condescendingly. "But having done his duty, you must not expect him to dance attendance on you all evening, you know."

Miranda could think of no suitably crushing reply to this speech and so merely smiled coolly. Inwardly, however, she was fuming. Some of her critics had been more or less well-intentioned, others were openly spiteful, but the consensus of opinion among the Upton Charnhurstites seemed to be that her dance with Lord Longworth had been a freakish incident such as could never happen twice. The worst of it was that Miranda herself was beginning to believe the same thing. To be sure, he had spoken of inviting her to stand up with him again, but it would be foolish to expect such an invitation to really materialize.

"I don't expect it," she told herself firmly. "I don't expect anything of him, not on my own account."

For Sylvia, of course, it was different. Sylvia was young

and pretty and charming. It would be no great wonder if Lord Longworth were taken with her attractions.

"They seem to be getting on all right," Miranda reflected, watching her sister and Lord Longworth go through the figures of the dance. "And they make a handsome couple." Strangely enough, this reflection made her feel no better, but rather caused her to turn away from the dance floor with a sigh.

Under the circumstances, she could only be glad when the foppish Mr. Phelps strolled over and addressed her with the laconic words, "Dance, Miss Strong?" He might be—undoubtedly was—a dandy, and Miranda suspected him of being an egoist as well. But his invitation represented a means of escape. Given the persecution she had endured since dancing with Lord Longworth, she would have taken any means of escape that offered.

The dance proved more enjoyable than she would have anticipated. Mr. Phelps was a good dancer and not so bereft of manners as he had first appeared. And though, as Miranda had expected, most of his conversation revolved around the subject of Mr. Phelps, he occasionally condescended to discuss his friend as well, a subject she found much more interesting.

"When Longworth said he was coming down here for six or eight weeks this autumn, I couldn't imagine what he was about. I mean, Brighton's one thing—with the Regent's parties, and the theaters and assemblies and all, one can generally depend on there being something to while away one's time. But the country's such a dead-and-alive kind of place. I suppose, owning a property here, Longworth might consider he has a duty to stop at the Hall now and then and see how things are going on. But to spend the best part of two months here! To my mind, that's carrying duty too far. What I mean is, that's what bailiffs are for, aren't they?"

Miranda smiled. "Bailiffs are useful things in their way,"

she said. "But I fear it is unrealistic to expect one to work well entirely unsupervised, Mr. Phelps. Lord Longworth is probably wise to take a personal interest in the management of his estate."

Mr. Phelps grimaced. "Wise he may be, but he's let himself in for one deuce of a dull six or eight weeks! Not that this party tonight isn't a decentish affair, as provincial assemblies go," he added condescendingly. "But what I mean is, you'll hardly be holding assemblies every night, will you?"

"I am afraid not," returned Miranda gravely. "Still, I doubt not you and Lord Longworth will be able to obtain a reasonable amount of diversion once you become acquainted with the neighborhood. There will be invitations to private dinners and dances now and then—and of course the weekly whist parties at the Stag, with which you are already acquainted."

"Yes, whist for three-penny points! That's not *my* idea of diversion."

Mr. Phelps looked and sounded so disconsolate that Miranda could not help laughing. "Well, if our local diversions do not satisfy you, Mr. Phelps, perhaps you can convince Lord Longworth to give a few of his own," she said. "You must know that all of us here in the village are dying to get a look inside Longworth Hall. It's been shut up for as long as I can remember."

"That's an idea," said Mr. Phelps, looking at her with respect. "A dashed good idea, by Jove. I'll tell Longworth he owes me a ball, at least, and a couple of rout parties as well. Seeing that I was good enough to immolate myself on the altar of duty and accompany him down here, I think it's his duty to keep me entertained."

Miranda expressed grave approval with this sentiment. Inwardly, she reflected with amusement that if Lord Longworth did indeed give a party for the residents of Upton Charnhurst, then she might claim at least partial credit. She was still smiling when the dance ended, but as Mr. Phelps led her back to her seat, her good mood left her abruptly. There was a man standing beside her chair, talking to Sylvia—a man whom she instantly recognized as her cousin Benedict. Miranda's face hardened. Benedict Strong seldom attended the village assemblies, preferring instead to entertain himself with noisier and less reputable gatherings at the local alehouse. The mere sight of his dissolute face always revived in Miranda the old resentment that such a man should be in possession of her family home.

"Good evening, Cousin," she said, giving him a cold and formal bow.

"Good evening, Cousin," he returned, smiling genially. He was a big man, running to fat, with a red face and coarse, straw-colored hair. "Thought I'd look in on your party here and see if there was anything doing. And what do I find but that our local nob's put in an appearance! Sylvia here's been good enough to introduce us."

He moved aside as he spoke, and Miranda saw to her dismay that Lord Longworth was also standing beside Sylvia, a polite smile on his face. It seemed to Miranda that if her dance with him had represented the evening's zenith, this was undoubtedly its nadir. To be forced to acknowledge a vulgar man like her cousin before him—and to hear that same cousin address him to his face as "our local nob!" What must he think of her?

"But it's on Sylvia's account I really mind it," she told herself. "Any man might balk at the prospect of such a relation." She could think of nothing to say to ease the situation, but fortunately Lord Longworth was more adroit. Turning to Mr. Phelps, he politely introduced him to Benedict Strong. Miranda winced a little as her cousin acknowledged the introduction with a loud "How d'ye do, sir?" but he said nothing worse during the few minutes of conversation that followed. She was thankful when he presently made an excuse and took himself off.

But though the incident might have been much worse, she still felt deeply humiliated. She glanced at Lord Longworth, expecting to see disgust on his face. He was looking at her rather quizzically, but his quizzical expression changed to a smile when he encountered her eye. "I am glad to see you again, Miss Strong," he said. "I was hoping you might be free to dance this next dance with me?"

Miranda was amazed and confounded. "Oh, yes, but—really, I did not expect such an honor, my lord," she said. "If you would prefer to dance with some other lady, I should be happy to make introductions."

Lord Longworth continued to smile with his lips, but when he spoke again his voice was rather cool. "That is very kind of you, Miss Strong. But if you do not care to dance with me, I shall not trouble you to perform any introductions. I would rather sit the dance out."

"But I do care to dance with you, my lord!" exclaimed Miranda. The words were true enough, but when she happened to glance at Sylvia she experienced a sudden qualm. Was it hurt or merely surprise that she read in her sister's eyes? And if it was hurt, was she really justified in selfishly accepting Lord Longworth's invitation, when her sister's happiness might depend on her refusing it? Miranda made a last, desperate attempt to rectify matters as she saw them. "Of course I will dance with you if you like, but I had supposed you meant to dance this dance with my sister, just as you did the last."

Lord Longworth looked surprised. "No, I don't think so," he began, but Sylvia interrupted him.

"Oh, no, Miranda, I am engaged to Henry for this dance," she said with a shake of her blond curls. "You go on and dance with Lord Longworth." And so Miranda, outwardly unwilling and yet inwardly pleased, accepted the arm that Lord Longworth extended to her and accompanied him onto the floor.

She noticed right away that his mood seemed graver and

less lighthearted than it had during their earlier dance. He said nothing at all for several minutes. Miranda was likewise silent, feeling she had made a mess of things but uncertain how she could have acted differently. She was also still feeling humiliated over the encounter with her cousin. Surprisingly, it was to this incident that Lord Longworth referred when he finally did speak.

"So does your cousin also live in the village, Miss Strong? Or is he merely visiting you and your sister?"

"Oh, no," said Miranda. She spoke emphatically, then sighed and went on with a forced smile. "Although I could better endure it if he *was* merely visiting us! The fact is that you have hit upon a sore point, my lord. My sister and I used to live in the house he lives in now, The Vineyard. I don't know if you are familiar with it—"

"Yes, I think I know the place you mean. That big, half-timbered house just opposite the church?"

"Yes, that's it. As I said, my sister and I used to live there, but when my father died a few years ago the place went to my cousin. Sylvia and I now live in a cottage on the outskirts of the village, just across the common from where you and I had our first, historic encounter."

She spoke lightly and tried to smile as she spoke, but Lord Longworth did not seem to be deceived. "I am sure losing your home must have been painful for you and your sister," he said quietly. "For what it's worth, you have my condolences, Miss Strong. I have often felt that the English law of entail left something to be desired, particularly in regard to its treatment of the female descendants. The French system is a good deal fairer in that respect."

Although gratified by his sympathy, Miranda was embarrassed at having betrayed herself. She turned the matter off with a little laugh. "But surely you yourself have profited by that system, my lord!" she said. "And in a sense we all have. There would be no magnificent estates like Longworth Hall in England if it were not for the laws of entail that kept them together generation after generation."

"That's true, of course. As you say, I have profited by the system. But that doesn't mean I am not alive to its inequities." In an abrupt change of subject, he added, "I noticed you dancing with my friend earlier, Miss Strong. It looked as though you were getting on very well."

The words themselves were neutral, but it seemed to Miranda that Lord Longworth's voice held almost a jealous tone. She looked at him in surprise. "Well enough, I suppose. Mr. Phelps was bewailing the lack of society here in Upton Charnhurst." With a glimmer of a smile, she added, "I am afraid you will shortly be solicited with demands to give a ball at Longworth Hall, my lord!"

"A ball at Longworth Hall?" repeated Lord Longworth, looking taken aback. "What nonsense is this?"

"I'm afraid it was my doing, my lord. I mentioned to Mr. Phelps that all of us in the village are longing to attend a party at Longworth Hall, and he was quick to seize on the idea. He feels a ball is the very least you owe him for dragging him down to such a dead-and-alive place!"

Lord Longworth snorted, but he also looked relieved. "So the idea was yours, was it, Miss Strong?" His face became suddenly thoughtful. "I hadn't planned to do any entertaining while I was down here, but it's not a bad idea, now I come to think of it. The main question would be whether people were willing to come. Even though I've owned the Hall for years, I'm virtually a stranger here."

"They'll come," Miranda assured him. She reflected cynically to herself that even if the high sticklers of Upton Charnhurst society were inclined to boycott Lord Longworth's ball, there would still be plenty of people like Mrs. Jordan who would jump at the chance to attend it. "Oh, yes, they'll come, my lord," she repeated. "I have no doubt you can fill your rooms as full as you like."

She spoke gaily, but there was nonetheless a touch of bitterness in her voice. Lord Longworth looked at her thoughtfully. "And I have no doubt you are right, Miss Strong—assuming that filling my rooms was my only object. But you see, I am rather particular about the company I keep. Merely filling my rooms would not satisfy me."

"Oh," said Miranda blankly. "Well, as to that, I am sure you can please yourself, my lord. If you really intend to give a ball, I expect anyone hereabouts would be glad to come."

"Perhaps so, but I would like to be more specific on that point before committing myself. Would you, for instance, be willing to come if I was to give a ball? You and your sister?"

He looked at Miranda searchingly. She was astonished by the question and rather flustered by it as well, but a moment's reflection served to calm her spirit.

"It is not my opinion but Sylvia's that he cares about," she told herself. "Of course he has been smitten by Sylvia, and it is on her account he proposes to give a ball."

Miranda was pleased to see that her cousin's boorish behavior had not served to entirely spoil her sister's chances with Lord Longworth. Of course she was pleased—but despite her sisterly pleasure, there was a pang in her heart as she answered his question.

"Why, certainly, my lord. I am sure both my sister and I would be pleased to come to your ball, if you give one."

She smiled as she spoke, and he smiled, too. "Very well, then, Miss Strong. I shall start making plans immediately for a ball at Longworth Hall."

The dance ended soon after this. Lord Longworth thanked her for the dance and politely accompanied her back to her seat. Miranda suspected he was hoping to intercept Sylvia for the next dance, but if so, his hopes were disappointed. Sylvia remained on the floor with Henry Ellis throughout the following dance. Lord Longworth stayed with Miranda for some time, chatting lightly on various subjects, but eventually Mr.

Phelps showed up to demand that his friend make a fourth in a game of whist that he had gotten up in the adjoining card room.

"I suppose I must humor him, Miss Strong," Lord Longworth told Miranda with a smile. "But I will hope to see you again soon." In a lower voice, he added, "Do you think I might call upon you and your sister, now that we are properly acquainted?"

"To be sure," Miranda assented. As she watched him walk away with Mr. Phelps, she reflected with gloomy pleasure that Sylvia had obviously made a powerful impression on him. As if to confirm these thoughts, she caught a few words that Mr. Phelps addressed to him as they went into the card room.

"By Jove, old fellow, I've never seen you so *épris*. To be sure, that Strong gel's a handsome piece—"

The door swung shut behind the two men just then, cutting off the rest of Mr. Phelps's words, but as far as Miranda was concerned, this was all the confirmation she needed. Of course Lord Longworth might not be serious in his intentions toward her sister, but his behavior and his friend's words proved he was at least interested. With proper management, that interest might be parlayed into an offer of marriage.

For the rest of the evening, Miranda was absorbed in planning how best she might further her sister's matrimonial chances. Several other ladies addressed catty or curious remarks to her about her capless condition and her dancing with Lord Longworth, but she brushed them aside with an absent smile that served to annoy her would-be critics more than any verbal retaliation could have done. Rather to her surprise, she also received several more invitations to dance. In the normal way she would have refused these invitations, but just in time it occurred to her that to dance with other gentlemen would make her dances with Lord Longworth seem less singular. So she accepted them instead, and contrived to have a very pleasant time in spite of the efforts of Miss Lattimer and others to make her feel abashed.

She was guiltily glad, however, when Sylvia turned her ankle midway through the seventh dance, necessitating an early departure. "I can't think how I came to be so clumsy," said Sylvia apologetically, as Miranda and Henry helped her out to the carriage. "But I'm sure it's only a mild sprain and will heal in a day or two. Indeed, there's really no reason why we can't stay at the assembly, Miranda. I may not be able to dance anymore, but my ankle's not painful at all when I'm just sitting."

Miranda, however, insisted on accompanying the sufferer home. During the drive, she watched attentively to see what her sister's relations with Henry Ellis might be. If Sylvia had been as taken with Lord Longworth as he had been with her, then she might betray it by a cooler manner toward her other beau. But as far as Miranda could tell, she and Henry were on the same affectionate terms as ever. This was disappointing, but Miranda told herself it was early days yet.

"I'll try to sound her out on the subject tomorrow, when Henry isn't around," she resolved. "Perhaps she doesn't realize that she has any chance with a nobleman like Lord Longworth. Sylvia is a very modest girl, in spite of being so pretty."

Accordingly, the next morning at breakfast, Miranda began sounding out her sister on the subject of Lord Longworth. "It was quite the party last night, wasn't it?" she remarked lightly. "I don't remember the village assemblies being so lively in the past."

She was pleased when Sylvia rose immediately to the bait. "Oh! That was because Lord Longworth and Mr. Phelps were there, of course."

"Yes, I daresay," said Miranda casually. "They seem pleasant gentlemen, especially Lord Longworth."

Sylvia gave a gurgle of laughter. "Yes, although it was rather awkward, our getting him mixed with Mr. Phelps! And then, my blurting it out to him and giggling like a schoolgirl afterwards! I thought I should sink through the floor with embarrassment."

"He didn't mind that," Miranda assured her. "In fact, I have reason to think he was quite taken with you."

Sylvia gave her an incredulous smile. "Taken with me? I should say rather taken with you, Sister! Everyone was buzzing about it. Why, he asked you to lead off with him! I am sure no compliment could have been more particular than that."

"That was nothing," said Miranda dismissively. "I'm sure he would have led off with you if you had been the eldest rather than me."

"And I am very sure he would not! Why, he danced twice with you, Miranda—and that's an honor he didn't bestow on any other girl in the room. Mrs. Jordan was green with envy. She'd hoped he would dance at least once with Maddy or Betsy."

Miranda dismissed Mrs. Jordan's envy with a contemptuous sniff and returned to her original subject. "I think Lord Longworth would have danced with you again, too, Sylvia, if you hadn't been so taken up with Henry Ellis," she said. "Don't you think he is a very fine gentleman?"

"Oh, yes, very fine," said Sylvia.

Her voice held no particular enthusiasm. "I thought you must be impressed with him," Miranda persevered. "He had such an air about him. I thought him quite the most gentlemanlike man in the room."

"I suppose he was very gentlemanly," agreed Sylvia, still with no noticeable enthusiasm. Miranda was exasperated.

"Sylvia Strong, how can you be so provoking? You stood up with an eligible nobleman for one whole country dance. And yet you act as though he was nothing out of the ordinary!"

Sylvia raised candid blue eyes to her sister's face. "Well,

the truth is, I thought he *was* quite ordinary, in spite of being a nobleman. He must be at least forty—quite middle-aged, you know, and not really what you could call handsome. Of course his manners were very pleasant and gentlemanly, but then, so are Colonel Comstock's and Reverend Winchell's. And I wouldn't get excited about dancing with them!"

Miranda could only stare at her, overcome by indignation at this slighting speech. Sylvia went on, oblivious to her sister's indignation. "I suppose many people would consider him eligible, merely because he is wealthy and a nobleman. But you know I don't care for such things, Miranda. The only man I care for is Henry Ellis, and I mean to marry him if he ever gets around to asking me. If he doesn't, I shall remain a spinster."

"Well, I think you are a very silly girl," snapped Miranda. "I suppose you'll be using Lizzie Bragg's love potion next, in order to get Henry to propose to you!"

"I've thought about it," returned Sylvia cheerfully. "In fact, I've almost made up my mind to try it next time he calls. I tasted it a few days ago, and nothing happened, so I'm sure it's not poison."

"Well, all I can say is that you're a very silly girl," repeated Miranda. Rising from the table, she left the room in a dudgeon.

It seemed to her quite unaccountable that Sylvia should prefer Henry Ellis to Lord Longworth. "To call Lord Longworth 'middle-aged,' and 'not handsome'!" she reflected incredulously. "And to speak as though his only attractions were his wealth and title! I could shake Sylvia for being so foolish. But perhaps she'll come around in time. No, she won't, though—she's always been a very obstinate girl in her likes and dislikes. And even without Lizzie Bragg's potion, I'm sure Henry means to propose to her. Oh, what a mess it all is.

"It is a mess, isn't it, Tomcat?" she said aloud, addressing her pet, who had just come in from the garden. Tomcat purred and rubbed his head against her hand. Miranda scratched him gently behind his ears as she pondered the situation. She was still pondering when Polly, the senior Cottage maidservant, burst into the room in a state of great excitement.

"Miss Strong, there's a gentleman to see you!" she exclaimed. "A gentleman—and he says he's *Lord Longworth!* Miss Strong, you might have knocked me over with a feather when he said that. I was that flustered that I almost put him in the parlor, but then I remembered in time I hadn't got the breakfast dishes cleared away yet. So I put him in the sitting room instead. Oh, Miss Strong, only think of Lord Longworth coming here! My mum and sister'll stare when they hear this, and no mistake."

"That will do, Polly," said Miranda, breaking in firmly upon these raptures. "Tell Lord Longworth I'll be down immediately. And tell Miss Sylvia to come down to the sitting room, too," she added, as an afterthought. Sylvia might have repudiated Lord Longworth earlier in speaking, but she might have more trouble doing so in person, as Miranda reckoned to herself. In any event, she should have one more chance to come to her senses before it was too late.

As she was going downstairs, Miranda caught a glimpse of herself in her bedroom mirror. She paused and studied her reflection with a frown. She was wearing her prettiest white muslin morning dress, which was all to the good, but she was also wearing a cap atop her head. Her hair, too, was dressed very plainly in a simple knot at the nape of her neck. Miranda felt an irrational urge to take off her cap and arrange her hair as she had worn it the night before. But of course it *was* an irrational urge, as she reminded herself. Last night had been one thing, and more or less forgivable under the circumstances. But there could be no possible reason to make herself fine on this occasion, or to eschew her habitual cap.

"I won't make a laughingstock of myself," Miranda told

herself obscurely. And having conquered her momentary impulse, she went resolutely downstairs to the sitting room.

Tomcat followed after her, so that they entered the sitting room together. Lord Longworth was seated there, on the room's rather shabby chintz-covered sofa. He rose to his feet with a smile.

"Ah, here is Miss Strong—and my namesake!" Having saluted Miranda's hand, he squatted down to offer his hand to the cat. "How are you, Tom? I hope you've been behaving yourself and not distressing your mistress with any more unauthorized nocturnal jaunts?"

"No, he has been an exemplary cat," said Miranda. She watched with some amusement as Tom, having sniffed the visitor's fingers carefully, allowed his fur to be stroked with the air of one conferring a great favor. "You must like cats, my lord. You seem to have a way with them, at all events."

"Yes, I do like them," said Lord Longworth, shooting her a quizzical, blue-eyed look. "I like dogs, too, of course, and I generally have several about me at any given time. But a man who depends solely on dogs for companionship runs a risk of becoming too set up in his own esteem, in my opinion. It takes a cat to keep one properly humble."

"I suppose so," said Miranda, smiling. "I never thought of it that way, but I can see how keeping a cat would tend to keep one's conceit at bay. They're such conceited creatures themselves."

"Yes, they put all human conceit in its proper proportion." Lord Longworth stroked Tom once more, then rose to his feet. His eyes swept Miranda with an admiring look that yet held a certain reserve in it. "You seem not to have suffered from your late hours last night, Miss Strong. You're looking very fresh and—and handsome this afternoon."

Miranda was sure he was noticing her cap. She felt her color rise but endeavored to answer with her usual composure. "You are very kind to say so, my lord. But in fact I did not keep such very late hours last night. My sister injured her ankle not long after you went into the card room, and we were obliged to leave early."

"Ah, that explains it. I looked for you later in the evening but did not see you." He hesitated a moment. "I trust your sister's injury was not serious?"

"No, merely a slight sprain, my lord. I bound it up with arnica last night, and she was well enough to come downstairs this morning. I have no doubt she will soon be here."

She smiled at him reassuringly. He smiled back but seemed at a loss for words. Miranda supposed it was merely the natural shyness of a man come a-wooing, who was unfortunate enough to be received by his sweetheart's sister rather than the lady herself. Accordingly, she pretended to pay no notice, but talked in a calm, rational way about village events and other neutral topics. A few minutes later Sylvia came in, bright, smiling, and lovely, and Miranda prepared to resign the conversation to her.

Sylvia, however, had clearly expected someone else. And it was all too clear, to Miranda at least, that the someone else was the ubiquitous Henry Ellis.

"Oh!" she said blankly, stopping short and gazing at Lord Longworth with consternation.

Miranda felt it an awkward moment. "You see Lord Longworth has come to call upon us, Sister," she said brightly. "Did not Polly tell you he was here?"

Sylvia murmured something about having misunderstood. "I am glad to see you, my lord," she said, addressing him with a slight curtsy. He returned the salute but seemed still constrained in his manner. Miranda could not blame him. "Do sit down, both of you," she urged. "I'll go order some tea for us."

Hurrying out of the room, she congratulated herself on her adroit management of the situation. Lord Longworth would now have opportunity to pay his gallantries in private. And though Sylvia seemed little disposed to receive them, still Miranda could not believe she was not a little flattered to be the object of his attentions. *"I* would be," she told herself, then put the thought hastily from her as something disloyal. As punishment, she forced herself to stay away from the sitting room twice as long as was really necessary to prepare the tea. But when at last she returned to the sitting room carrying the teapot and cups and accompanied by Polly bearing a tray with cake and bread and butter, she found matters not far advanced.

Sylvia was seated stiffly on a chair near the fireplace, at the furthest possible distance from where Lord Longworth sat on the sofa. She was talking in a determined way about the weather. Lord Longworth was listening politely, but both he and Sylvia appeared glad to see her with the tea. They both sprang to their feet, Lord Longworth to assist her with her tray and Sylvia to assist Polly with hers. "Sister, will you pour?" said Miranda. "I must just run out to the kitchen and get more sugar."

As she hurried away, she reflected with satisfaction that food and drink ought to have a relaxing influence on the two of them. Hoping to further their courtship, she dallied as long as possible about her errand, only returning to the sitting room after some ten or twelve minutes. This time, she found its two occupants in a more promising attitude. They were both seated at the table, and Lord Longworth was saying something to Sylvia in a low voice, which he broke off hurriedly at Miranda's entrance.

"There you are, Miss Strong," he said. "We were just talking about you."

Miranda was disappointed. She had hoped her absence was encouraging a romantic *tête-á-tête*. "I am sure you could have found some more interesting topic than me to discuss," she said lightly. Tomcat, who in her absence had made himself comfortable on the hearth rug, yawned as though agreeing with her. Lord Longworth smiled.

"No, indeed, Miss Strong. Our conversation was sufficiently interesting, I assure you. May I help you to cake and bread and butter?" He filled a plate with these dainties while Sylvia poured her out a cup of tea.

Miranda still had hopes she might salvage the interview. She had already absented herself twice from the sitting room, and it seemed a little obvious to do it a third time, but she was determined to do all she could to assist in her sister's courtship by this most desirable suitor. Sylvia, however, had other plans. "I am afraid the two of you must excuse me," she said, as soon as she had finished drinking her tea. "I have an engagement this afternoon, and I must go change my dress." Looking at Miranda, she added, "Henry is taking me out driving this afternoon, as usual."

*Now why did she have to put in that "as usual"?* Miranda reflected with vexation. *Bad enough that she should speak of driving out with another man, without making it clear that it is a habitual engagement.* She glanced at Lord Longworth. He seemed not unduly distressed—in fact, he was smiling— but Miranda supposed that was only politeness. She was sure he would not want to come to the Cottage again, after receiving such a deliberate snub.

The thought depressed her more than she would have thought possible. Somehow it seemed an end to all her hopes and dreams—to hopes and dreams that she had not even acknowledged, apparently. Why else should she have felt a stinging of tears behind her eyes? On the hearth rug, Tomcat was chasing his own tail, circling madly round and round after that tempting quarry that was always, inexplicably, just beyond his own reach. Miranda felt suddenly that she had been doing the same thing, ever since the night she had met Lord Longworth at the park palings. It was clearly fated that Sylvia should marry Henry Ellis. It was equally fated that she herself should live out the rest of her life as a lonely, penurious old maid. In trying to avert her own and her sister's fates, she had been engaged in a pursuit as futile as Tomcat's. The thought made her eyes suddenly brim over with tears. Hastily, she rose to her feet.

"I beg you will excuse me also, my lord. I must—I must see to some things about the house."

Lord Longworth, who had been watching Tomcat's antics with an appreciative smile, turned to look at her in surprise. Miranda felt his look but did not dare meet his eyes. She felt at that moment that she would willingly sacrifice everything else if only she might get out of the room without disgracing herself. It might be done politely, or it might be done brusquely, but it must be done soon—and perhaps brusquely was the better way, as being the least likely to betray her true state of mind. Miranda drew herself up, dropping a stiff curtsy and speaking with a semblance of proud indifference. "Good afternoon, my lord," she said, and swept from the room without a backward glance.

# FIVE

By the time Sylvia returned from her drive with Henry, Miranda was in a calmer state of mind.

She was still deeply ashamed of having treated Lord Longworth so rudely. Even as she left the room she was ashamed, and later, when she heard his footsteps going down the hall and the door shutting behind him, she was so overcome with shame and remorse that she had wept. Yet ashamed as she was, she knew she would have been even more ashamed to have wept in front of him. Of the two alternatives, it seemed better that he should tell people what a cold, haughty, disagreeable woman the eldest Miss Strong was rather than that he should laugh at her as a wet-goose. There were already people in the village of Upton Charnhurst who thought her cold, haughty, and disagreeable. Miranda told herself that one more could hardly matter.

So she greeted Sylvia with very much her usual composure and asked her how her drive with Henry had gone. Sylvia did not notice anything amiss in her manner, but then, given the circumstances, it was doubtful whether Sylvia would have noticed anything amiss even had her sister been in a full-blown fit of hysterics. She was wholly and exultantly intent on her own affairs.

"Miranda, look!" she demanded, stripping off her glove and displaying her left hand. Miranda looked, and observed a glittering diamond ornamenting the third finger. Sylvia laughed joyously, turning her hand from side to side to admire the play of light on the stone.

"Henry?" said Miranda, though she already knew the answer. Sylvia nodded with an expression of blissful content.

"Yes, Henry," she said. "We are to be married at Christmastime. Oh, wish me joy, Sister!"

"Of course I wish you joy," said Miranda, enfolding her in her arms. In a voice that shook slightly, she repeated, "Of course I wish you joy. But oh, Sylvia, I can hardly believe that you are to be married. It seems only yesterday that you were a little girl."

Sylvia laughed again. "Silly Miranda! I have been grown up for several years now. It's just that you've been taking care of me so long that you can't see it." More soberly, she added, "Don't think I'm not grateful for all you've done for me, Miranda. I *am* grateful—and I intend to show you how much by turning the tables and taking care of you for a change! I talked it all over with Henry today, and it's all settled."

"What's all settled?" said Miranda in puzzlement.

"Why, that you should live with us after we are married. Henry quite agrees that I cannot go off and leave you alone."

Miranda could only stare incredulously. Sylvia went on, her voice buoyant yet deeply earnest. "I have it all planned out. There's plenty of room for you at Elliston House. You can have your own rooms and come and go as you please. I am sure we will all be very happy together, much happier than we have been living in this nasty little cottage."

"I wouldn't call it a nasty little cottage," said Miranda. She said it absently, however, for her thoughts were engaged in considering her sister's offer. She was deeply touched that Sylvia should have thought of her in the midst of her own happiness. Henry, too, seemed to have behaved very well, she grudgingly admitted to herself. It was not every man who would allow himself to be saddled with a spinster sister-in-law when he doubtless wished to be alone with his bride.

Altogether, the offer seemed like an answer to a prayer. It was therefore very odd how curiously disinclined Miranda was to accept it. When Sylvia pressed her for an answer, saying, "Do say you will come live with us, Miranda," she evaded making any firm commitment.

"You may tell Henry that I greatly appreciate his and your generosity, Sylvia. But all this has taken me greatly by surprise. I shall have to think the matter over before I will know what is best to do."

Over the next few weeks she did think the matter over, hundreds and hundreds of times. The sum of her reflection was rather surprising. Much as she loved Sylvia, much as she had dreaded the prospect of living without her, she could not feel comfortable or happy with the idea of living with her and Henry at Elliston House.

"It's not right and it's not natural," Miranda told herself. "For me to go on living with Sylvia after her marriage would be to act as though things hadn't changed between us. Yet they would be changed—changed in nearly every particular. Such a situation would tend to breed resentment in both of us, and I imagine Henry would be resentful, too. No, it's better that I should let Sylvia and Henry go off to Elliston House, while I pursue my own life independently and see what I can make of it.

"It's odd, but I can't rid myself of a conviction that this is one of those situations that's meant to be a test of character." Miranda spoke the thought aloud to Tomcat, who was reclining lazily in her lap as she mused over her dilemma. "I've a choice now between the easy downhill road and the difficult uphill path, just as Reverend Winchell was preaching about in his sermon last Sunday. If only I continue to struggle upward against adversity, I ought to be rewarded in the end. But oh, the end seems a long way away, and I can't imagine any reward being worth the trouble of getting there. Can you, Tom-cat?" She stroked the cat's ears. Tomcat yawned and rolled a sleepy golden eye at her, as though to say that all such philo-sophical mysteries were an open book to an intelligent cat like himself. Miranda laughed.

"What would you know about adversity, you lazy beast? You take life 'aisy,' as Polly says. I don't suppose life without Sylvia will be 'aisy' for me, but I'll trust that it will bring its own consolations in due time. And in the meantime I do have you, Tomcat." She stroked the cat affectionately. "I must go and thank Lizzie Bragg for you one of these days. I never would have believed when she first gave you to me that you would end up being such a comfort to me, Tomcat. Though you didn't bring much comfort to me when you engineered my introduction to Lord Longworth!" Miranda sighed at the remembrance. "It would have been better if I'd never met him rather than have things turn out as they did. I heard the Jordan girls saying last night that he is definitely planning to give a ball at Longworth Hall in a few weeks. I don't believe they know what they're talking about, but even if Lord Longworth does mean to give a ball, I don't suppose he will be inviting the Misses Strong to attend!"

In this she was wrong, however. The invitation from Lord Longworth arrived two days later and was undeniably ad-dressed to both Miss Miranda Strong and Miss Sylvia Strong. "An All Hallow's Eve ball!" said Sylvia, perusing the invita-tion with delight. "Fancy dress, too! This is doing things in a proper style. How nice of Lord Longworth to invite us."

"Are you sure he invited us?" said Miranda incredulously.

"Oh, yes, here are both our names, Miranda. Why should he not invite us?" She looked at her sister curiously. "If he was not too top-lofty to visit us here at the Cottage, he could certainly have no objection to inviting us to a ball along with dozens of other people."

"I suppose not," said Miranda, but she was still surprised.

A fancy dress ball! The Upton Charnhurstites would be wild with excitement, as she reflected with a bitter smile.

"No doubt the Jordans are in the seventh heaven," she told herself. "But I still can't believe Sylvia and I received invitations, after the way both of us snubbed Lord Longworth. Is it possible he still hankers after Sylvia, even after her making it clear that she cares only for Henry? Perhaps he has not seen the papers and does not realize she is engaged."

Miranda had taken care that notice of the engagement should be inserted in the London papers as well as the local gazette. If Lord Longworth was too superior to look at the one, he surely must have seen it in the other, she reasoned. "But he might have missed the notice, I suppose. Really, it's the only explanation. Well, he's doomed to disappointment if he gave this ball with the idea of making up to Sylvia. But there's nothing I can do to avert his disappointment."

"I wonder what I should wear?" said Sylvia, breaking in upon her sister's reflections. "Miranda, do you have any ideas? It would be sweet if Henry and I could find costumes that went together."

"You mean to go then?" said Miranda, looking at her in surprise.

"Yes, don't you? Surely you do not mean to miss this party! It will be the most exciting thing that's happened in Upton Charnhurst in ages."

Miranda had to admit that this was true. And though any further meeting with Lord Longworth would doubtless be accompanied by awkwardness, still she could not overcome a sneaking desire to attend the masquerade. "If I am in costume, it's likely he won't even know I'm there, at least not till after the unmasking," she told herself. "Perhaps I could leave early, so as to keep my identity a secret."

The idea cheered her so much that she allowed Sylvia to accept the invitation in both their names with only a token show of reluctance. Costumes were the next question. A certain trunk in the attic, full of relics from past fancy dress occasions, was ransacked by both sisters. It proved to contain any number of false beards, dominoes, masks, and other useful items. "Here's a charming shepherdess's dress," said Sylvia, regarding it with pleasure. "I can be a shepherdess, and Henry can be a shepherd. I expect he can get a costume made locally or buy one ready-made in Winchester. What will you wear, Miranda?"

Miranda flipped dubiously through the stock of camphor-scented clothing. "I don't know. Perhaps I will merely wear a mask and domino."

"But that's so tame," objected Sylvia. "I can think of a better idea than that. Why don't you be Undine? You could get a dress with floating greenish draperies and wear your hair down and carry a bouquet of water lilies. You'd make a lovely water sprite."

"A superannuated water sprite," scoffed Miranda. "I'm too old for such a costume, Sylvia. People would laugh at me for wearing it."

"No, they wouldn't. You'd look very well in it. And I don't know why you like to pretend you're so very elderly. You're only twenty-nine, after all, and you haven't a gray hair or a line in your face. I overheard old Colonel Comstock say at the assembly the other night that you were still as handsome as when you first came out."

"Did he?" Miranda was pleased at this praise but still dubious. "I don't know, Sylvia. I hate to go to so much trouble and expense for a costume I'll wear only once. And with your bride clothes to think of—"

"All the more reason you should have something for yourself now," said Sylvia firmly. "There's plenty of time to think of bride clothes. You go on and get yourself a proper costume, Miranda. I shall never forgive you if you don't."

The excitement of preparing for the ball absorbed Miranda fully for the next week or two. Feeling still rather guilt about spending money on herself at such a time, she assuaged her guilt by making her costume herself in the most frugal manner possible. Fortunately, the thinnest gauze was also the cheapest and lent itself splendidly to the creation of floating, Undinelike draperies. Likewise, there was no need for expensive laces or other rich trimmings when a total lack of ornament seemed more in keeping with a water sprite's toilette. Water lilies were a trifle out of season, but a circlet of plain green leaves did admirably as a headdress. It was a simple thing when done, but Miranda thought it rather effective. Sylvia thought the same.

"That pale green gauze over the darker green looks just lovely. I like the trailing sleeves, and the way the layers of the skirt float out when you turn quickly. It ought to look a dream when you're dancing. Do you suppose Lord Longworth will ask you to lead off again?"

"Oh, no," said Miranda quickly. "I'm sure he will not."

Sylvia looked roguish. "You can never tell. I know you thought he admired me, but if you ask me, it was you he really liked. I could tell by the way he went on and on about you when we were dancing at the assembly. And when he came to call on us the next day, he as good as admitted it while you were out of the room. Truth to tell, I'm surprised he hasn't been back to call since then."

Miranda looked at her sister. She appeared to be in earnest. "Nonsense, Sylvia," she said, in a voice that was the slightest bit unsteady. "It cannot be that Lord Longworth likes *me*."

"Why not? You liked him, didn't you?" said Sylvia, firing up with sisterly indignation. "Why shouldn't he like you in return, I should like to know? And I notice that when you still thought he was Mr. Phelps, you were ready enough to get him. It was only when you found out he was Lord Longworth that you tried to foist him off on me."

Miranda was silent, trying to adjust her mind to this new possibility. For a brief moment, hope and longing soared within her heart—a hope and longing that had lain there un-acknowledged ever since she had first made Lord Longworth's acquaintance. But the next moment, realization brought her hopes crashing down to earth again. "Even if what you say is true, Sylvia, it doesn't matter now," she said flatly. "Lord Longworth may have been inclined to admire me once, but I am sure he no longer does."

Sylvia attempted to dispute this statement, but Miranda turned the subject off by telling her brusquely that she needed to hurry and get into her own costume if she was to be ready by the time Henry arrived with the carriage. Sylvia, with a glance at the clock, flew to her bedroom to dress, and Miranda sank down on the stairs and buried her face in her hands.

She felt cold and sick and utterly miserable. She tried to tell herself Sylvia must have been mistaken in thinking Lord Longworth had admired her. There was little comfort to be gained in that thought, but it was better than believing that he *had* admired her, and that she had destroyed his admiration through a mixture of pride and short-sightedness. Miranda tried hard to dismiss this latter notion as folly, but when she looked back over her short acquaintance with Lord Longworth, remembering the things he had said and the way he had looked at her, she felt a sickening conviction that her sister was right.

"What have I done?" she asked herself in despair. "Oh, what have I done?"

It was impossible that she should go to the party now. Miranda felt she could not bear to face Lord Longworth while the realization of her folly was still fresh in her mind. Indeed, she questioned whether she would ever be able to bear seeing him again. "But of course, he'll be going back to London soon," she comforted herself. "Mr. Phelps said he only planned on staying for six or eight weeks. It's been nearly six weeks now."

She continued to sit hunched on the stairs, overcome with

depression and despair, until Sylvia presently reappeared, smiling and lovely in her guise of a shepherdess. Miranda addressed her abruptly. "Sylvia, I've changed my mind about attending the party tonight. Please make my apologies to Henry, and to Lord Longworth."

Sylvia's smile turned at once into a look of dismay. "Not going! Oh, Miranda, why ever not? Do you feel unwell?"

"Very unwell," said Miranda, with heartfelt sincerity. "But I shall be better presently, I'm sure. And there's no reason you and Henry can't go on and attend the ball, Sylvia. I should feel even worse if I thought I was spoiling *your* evening."

Sylvia protested, declaring that she would certainly stay home if Miranda was feeling unwell. But Miranda, who longed inexpressibly for solitude, was firm in rejecting her sister's offers of assistance. She saw her go off to the party with a feeling of gloomy satisfaction. The maids and manservant had been given the evening off, in expectation of her and her sister's absence, and she was now perfectly alone in the house.

"Alone except for you, Tom," she told the cat, who had come over to rub his head against her ankles. "Let's go outside and sit in the garden."

Tomcat purred his approval of this idea. Miranda rose to her feet, pulling off the wreath of ivy leaves that she had donned for the party. For a moment she held it in her hands, looking at it regretfully, then tossed it on the hall table with a sigh. Her shawl was lying nearby. Miranda picked it up, threw it over her shoulders, and went out into the garden with Tomcat following after her.

It was a fair, moonlit night, cool but not unduly chilly for late October. Miranda did not mind the chill. She sat on the steps, her hands clasped in her lap and her thoughts miles away—three miles away, to be exact, with the revelers at Longworth Hall.

She wondered if Lord Longworth had missed her among

his other guests. It hardly seemed likely. Such a man as he could have his pick of the eligible women in the kingdom, let alone the little village of Upton Charnhurst. If by some unlikely contingency of events he still felt the sting of being snubbed by Miss Miranda Strong, he could doubtless find ready consolation elsewhere.

Miranda sighed and pushed away a strand of hair that a gust of wind had blown across her face. Another gust came, rattling the dead and dying leaves in the trees overhead. Several went swirling to the ground, and Tomcat dashed after them, pouncing on first one and then another. Miranda watched him with wan amusement. His gambols took him farther and farther from the house, and she, well aware of the difficulties of finding a black cat in the dark, stirred herself to call him back.

"Tom, come here! Come back, you vexatious creature."

"That's a nice way to greet a fellow," said a reproachful voice in her ear. Miranda jumped. Turning, she beheld Lord Longworth standing beside the cottage steps, regarding her with a diffident smile.

"Oh, but you startled me!" said Miranda. Her heart did seem to be beating uncommonly fast, and it was convenient to blame it on shock. Besides, she had every reason to be shocked at the sight of Lord Longworth, when she had just been imagining him several miles away.

This point had no sooner occurred to Miranda than she found herself voicing her puzzlement aloud. "What are you doing here?" she asked. "Why aren't you at your party?"

"Why aren't *you* at my party?" he countered. "You said you would come."

His voice was more reproachful than ever. Miranda stared at him. "Did you come over here merely to ask why I didn't come to your party?" she demanded incredulously.

"Yes, I did," he said. "At least, your sister told me you weren't feeling well—and that naturally concerned me. I thought I would come over and see how you were. But you don't look ill." His voice was accusing.

Miranda stared at him a moment longer. Several widely divergent thoughts flitted through her mind, among them the thought that consolation might not be so far to seek as she had supposed. A smile began to curve her lips. "I think—I really believe—that I am feeling better now, my lord," she said.

"Are you? Well, then, get your things and let's go. We still might make it in time for the first dance." Miranda stood up, and he looked appreciatively at her gauzy green robes. "Is that your costume? It's very becoming. You must have taken my suggestion and decided to impersonate Titania!"

"Indeed I did not," said Miranda robustly. "I'm supposed to be Undine, not Titania."

"Well, you look a veritable Titania to me! Very lovely, and very alluring." He hesitated a moment, looking down at her. "Perhaps I've no business asking this—but you must know I was very taken with you from the first moment I saw you, Miss Strong. And though there've been times I've fancied the feeling might be mutual, there've been other times when I've felt as though you've been trying to hint me away! Can you—do you think you might be able to think of me as more than a friend someday, if you were given time to get used to the idea?"

Miranda could hardly keep from laughing aloud, partly from joy and partly at the absurd idea of needing time to recognize him as the man of her dreams. What she actually said, in a very demure voice, was, "Yes, Tom, I think perhaps I could."

He smiled, a slow smile of bemusement and pleasure. "You called me Tom," he said.

"You don't mind, do you?" countered Miranda.

"No, indeed! In fact, it almost encourages me to make so bold as to—kiss you."

Catching one arm about her waist, he drew her toward him.

But just as he was lowering his lips to hers, Miranda caught sight of Tomcat moving toward the open cottage door with what looked alarmingly like a still squirming mouse in his mouth. Forgetting all else except the need to keep additional rodents out of the cottage, she cried out, "No, Tom! No!"

"No?" said Lord Longworth, opening his eyes and regarding her with bewilderment.

Miranda laughed and gestured toward the cat. "I was talking to the other Tom," she said. "Not to you." Having shut the cottage door and forced the protesting cat to release his prey, she returned to where Lord Longworth was standing. "To you, I would say rather—yes, Tom!" She smiled at him invitingly.

An answering smile spread across Lord Longworth's face. "That's exactly what I hoped you'd say," he said, and proceeded to kiss her soundly.

# More Zebra Regency Romances

# Merlin's Legacy

## A Series From
## Quinn Taylor Evans